ROLLING THUNDER

ROLLING THUNDER

A JOHN CEEPAK MYSTERY

Chris Grabenstein

PEGASUS BOOKS
NEW YORK

ROLLING THUNDER

Pegasus Books LLC
80 Broad Street, 5th Floor
New York, NY 10004

Copyright © 2010 by Chris Grabenstein

First Pegasus Books cloth edition 2010

Interior design by Maria Fernandez

Library of Congress Cataloging-in-Publication Data is available.

ISBN: 978-1-60598-089-8

10 9 8 7 8 6 5 4 3 2 1

Printed in the United States of America
Distributed by W. W. Norton & Company, Inc.

For
Eric R. Myers

1

THE DAY STARTS LIKE SO MANY OTHERS WITH JOHN CEEPAK: We bust an eight-year-old girl for wearing high heels.

"She wants to ride the ride!" says the kid's mother, who, I'm assuming, was her accomplice in the beat-the-roller-coaster-height-requirement scam. The ponytail piled up on top of the short girl's head (which makes her look like one of the Whos from Whoville) was, no doubt, another part of the plan.

"The rules regarding the minimum height requirement are in place to protect your daughter," says Ceepak.

"I wanna ride the ride!" The little girl stamps her foot so hard she snaps off a heel.

"This way," says Ceepak, indicating how mother and daughter should exit the line snaking about a mile up the boardwalk from the entrance to Big Paddy's Rolling Thunder, the brand-new, all-wood roller coaster rising up behind us like a humongous hump-backed whale made out of two-by-fours.

It's the Saturday of Memorial Day weekend. The unofficial start of another Fun-in-the-Sun season down the shore in Sea Haven, New Jersey. Opening day for Big Paddy O'Malley's Rolling Thunder roller coaster.

Ceepak and I are working crowd control with half the Sea Haven PD. The other half is inside on security duty for the dignitaries about to take the first ride around the heaving mountains propped up on wooden stilts. You step far enough away, the Rolling Thunder looks like a K'NEX construction kit sculpture. Or one of those summer camp Popsicle stick deals on steroids.

Ceepak and I walk up the line. He's staring at short people's feet.

"Young man?"

This is directed at a boy, maybe seven and very ingenious: He's duct-taped a pair of flip-flops to the soles of his sneakers.

"Please step out of the line."

"What?" says a very hairy man in a sleeveless AC-DC Rolling Thunder T-shirt, the one with the monkey skeletons banging Hell's bell. AC-DC's munching on fried zeppole wads, showering so much powdered sugar down the front of his black tee it looks like his curly chest has dandruff. "What's your freaking problem, officer?"

"Your son's shoes," says Ceepak. "Clearly you are attempting to circumvent the ride's forty-eight-inch height requirement."

"Huh?" father and son say at the same time, because I don't think "circumvent" is a vocabulary word either one of them has learned yet.

"It appears," Ceepak clarifies, "that you are encouraging your son to cheat."

That settles that.

No way is John Ceepak cutting Shorty a break because, as annoying as it sometimes is, my partner—an ex-military man who looks like he could still jump out of a helicopter with a Humvee strapped to his back—lives his life in strict compliance with the West Point Cadet Honor Code: He will not lie, cheat, steal, or tolerate those who do.

"Please step out of the line, sir."

"We're not steppin' nowheres," says the boy's father. "Is it our fault the rules are so freaking stupid?"

"Actually," I chime in, "the rules are there for a reason."

AC-DC Man sizes me up. He's bigger than me. Heck, his beer gut is bigger than me. But I've got a badge on my chest and a gun on my belt. He doesn't. Well, not that I can see. Like I said, he has a laundry bag belly sagging all the way down to the tip of his zipper.

"Come on. Don't youse two have something better to do than ruin a kid's day?"

"The roller coaster isn't going anywhere," says Ceepak. "Perhaps you and your son can come back and ride it later in the summer after he's reached the required height."

"He's riding it today!"

"No, sir. He is not."

"What? You gonna arrest him?"

"Of course not. If you wish to remain in line, that is your prerogative. However, rest assured, an hour from now, when you finally reach the front, your son will not be allowed to enter the ride. Danny?"

We move on.

The crowd is amazing. I know Memorial Day is considered the unofficial start of summer, but here in Sea Haven things don't usually get this crowded until after the schools let out near the end of June. Then the population of our eighteen-mile-long barrier island swells from twenty thousand to a quarter million, and we have to hire all sorts of part-time cops just to deal with the traffic and crosswalk congestion—especially near the Rita's Water Ice stands.

So it's incredible to see how many people have shown up on the last weekend in May to ride the new roller coaster erected on the recently refurbished Pier Four. Big Paddy O'Malley, the father of this kid Skip I knew in high school, and his partners bought the whole pier late last summer after a boarded-up ride called the Hell Hole burned down, almost taking Ceepak and me with it.

It's a long story. Remind me. I'll tell you about it sometime.

Anyway, Big Paddy O'Malley and company gutted the old pier down to its pilings, tore out the rusty old rides, hauled away what was left of the Whacky Wheel and the Chair-O-Planes, and built this 100-foot tall, 3,458-foot-long wooden roller coaster with an eighty-foot drop and a top speed of fifty miles per hour.

"I'm afraid that father and son will have a long wait," says Ceepak. "With two thirty-seat trains, the ride has a maximum capacity of only one thousand passengers per hour."

I think Ceepak is a member of the American Coaster Enthusiasts, just so he can memorize stats like that from their bimonthly newsletter.

Of course, all thirty seats in the first train to hurl (pun intended) around the track will be filled with members of the O'Malley family plus assorted state and local dignitaries—not to mention my buddy Cliff Skeete, a disc jockey at W-A-V-Y who will be doing a live remote broadcast so we can all listen to him scream like a terrified two-year-old into his cordless microphone.

"*One minute to blastoff!*" Cliff's voice booms out of the giant speakers they've set up near the ride's entrance so everybody on the boardwalk (or anywhere else in a hundred-mile radius) can hear. Over the entryway, there's this cool neon sign with retro red letters spelling out R-O-L-L-I-N-G, then T-H-U-N-D-E-R, with jagged blue lightning bolts flashing on both sides.

"*Let me tell you, folks,*" croons Cliff, who calls himself the Skeeter when he's on the air and plays this annoying mosquito buzz every time he mentions his name, "*this job has its ups and downs. And today, its gonna have it's ups and downs and ups and downs—not to mention a few twists and turns. Riding in the front car we have Mrs. and Mr. O'Malley—Big Paddy himself. Their sons, Kevin, Skip, and Sean. Daughter Mary—who's sitting right in front of me. You ready to roll, Mary?"*

Dead air.

Now I remember what the mean kids used to say about Mary O'Malley: she rode the short bus to school. I believe she is mentally challenged. Slashed her wrists in the bathtub a couple times.

"Oh-kay. Thanks, Mary," says Cliff, because that's what good deejays do: they keep calm and blather on, no matter what. *"Thirty seconds until blastoff."*

Ceepak and I are up near the front of the line now. I can see the "You Must Be This Tall to Ride This Ride" sign. It's a leprechaun holding out his hand. The O'Malleys are major-league Irish.

Ceepak motions to the kid in a green polo shirt checking heights.

"Be aware that some people in this line are attempting to cheat your height requirement."

"For real?"

"Totally," I say, because Ceepak is over thirty-five and wouldn't know how to say it.

The guy returns to his measuring stick task with renewed zeal.

There are other warning signs posted near the entrance. My favorites are the graphics suggesting that this attraction is not recommended for guests with broken bones, heart trouble, high blood pressure, pregnancy, or "recent surgery."

Sure. The day after my appendectomy, the first thing I'm gonna do is climb on a roller coaster.

"Ten, nine, eight . . ." D.J. Cliff is swinging into his Apollo 13 impression. The thing is—roller coasters don't really blast off; they more or less lurch forward, then chug up a hill.

". . . three, two, one . . . here we go, folks!"

The crowd crammed into the Disney World–style switchbacks cheers because, as the first train crammed with dignitaries pulls out, the second one finally slides forward. Thirty non-VIPs scamper onto the loading dock and jump into the next train's seats. The impossibly long line is actually moving.

Ceepak and I step back, gaze up.

From underneath the latticework of planks, we can see the first train rumbling forward, clicking and clacking on the steel tracks.

"We're on our way," Cliff commentates. *"Here comes the first hill! It's a big one!"*

Now comes the clatter of the chain running down the center of the track as it grabs hold of the coaster cars and hauls them skyward. This is the part of a roller coaster ride that always scares me the most. The anticipation of what's to come when you finally reach the top. The thought that you could so easily climb out, walk back down, call it quits. And, near the top, it always sounds as if the chain is getting tired, that it's stuttering, that it may not be able to hoist the train *all . . . the . . . way . . . up.*

But, of course, it always does.

The clacking stops. The first car has reached the summit.

"This is it!" booms Cliff. *"Here we go!"*

There is no sound for a long empty second.

And then the screams start.

"Oh my gawd!" cries Cliff, momentarily forgetting that he is on the air. *"Whoo-hoo! Yeaaaaaah! Whoo-hoo!"*

The train rattles down that first hill in a flash.

Now everyone is screaming. The mayor, the O'Malley family, the chamber of commerce, Cliff the D.J.—plus all the people on the ground waiting for their turn to scare themselves to death. It's a screechfest.

They're rolling through the first banked curve. The initial screams subside—just long enough for everyone to catch their breath for the second hill—not as steep but just as exciting.

"Whoo-hoo!" Cliff has 86'd any scripted commentary. He's barely using words anymore. *"Boo-yeaaaaaah!"*

The train rattles up and down a series of knolls, shoots into a wooden tunnel, zooms out the other side.

"Oh my God!" somebody shouts. *"Stop the train!"*

"Huh?" Cliff. Confused.

"Stop the train!" It sounds like Skippy. *"Stop it!"*

Some kind of alarm buzzer goes off.

"Stop it!" That was Skip's dad. Big Paddy. *"Stop the damn train!"*

In the distance I hear the screech of brakes. Steel wheels scraping against steel rails. Cars bumpering into each other.

Then an awful quiet.

"Oh my god!" Mr. O'Malley again. *"Hang on, honey. Oh my god! It's her heart!"*

2

"WE NEED SOMEONE TO CALL NINE–ONE–ONE! NOW! OMIGOD! She's in bad shape! I think she's having a heart attack! Call nine–one–one. We need an ambulance!"

Cliff Skeete sounds panicky. His remote roller coaster broadcast has suddenly turned into a breaking news bulletin.

"Go to music! Go to music!"

Bruce Springsteen's "Lucky Town" starts rocking out of the giant loudspeakers. Not the best choice.

"Danny?" Ceepak hops up and over the metal railings penning in the crowd. I hop over after him.

We're in full uniform—radios, batons, guns, handcuffs rattling on our utility belts. People scoot out of our way.

"Ticket booth," Ceepak shouts.

"AED?" I shout back.

"Roger that."

Ceepak's hoping Big Paddy was smart enough to equip his thrill

8

ride with an Automated External Defibrillator, a portable electronic device that can revive cardiac-arrest victims—if you jolt
them soon enough.

Ceepak barrels over the final barricade, scopes out the small hut
where the ticket seller sits.

"AED!" he shouts to the girl sitting stunned behind the
window. She doesn't flinch so Ceepak shouts again: "AED!"

Meanwhile, on WAVY, Bruce is singing, "When it comes to
luck you make your own." Springsteen. The soundtrack of my life.

"On the wall!" I shout. I have a lucky angle and can see the
bulldozer-yellow box mounted on the wall behind the petrified
teenage ticket taker.

Ceepak dashes in, yanks the defibrillator off the wall, then darts
out of the booth, AED in one hand, radio unit in the other.

"This is Ceepak," he barks as he dashes up the empty exit
ramp. I dash after him. "Request ambulance. Pier Four. Possible
cardiac arrest. Alert fire department. Potential roller coaster
rescue scenario."

"Ten–four" squawks out of his radio as he clips it back to his
belt.

"Danny? You know the family?"

"Yeah."

I guess I know just about everybody in Sea Haven. I grew up
here. Ceepak? He grew up in Ohio, where they don't build roller
coasters jutting out over the Atlantic Ocean. He only came to
Jersey after slogging through the first wave of hellfire over in Iraq
as an MP with the 101st Airborne. Saw and did some pretty ugly
stuff. Then an old army buddy offered him a job down the Jersey
shore in "sunny, funderful Sea Haven," where nothing bad ever
happens.

Yeah, right. Tell it to whoever's having the heart attack.

"When we reach the roller coaster cars, keep everybody calm
and seated," Ceepak shouts over his shoulder as we race up the

steep ramp. "I'll administer CPR. Wire up the AED. Time is of the essence."

"Okay," I say.

We reach the unloading platform, between the control room and the train tracks.

Ceepak scans the horizon.

"There!" He spots the stranded roller coaster train—on top of a curved hill about a quarter mile up the track. He hops off the platform. "Keep to the walkboard!"

There's a wooden plank paralleling the train tracks. A handrail, too. This must be how the maintenance workers inspect the tracks every morning.

"Use the cleats, Danny."

I notice wood slats secured to the walkboard.

"They act as a nonslip device."

Good. Nonslipping off a giant wooden scaffold eighty feet above the ocean is an excellent idea.

"Short, choppy steps, Danny. Short, choppy steps."

Ceepak takes off, looking like a linebacker doing the tire drill at training camp. I hop down to the narrow walkway plank and, like always, try to do what Ceepak is doing.

Except, I grab the handrail, too.

We're going to have to run down a slight hill, the straightaway where the roller coaster slows down before coming to its final, complete stop in the loading shed. After that comes an uphill bump and a downhill run to a steeply banked inclined turn sloping up to the crest of another much higher hill where the roller coaster train is stuck.

"They should've brought the car down to the finish," I shout, the words coming out in huffs and puffs as I chug up what is basically a 2-by-12 board.

"Roger that," says Ceepak. "I suspect they panicked." He's not even winded. Cool and calm as a cucumber on Xanax.

I'm not surprised.

When he was over in Iraq, Ceepak won all sorts of medals for bravery, valor, heroism—all those things I only know from movies.

Of course, Ceepak never brags about the brave things he's done. I guess the really brave people never do. In fact, I only learned about the Distinguished Service Cross he won for "displaying extraordinary courage" last summer when Ceepak, his wife, Rita, Samantha Starky, and I went swimming at our friend Becca's motel pool. In his swim trunks, I could see that Ceepak has a huge honking scar on the back of each of his legs—just below his butt cheeks.

"I took a few rounds," was all he said.

Then I went online, looked up his citation. It happened during the evacuation of casualties from a home in Mosul "under intense enemy fire." Although shot in the leg, "Lieutenant John Ceepak continued to engage the enemy while escorting wounded soldiers from the house."

When the last soldier leaving the house was nailed in the neck, Ceepak began performing CPR. That's when the "insurgents" shot him in the other leg, gave him his matching set of butt wounds.

Didn't stop him.

According to the official report, he kept working on the wounded man's chest with one hand while returning enemy fire with the other. He brought the guy back—even though he was "nearly incapacitated by his own loss of blood."

Yeah. The O'Malleys don't know how lucky they are John Ceepak was on roller coaster duty today.

3

WE'RE ALMOST TO THE STRANDED TRAIN.

A forest of wooden trestles and trusses rises around us: a maze of slashing horizontal, vertical, and diagonal pine lines.

"Ceepak!" It's Skippy. "Help!"

"Who's in cardiac arrest?" Ceepak asks as he crests the hill. I'm twenty paces behind him.

"My wife!" shouts Mr. O'Malley from the first car. "Help her!"

He struggles to right Mrs. O'Malley, who has slumped forward. Her long hair is dangling over the front panel of the coaster, blocking out half the Rolling Thunder lightning-bolt logo. Mrs. O'Malley's plump body is locked in place by the roller coaster safety bar.

Behind Mr. O'Malley, I see Skippy and his older brother, Kevin. In the second car, sister Mary and Sean—the youngest son. The fourth O'Malley boy, Peter, isn't in any of the cars. Skippy told me once that Peter is gay. His father and mother don't approve. Hell, they don't even invite him to roller coaster openings.

Behind Sean and Mary, I see my D.J. buddy Cliff Skeete, who sticks out like a sore thumb because, one, he's wearing big honking headphones and holding a microphone, and two, he's the only black dude on this ride. Next to Cliff is our mayor, Hugh Sinclair. Behind them: all sorts of big shots I didn't go to high school with.

"Quick!" Mr. O'Malley cries. "Help her. Do something!"

"I need to access her chest!" says Ceepak, hopping off the walkboard, landing on the track.

"Do it!" says Mr. O'Malley.

Ceepak braces his feet on the tie beam in front of the stalled coaster car.

"Help me lean her back," he says to Mr. O'Malley.

Mr. O'Malley, who is a big man with a ruddy face, grabs hold of his wife's shoulders and, with Ceepak's help, heaves her up into a seated position.

Now Ceepak props the mustard-yellow AED box in her lap. Lifts a wrist to check her pulse.

"She's not breathing!" screams Mr. O'Malley.

"No pulse," adds Ceepak, matter-of-factly. He tears open her blouse and slaps the two adhesive pads where they're supposed to go: negative pad on the right upper chest; positive electrode on the left, just below the pectoral muscle.

The AED will automatically determine Mrs. O'Malley's heart rhythm, and if she's in ventricular fibrillation—which means that even though there isn't a pulse, the heart is still receiving signals from the brain but they're so chaotic the muscle can't figure out how to bang out a steady beat—it'll shock the heart in an attempt to restore its rhythm to normal.

You work with Ceepak, you learn this stuff.

He switches on the machine.

"Clear!" he shouts.

Mr. O'Malley lets go of his wife's shoulders.

Ceepak pushes the "Analyze" button.

13

Waits.

If she's in v-fib, it'll tell him to shock her.

I glance over his shoulder, read the LED display.

No Shock.

That means Mrs. O'Malley not only has no pulse, she is not in a "shockable" v-fib rhythm.

"Initiating CPR," says Ceepak.

"You should step out of the car, Mr. O'Malley," I say, extending my hand. "We need to put your wife in a supine position."

He climbs out.

Ceepak finds the roller coaster's safety bar release and slams it open with his foot. All the bars in all the cars pop up. Now he can maneuver Mrs. O'Malley across the two seats so he can more easily administer CPR.

"Time me, Danny!"

"On it."

After one minute of CPR, he'll use the AED to reanalyze Mrs. O'Malley's cardiac status.

While he thumps on her chest, I glance at my watch and wonder why nobody in the roller coaster car started doing CPR while they waited for us to charge up the hill. Skippy should have known how to do it. We learned it when we were part-time cops. Well, we were supposed to. Maybe Skippy thought he could skate by without doing his homework.

"One minute!" I shout.

Ceepak goes to the AED machine. "No shock indicated. Time me!"

He pumps his fists on Mrs. O'Malley's chest again. She's a large woman. Very fleshy.

It's so eerily quiet up here on the wooden train track. Just the wet, flabby sound of Ceepak's fists pumping down on Mrs. O'Malley's chest. Nobody's talking. Hell, they're barely breathing. There's nothing up here but the wind whistling through the squared-off beams. They surround us like crosses on Calvary.

And then Cliff Skeete starts yammering into his microphone.

"This is the Skeeter with a live W-A-V-Y news update. Officers John Ceepak and Danny Boyle, two of Sea Haven's finest, are currently on the scene administering CPR to Mrs. O'Malley."

"Danny?" This from Ceepak who doesn't even look up from his chest compressions.

"Cliff?" I slice my hand across my neck, give my buddy the cut sign.

"And now back to more sizzling sounds of the Jersey shore. Southside Johnny and the Asbury Jukes. 'I Don't Want To Go Home.'"

I do. But I'm busy staring at my wrist, timing Ceepak's CPR. "One minute!"

Ceepak goes back to the yellow box. "Reanalyzing cardiac status."

He doesn't bother to report what the LED on the AED unit says.

He simply swings back to Mrs. O'Malley's chest, starts thumping it again. Off in the distance, I can hear the approaching whoop-whoop of a siren. The rescue squad ambulance. The whoop-whoop is shattered by the blast of an air horn. The fire department.

All the first responders are racing to the scene.

But it's too late.

Mrs. O'Malley's brain isn't sending signals of any kind to her heart any more. It isn't beating.

We ran up here as fast as we could.

But it took us too long to reach her.

Ceepak keeps pounding on Mrs. O'Malley's chest.

"Dammit," he mutters.

He has to keep administering CPR until the paramedics or a doctor shows up. Those are the rules.

But I can tell we're not winning any life-saving merit badges today.

4

A TEAM OF PARAMEDICS CLIMBS UP THE TELESCOPING LADDER off the back of a fire truck.

They administer some drugs to see if they can get Mrs. O'Malley's heart to quiver a little, stimulate some kind of shockable rhythm.

It doesn't work.

One of the guys takes over for Ceepak. The other one radios the hospital.

The doctor at the other end calls it.

Mrs. O'Malley is officially dead.

The paramedics climb back down the steep aluminum ladder to the fire engine below.

We don't want the civilians trying to do that, so Ceepak and I will stay up here with the stranded roller coaster train until it starts rolling again.

Why'd they throw the emergency brakes?

This is what I'm thinking as Mr. O'Malley, with Ceepak's assistance, slowly climbs back into the first roller coaster car so he can cradle his dead wife's head in his lap.

They should've let the damn train keep going till it reached the end of the line. It would've saved us five minutes.

It could've saved Mrs. O'Malley's life.

"Mommy's dead?" This from Mary O'Malley, squirming in the first row of the second car. She's the oldest of the five O'Malley children, maybe thirty-five, but she sounds like she's six.

I nod because I'm closer to her than Ceepak. "Yeah."

Believe it or not, Mary giggles.

"What are you gonna do now, Momma's Boy?" she leans forward to tease Skip in the car in front of hers.

Skip glares over his shoulder. Hard. I see tears in his eyes.

"She didn't want to ride this stupid ride! Kevin made her!"

"Shut up, Skippy," says big brother.

"She was afraid of roller coasters."

"I said shut up."

Skippy sniffles. Poor guy. He has a hard time hiding his emotions. Doesn't make you prime police cadet material, something I know Skippy still wanted to do, even though his summer as an auxiliary cop didn't end with a job offer. Friends tell me he signed up for one of the New Jersey police academies, paid his own tuition. I guess that didn't pan out, either. He never graduated. Still works at his dad's miniature golf course.

"Momma's Boy, Momma's Boy!"

"Okay, you guys," I say as I work my way up the walkboard. I need to be closer to Mary, who's rocking back and forth in her seat. A side effect of her meds, I'm guessing. "We should probably lower those safety bars."

"Good idea," says Mayor Hugh Sinclair, who's seated beside Cliff Skeete in the second row of car number two. They lower their safety bar. So does just about everybody else. I hear the crickety-clink-clicks all around me.

Except in Mary's row.

"What can I tell ya, Danny Boy?" says her snotty brother Sean seated beside her. "Me and Mare be lunchin', livin' on the edge." From six feet away, I can smell his breath. It reeks of booze. And it's ten o'clock in the morning.

"Lower your damn safety bar, Sean!" This from Kevin O'Malley. He's the oldest boy. Sean's the youngest.

"Yo, bizzle. Chill."

"Lower it!"

Meanwhile, up front, Mr. O'Malley is still sobbing and stroking his dead wife's hair.

"Officer?" Uh-oh. The mayor. Talking to me.

"Yes, sir?" I say.

"Is it possible for us to ride this thing down to the finish line? Now?"

"Hang tight," I say. "We're working on getting everybody down safely."

"For rizzle?" says Sean, who, I'm remembering, is a major-league butt wipe. "From over here it looks like you popos be doing shiznit." He pulls out his cell phone. Starts thumb-texting someone.

I turn to face Ceepak who has climbed off the track and is back up on the narrow-gauge walkboard.

"What's our play?" I ask.

And that's when I hear Mary stumble up and out of the roller coaster.

"Whoa!" says her drunken brother as their car rocks like a canoe.

"I'm a little birdy," says Mary, flapping her arms.

She's teetering on the walkboard. Three feet in front of me. Fifty feet above the pier below.

"Danny?" This from Ceepak. Behind me.

"Give me your hand, Mary."

"I'm a little birdy." More arm flaps.

"Mary?" Mr. O'Malley shouts. "Sit down! Now!"

"Sit," echoes Kevin.

She doesn't. She skips backward. Doesn't hold on to the handrail. She's too busy fluttering her arms up and down.

"Okay, Mary," I say with a smile. "Time to fly back to the nest."

We're about four cars up the coaster now. Everybody who isn't staring at crazy Mary is staring at me, the crazy cop about to plummet with her off a rickety track propped up by knotty pine chopsticks.

We clear the train completely. Keep climbing up the steep incline.

I glance over my shoulder.

Ceepak is maybe twenty yards away, now. He needs to stay with the others. Stop anybody else from going for a stroll. I glance down at the fire truck. Fortunately, they're not sending up the ladder again because it would probably just freak Mary out.

I'm on my own.

But maybe the fire guys have one of those trampoline-type nets from the circus to catch us when we fall.

"Careful!" I say because Mary is about to bang her head on a crossbeam because she'd have to turn around to see it.

She stops. Glares at me. I can see white flecks of dried spittle in the corners of her crooked smile. Her glasses are so thick they're magnifying lenses that turn her brown eyes into giant hamburger patties.

"I can fly!" She looks over the edge. We're way high up. Down below, there's nothing but a crazy crisscross of wood.

Mary grabs one of the chaser-lightbulbs that line the railing. Squeezes it. Crushes the glass globe like it's an eggshell.

She giggles when it shatters. I see blood in her palm.

She reaches for the next lightbulb down the line.

"Hey," I say, "remember Ken Erb?"

Mary tilts her head sideways like a sparrow contemplating sunflower seeds. "Ken Erb?"

"He always had those bird kites. Remember? He'd bring 'em to Oak Beach. You were there. I remember. With your brothers. Watching Ken fly his kites."

Mary smiles. "Pretty colors."

"Yeah. And the white dove. Remember the white dove? How about the eagle? Oh, man, the eagle was awesome!"

Mary nods.

"You wanna go see 'em? You wanna go see Ken's kites?"

Another nod.

"Okay. Here. Take hold of my hand."

She takes it. Smiles.

"We're going down to Oak Beach to see Ken's kites, okay?"

"Okay."

"But first we have to get back in the roller coaster."

"Can we get ice cream, too?"

"Sure." I grip her hand. It's sticky where it's bloody. "What's your favorite ice cream, Mary?"

"Chocolate. With sprinkles."

Now I'm the one walking backward. "Cool. I like sprinkles, too."

"Really?"

"Yeah."

"Jesus, you're a fucking pussy." Her voice is straight out of *The Exorcist*.

Okay. That caught me off guard. But Mary is still holding my hand, we're almost back to the roller coaster car, and neither one of us is dead.

She can call me anything she wants.

———

The controller at his computer console down in the operations trailer was able to manipulate the track brakes in such a way that he can safely roll the coaster down to the unloading shed.

It's like a funeral train now. Carrying the corpse of Mrs. Jackie O'Malley and twenty-nine mourners. Since there were no empty seats, Ceepak and I decide to walk down the tracks.

Okay, we could've climbed down that fifty-foot-long ladder to the fire truck, but I kind of voted against that option. I hate climbing a ladder to clean leaves out of a gutter.

"You handled that quite well, Danny," Ceepak says over his shoulder as we tiptoe down a hill on the walkboard.

"Thanks. I was scared."

"You didn't show it."

"Well, inside, I was freaking out."

"Me, too."

I laugh. "No way."

"Trust me," he says. "My adrenaline was pumping when Ms. O'Malley headed up that hill. I was afraid we might have two deaths to deal with this morning."

Wow. Who knew? The big guy is human. He just knows how to hide it.

By the time we make it down to the bottom, the medics are already zipping up Mrs. O'Malley's body bag.

A nurse of some sort—she's dressed in those cartoon cat-and-dog scrubs pediatric nurses wear so kids don't bawl their eyes out when they see a needle—is bracing Mary O'Malley by the elbow. Must be her full-time caregiver except for when Mary is asked to pose in happy family portraits for PR purposes.

"Well done, men," says Mayor Sinclair, striding over to me and Ceepak. "You two handled a very difficult situation extraordinarily well. I'll be sure to put in a good word with Chief Baines."

He winks. Ceepak nods.

The mayor folds a stick of gum into his mouth. "We'll close down the ride for a week. Have the grand reopening next weekend when all this is behind us."

He flips a hand toward the roller coaster cars.

By "all this" I guess he means Mrs. O'Malley dying.

"And," says the mayor, lowering his voice, "let's not talk to the media today. Fortunately, most of the folks in line were locals. This thing will blow over pretty quickly. Shouldn't impact our summer season."

The mayor smiles. Waiting for Ceepak and me to say, "Sir, yes, sir," or lick his boots or something.

We just stand there. Kind of grim-faced.

Somebody died this morning.

"Okay. Glad we had this chat." The mayor surveys the small crowd clustered near the exit ramp. "Cliff? Skeeter? Hey, buddy, got a second?"

He rushes over to the DJ, who twirls around and jabs a microphone in his face.

"Mayor Sinclair. You were up there with me on the roller coaster. How did it feel to be stranded like that?"

The mayor swats at the mic as if it were an annoying little gnat.

"Turn that goddamn thing off!"

Five seconds later, on the big outdoor speakers, I hear an echo of the mayor's words, only the "goddamn" is gone. Thank goodness for the five-second delay. Something Cliff and I could've used back in high school when we ran our DJ business and I dropped an F-bomb at a birthday party when an amplifier unexpectedly shocked me. It was the kid's sixth. We were supposed to be spinning discs so he and his buddies could dance the Hokey Pokey and play musical chairs. We had not been hired to give adult vocabulary lessons.

"We should head back to the house," says Ceepak. "Write this up."

He's right. There's no longer any need for crowd control. That long line? It's gone. The ride is shut down. Those kids wore high heels and duct-taped sandals to their shoes in vain.

We wait for the paramedics to carry Mrs. O'Malley's body down the exit ramp to the waiting ambulance. It looks like Mr. O'Malley will ride in the back with his wife.

I see Skippy take Mary's other elbow as he helps the nurse escort her to a parked SUV for the ride home.

"Don't worry—I'll handle things here," I hear Kevin O'Malley tell his dad as the paramedics close up the barn doors on the back of their vehicle.

Ceepak and I march down the exit ramp.

"Hola, babe!"

When we hit the boardwalk, we see Sean O'Malley swilling a beer out of a brown paper bag as a hot Hispanic chick in a skimpy black bikini sashays over to join him. Sean, who has the tightly bloated look of somebody who drinks beer for breakfast, tosses his empty can into a trash barrel and wraps his arm around his hot date so he can goose her booty.

"I got your text!" says the girl.

"Cool."

The girl swirls her tongue around inside Sean's ear.

He grins. Maybe belches.

Bikini Babe clutches Sean's shirt with two greedy hands. "Ding dong, the witch is dead," she purrs.

Sean's grin grows wider.

"Totally."

5

I'M FIGURING YOUNG SEAN O'MALLEY HAS MAJOR MOMMY ISSUES.

He and his date stroll across the boardwalk, hand on butt cheek instead of the more traditional hand in hand. They're heading for a Fried Everything stand. Fried Twinkies, Fried Snickers, Fried Oreos. I think they'll even batter and fry your flip-flops if you ask 'em to.

To my surprise, Ceepak is following the sashaying couple—and it's not because he enjoys watching bikini bottom grip-and-gropes.

"Excuse me? Mr. O'Malley? Miss?"

Sean and his hot date turn around. He's wearing a Donegal Tweed flat cap that he must think makes him look cool. I think it makes him look like a cab driver. Maybe a newspaper boy from 1932.

"Yo, po-po. What up?" says Sean.

"My name is Ceepak. Officer John Ceepak."

"I remember you, dude. From up on the roller coaster of death!"

"I'd like to have a word with you and your lady friend."

"'Bout what?"

"Disrespecting the dead."

"Huh?"

I jump in and help out: "Ding dong, the witch is dead?"

"Whoa. You dudes have us under surveillance or sumptin'?

"Mr. O'Malley," says Ceepak, "your mother just died."

He shrugs. Stuffs a cigarette in his mug. "So?"

His girlfriend shifts her weight to her left hip. "Yo—I'm the one who said it. You got some kind of issue with it, talk to me. Fo real. I'm serious."

Now she pouts. She has the lips for it: glossy, puffy ones.

Meanwhile, Ceepak's jaw joint is popping in and out under his ear. It does this from time to time, usually whenever he'd like to rip someone's head off. You see people die like Ceepak did over in Iraq, or like I've seen on the job, it does something to you. They aren't just bonus points on a game screen anymore.

"Ma'am," says Ceepak, "it might be best for all concerned if you were to refrain from making any more derogatory comments regarding Mrs. O'Malley in public."

Sean blows cigarette smoke out his nose holes like a cartoon bull.

"Why? Why can't she say that? Hell, I'll say it too. Ding dong, the witch is dead. How's that?"

"Great," I say. "Makes you sound like a total a–hole, Sean."

Ceepak cocks an eyebrow.

He does not, however, chastise me for my poor word choice while in uniform. If the a–hole fits . . .

"Aw-ite, Danny Boy, ease up, foo. Is it against the law for us to speak true?"

"Of course not," says Ceepak. "You are both well within your First Amendment rights to say anything, no matter how offensive I and others might find it. I am simply suggesting that, as a matter of respect, you both should exert some semblance of self-control."

"Then, let me school ya, Officer John Ceepak: my moms was one fat, cold-hearted witch. Hell, I'm surprised she could even have a heart attack because that would mean she had a heart instead of a chunk of black ice rattlin' around underneath all that whale blubber."

Sean, thinking he was just pretty damn clever, gives his cigarette a self-satisfied smack.

"She never did like me," says the girl with a head toss. "Didn't think I was the right kind of people for her boy, you know?"

"It's true," says Sean. "My mom did not dig Daisy—because she's from Puerto Rico and smokin' hot."

"Mrs. O'Malley?" says Daisy. "She was a racist. A bigot."

"Homophobic, too," adds Sean. Just ask my brother Peter, who was officially disinvited from this morning's festivities. How twisted is that?"

Daisy zips her manicured hand back and forth in a flying Z formation. "You think about that, officers, aw-ite? We done here. I'm hungry, Sean. You said you were gonna buy me a Snickers bar, baby."

"Yeah." Sean winks at us. "Laters, po-po. Laters."

They saunter up to the food stand.

I can hear a rush of bubbles popping around a candy bar recently dunked into a vat of boiling oil.

Or maybe that's Ceepak.

I know he tries to keep a lid on his rage at all times but sometimes he's a lot like that Springsteen song "The Promised Land": He just wants to explode.

We head back to the house, which is what we call police headquarters over in the municipal complex on Cherry Street.

All the east-west streets in Sea Haven are named after trees, even though, with all the sun and sand and salt water, we don't really have that many trees—just a few scrubby evergreens and rows of telephone poles that used to be trees in their youth.

"You think Sean had anything to do with his mother's death?" I ask Ceepak as our Crown Vic Police Interceptor cruises south on Ocean Avenue.

We just passed Pizza My Heart, one of at least three dozen Italian restaurants in Sea Haven. The parmigiana, manicotti, and fried calamari on their menus probably cause more heart attacks than all our boardwalk rides combined, but the menus don't come with any warning signs and there's no minimum height requirement; they'll even give the kids a booster seat.

"Is there some way Sean could've killed her and made her death look like a heart attack?"

"It's a possibility," says Ceepak. "However, we'll soon know if foul play is indicated. By New Jersey state law, the medical examiner is required to investigate all cases of human death that occur under suspicious or unusual circumstances."

I guess death by roller coaster is pretty unusual.

"If memory serves," Ceepak continues, "only four Americans die each year in roller coaster–related incidents."

"Heart attacks?"

"Often. The rides are designed to send heart rates soaring. In a recent study . . ."

Did I mention that Ceepak reads recent studies on just about everything? Last week, it was oysters and water pollution.

". . . German researchers noted that the heart rates of test participants climbed from ninety-one to one-fifty-three while riding a coaster with a maximum speed of seventy-five mph."

I nod and hope none of this is on the final.

"However, it wasn't the speed that caused irregular heart beats; it was the fear and stress of the ride."

"So Mrs. O'Malley scared herself to death?"

"She may have had a preexisting, undiagnosed heart condition. Perhaps high blood pressure. Or she may have been under some form of stress brought on by a life-altering event."

"Huh," I say. I guess Mrs. O'Malley could've been stressed about her daughter, Mary (who almost gave me a heart attack this morning), and her sons Sean and Peter. I think sons Kevin and Skip are pretty stress-free: hard-working, level-headed boys who don't drink Bacardi for breakfast, date San Juan hotties or, you know, other boys.

"Interestingly," says Professor Ceepak, "the 1994 earthquake in Los Angeles resulted in a four-fold increase in sudden deaths due to heart attacks. In 1991, when Iraq launched scud missiles at Israel, heart attacks doubled. A widow grieving the loss of her husband will see a fifty percent increase in her chances of sudden death due to a heart attack."

Stress. It's why I still surf, boogie board, and drink beer on a regular basis. It's all part of my heart-healthy lifestyle.

But I remember what Skippy said: his mother didn't want to ride the Rolling Thunder. She was afraid of roller coasters.

But Kevin probably convinced her she needed to be there for PR purposes, the same way political wives have to be there when their husbands call a press conference to confess that they've just had an affair with a hooker they met on the Appalachian Trail.

But what if Kevin O'Malley, for whatever reason, wanted to scare his mother to death?

Pretty easy way to get away with murder.

You don't need a gun or knife or poison or any kind of weapon at all.

You just need to build a big, honking roller coaster.

6

WE PULL INTO THE PARKING LOT BEHIND THE HOUSE.

There are about a dozen white cruisers (detailed in beachy turquoise and flamingo pink) angled into slots on the hot asphalt. The cop cars are flanked by assorted civilian cars, including my Jeep. Ceepak, on the other hand, rides his trail bike to work, lets his wife Rita have their one car, a dinged-up old Toyota.

The Sea Haven PD building looks like a sprawling split-level suburban home where the world's biggest ham radio operator lives. We have this huge antenna tower with all sorts of booms and masts angling off it—and still, our TV reception in the break room stinks.

When we hit the lobby, Chief Buzz Baines, who looks like a handsome TV anchorman back when they all used to have mustaches, is escorting a lumbering Italian bear through the gate in the wooden railing that separates the police from the public.

Bruno Mazzilli. The baron of the boardwalks. He now owns all four of the amusement piers jutting out into the ocean, including

Pier Four, which he purchased at a steal according to what Samantha Starky's mom told me. Mrs. Starky works in real estate. She knows who owns everything and how much they paid for it. Makes me nervous sometimes. Then again, I don't own anything except my Jeep, and I sort of share that with PNC Bank.

"Ceepak! Boyle!" The chief sees us. "Awesome work out there this morning, guys. Awesome."

"I only wish we had reached the roller coaster car sooner," says Ceepak.

"Hey," says Bruno Mazzilli, "your number's up, it's up, am I right?"

Ceepak does not answer.

Mazzilli turns to the chief. "So, you'll lean on the M.E.?"

The chief's mustache twitches. "I will ask Dr. Kurth to make her findings public ASAP."

"Good, good. That's all I'm askin'. Sooner people hear my partner's wife had a heart attack because, you know, she had a bum ticker or whatever, the sooner they know it wasn't our fault. We spent a fortune making sure Rolling Thunder is one hundred per-cent safe." He turns to us. "Thanks again, boys. You made the whole town look good, runnin' up the roller coaster like that and all. Makes tourists feel comfortable coming down here knowin' we got a world-class police operation. The roller coaster reopens next weekend. Let me know if you guys need free tickets. I'll fix you up with a stromboli, too."

Mmm. Stromboli. A rolled-dough sandwich stuffed with salami, provolone, pepperoni, peppers, garlic, and onions, then baked so the grease soaks into the crust. If you don't puke it up on the first hill of your roller coaster ride, you'll fart it out on the second.

"See you 'round, Buzz."

Mazzilli leaves.

"You guys hungry?" asks the chief, maybe picking up on that whole stromboli thread.

Truth be told, I'm starving. I skipped breakfast, figuring I might snag some fried chicken fingers rolled in Cap'n Crunch on the boardwalk. But then we had to run up a few scaffolded hills, instead.

Ceepak? The man could live on bran flakes, fruit, and power bars.

"Sam Starky brought in doughnuts," the chief adds.

Ceepak must see the starved-puppy look in my eyes.

"Doughnuts sound good," he says.

I shrug. Try to not drool.

Ceepak smiles. "After you, Danny."

I lead the way to the break room and I hear this playful little chuckle behind me.

Ceepak. I think me and my stomach amuse him.

"You guys were incredible! I heard the whole thing on the radio, and then Cliff dedicated that Springsteen song, 'Local Hero,' to you two, and I said to my friend Kim, 'I know those two guys, in fact, one's my boyfriend.' Here, Danny. This one is the Vanilla Kreme, the kind with the wedding cake white frosting you like in the middle, not the custardy yellow gunk you don't like because it reminds you of . . ."

She almost says snot because I think I said it on one of our Sunday-morning-after-Saturday-night Dunkin' Donuts runs. The Bavarian Kremes. Who wants to see that much mucus in the morning?

Sam bubbles on. "You want some coffee, Ceepak? This box is regular, this box is French vanilla."

Why do I think there was a third box of hazelnut that Starky has already guzzled? Then again, maybe not. Samantha Starky is a lot like a Colombian coffee bean: naturally caffeinated. She was a part-time summer cop last year, took a bunch of criminology classes at the nearby community college, then decided she'd rather be a district attorney than a police officer, so now she's cramming for her LSATs.

Her naturally percolated state? Very conducive to good grades.

"So, Danny, how's Skippy holding up?" she asks.

"Okay, I guess."

"He looked rather shaken," adds Ceepak. "I think he blames his brother Kevin for insisting their mother ride the roller coaster this morning. Apparently, she was somewhat reluctant to do so."

"Wow," says Sam. "The whole family must feel horrible."

No, I want to say, not the youngest son. He's all kinds of happy. And Peter. We haven't heard from him yet because he's gay and they wouldn't let him ride the ride.

"My mom heard that the funeral will probably be this Friday at Our Lady of the Seas. Poor Skippy." Sam has met Skip. On one of our dates, we played miniature golf at King Putt, the course he works at for his father. "I bet this is tearing him up."

"Yeah." I say. "He always gets kind of emotional."

Actually, Skippy cries a lot. Has ever since elementary school when he was the kid you'd see bawling his eyes out when he missed the ball in kickball.

I don't hang out with Skip O'Malley too much anymore, not since this one time at the Sand Bar when we were all sharing a couple of pitchers of draft and, as a joke, my buddy Jess played that Garth Brooks song on the jukebox, the one about lives left to chance and how he didn't want to miss the dance, and Skippy couldn't take it. The guy sobbed through a whole stack of paper napkins.

"He really wanted to be a cop," says Starky.

"Indeed," says Ceepak. "Unfortunately, if I'm honest, he did not display a genuine aptitude for the job."

He must be remembering busting Skippy's chops for yammering on his cell phone in the middle of Ocean Avenue a couple of summers ago when he was supposed to be directing traffic around a sewer excavation.

"Yeah," says Sam. "And then, of course, last fall he cheated."

"Come again?"

Okay. Sam's got Ceepak's interest. Mine, too.

"Oh, jeez. I thought you guys knew. And here I am, blabbing my big mouth. I shouldn't have said anything."

"Come on, Sam," I say. "What happened?"

"You promise you won't tell a soul?"

"Scout's honor," I say.

"You have my word," adds Ceepak.

"Well, you know he was in the Alternate Route Program, paid his own way to the Cape May County Police Academy. Anyway, they have this weekly exam every Friday, and I guess the teacher left the answer key on his lectern on Thursday, and Skippy copied it and even tried to sell the cheat sheet to this other guy who turned him in because, well, it's really not right to cheat on a test about important stuff like how to deal with death notices and what's the legal alcohol limit. I sure wouldn't want a brain surgeon who cheated on his anatomy exam and thought my brain was, I don't know, in my elbow or something."

Ceepak and I just sip our coffees and nod.

"Hey—you guys want to go out and celebrate your heroics tonight? You're not working tomorrow—I checked the duty roster. You both have the day off. We don't have to stay out too late."

"I can't," says Ceepak. "I promised T.J. I would watch some DVDs with him tonight. *In Harm's Way, The Caine Mutiny.*"

I nod.

Navy movies.

Ceepak's adopted son T.J. Lapczynski-Ceepak (yes, his name sounds like something you need an ointment to cure) is shipping off to Annapolis soon, made it into the United States Naval Academy. He's already cut off all his dreadlocks and is working on having a few tattoo sleeves erased from his arms.

"Well, we're not doing anything else tonight, are we, Danny? We could hit Big Kahuna's, Dance Club. They have this awesome band tonight. Steamed Broccoli."

We.

Over the winter and spring, without even realizing it, I gradually became part of a We, which is much more complicated than a Wii, the cool video game where you get to sprain your wrist playing tennis in your underwear.

Samantha Starky and I are a couple. I guess. We don't live together or anything, but we have passed the sixth-date mark and I now know that she stows her toothbrush in a souvenir Pocahontas glass from Burger King.

"Big Kahuna's sounds like fun," I say.

One of Ceepak's cell phones chirps on his utility belt.

He wears two: one for business, one for family.

"Hello?"

It's the family phone. When it's business, he answers, "This is Ceepak. Go."

He puts down his coffee cup.

"Are you injured? Okay. No. Stay there. We're on our way."

He snaps the clamshell shut.

"What's up?"

"Rita. Somebody crashed into her car in the parking lot of the Acme grocery store."

"She need us to write up the accident report?"

"Apparently, it wasn't an accident. Rita suspects the other driver rammed into her car on purpose."

7

"I WAS OVER THERE, PUTTING AWAY MY GROCERY CART."

Mrs. Ceepak points to the cart corral structure about twenty yards away from her Toyota. While she was off doing what any Ceepak would do (stowing an empty grocery cart in its proper parking spot as opposed to, say watching it roll downhill toward Ocean Avenue where it almost causes a wicked motorcycle wipeout), somebody else was banging into the rear end of her 1995 Toyota Corolla hatchback.

We're in the parking lot of the Acme, the biggest grocery store on the island. In the summer months, it's basically a giant Cookout Depot stocked with hamburgers, hot dogs, matching buns, marshmallows, chocolate bars, and graham crackers. You can buy potato chips in bags the size of pillows. Salsa or pickles in five-gallon drums.

Ceepak crouches down to inspect the damage.

The right rear bumper is kind of crumpled. The plastic

red-and-yellow brake light casing is cracked. There's a streak of red paint slashing across the fender.

"It was a red vehicle?" says Ceepak.

"Yes," says Rita. "A red pickup truck. An older Ford. It had Ohio license plates."

"And you say this wasn't an accident?"

"He rammed into our car on purpose, John. I saw him. He aimed his wheels at the bumper, then stepped on the gas and— boom! I'm just glad I wasn't in the car."

Rita rubs the back of her neck. Sympathetic whiplash.

"You saw that the driver was a man?" Even though Rita is his wife, Ceepak is giving her the same "just the facts, ma'am" treatment Joe Friday from *Dragnet* probably gave Mrs. Friday when he was off-camera.

"Yes. I think so. I didn't see a face, just a silhouette, but I'm confident the driver of the red truck was an old man with scraggly hair. Oh—he was a smoker, too. Had a cigarette stuck in his mouth the whole time he was lining up his shot."

"You make an excellent eyewitness, Mrs. Ceepak," my partner says, an uncharacteristic hint of playfulness in his voice.

"Why, thank you, Officer Ceepak. Nice of you to mention it."

The two of them are grinning like high school kids flirting over their Bunsen burners in chemistry class.

Mrs. Ceepak is in her early thirties, a little younger than her husband. Her hair is blond and slightly old-fashioned in the styling department because, I think, if she ever had fifty bucks, she'd rather give it to one of her favorite charities instead of the Shore to Please Hair Salon. Her face is Jersey fresh with gentle eyes— though the crow's-foot corners hint at the wear and tear from the fourteen years she spent working two jobs to raise her only son on her own.

Their playful grins quickly fade as they go back to surveying the new damage to their seriously dented car.

"Are you sure you're all right?" Ceepak asks.

"Fine," Rita sighs. "Just a little, you know, shaken up. Who would want to kamikaze into Silverado?"

I'm guessing the Ceepak's give their vehicles names. People do that, I'm told. I, on the other hand, call my Jeep "my Jeep."

"Perhaps a tourist from Ohio who wanted your parking spot?"

"I don't think so. The spot next to me, the one closer to the store, was wide open. I think this was somebody who wanted to hurt us."

Ceepak nods.

Unfortunately, sticking to his code, not tolerating lying, cheating, and/or stealing has earned my partner a few enemies. Locals and Bennies—Benny being a derogatory Jersey shore term for tourists. Why? I don't know. Some say it stands for Bayonne, Elizabeth, Newark, and West New York, all towns north of here.

We take some digital photographs of the damage and write up the incident as a "leaving the scene of an accident."

"That's a violation of N.J.S.A. 39:4–129," says Sam Starky when I pick her up around nine for our date at Big Kahuna's Dance Club.

"If you're convicted, your driver's license will be suspended—that's mandatory for the first offense. Of course, the state has to show that the driver was knowingly involved in the accident. 'Knowingly' means that the driver was actually aware that he was involved in an accident, or that, given the circumstances, he reasonably should have been aware that an accident had occurred."

Sam, my future D.A., finally takes a second to breathe, so I jump in edgewise: "Wow. I'm impressed."

"Well, I want to practice law in the State of New Jersey. Stick close to home and the people I love."

"Yeah," I say as we pull into Big Kahuna's parking lot, avoiding saying the "L" word myself. Sam seems to toss it out with reckless abandon. Me? Well, let's just say I'm not completely over the whole Katie deal.

Multicolored light ropes outline the nightclub's long roof. The parking lot is edged by fake palm trees and old surfboards stuck in the sand where other places might have flowerbeds.

We head up the ramp and join the line of tanned beach babes and their lucky dates. I feel like I'm at a cleavage convention.

"Danny?"

I turn around.

It's Gail, a drop-dead gorgeous girl who works at The Rusty Scupper, this grease pit over near the public marina where the waitress in her bathing suit is much more appealing than anything that crawls out of the kitchen on a plate.

I remember that Gail was the girl Skippy O'Malley was dating back when he was a part-time cop. Tonight, however, she's flying solo, traveling with her girl posse—six other incredibly beautiful women, none over the age of twenty-seven, all in party dresses that show off their cocoa butter tans, belly button jewelry, and what I'd either call their large, prominently supported breasts or their double lattes.

"Are you alone?" Gail asks, even though I'm standing next to Sam. Gail Baker has always been a few fries short of a Happy Meal.

"This is my friend, Sam. Samantha Starky."

"Hi!" says Sam.

We all shuffle a few feet closer to the doormen checking IDs. The smell of Axe body spray and Calvin Klein's Obsession wafts through the air. "So, how about you? Seeing anybody"

"Not tonight. Tonight is girls' night! My treat!"

Her six friends give up a wild chorus of whoo-hoos.

"You're treating?"

"Yunh-huh!"

"Tips must've been amazing at the Scupper this week!"

"Something like that! Catch you later, Danny Boy!"

We all fish out our entrance fees, get hand-stamped and wrist-banded by the thick-necked bouncer, Phil Lee (an old friend of mine from when I worked at the Pancake Palace). Some of the girls in Gail's crew have to show Phil their driver's licenses, and he takes his time studying them, matching photos with faces. He uses a little flashlight that lingers at the halfway point on the way down from the face to the ID, if you catch my drift.

The band, Steamed Broccoli, is extremely loud.

"You want a drink?" I shout at Sam when it's our turn to move beyond the bouncer station and wade through the mob flooding the barn-size dance floor. The joint is jumping, as they say. Some of the dancers, too.

"Sure!"

We head over to the main bar, which is set up like a horseshoe with maybe twenty stools, even though very few horseshoes have stools. I can see Gail and her girlfriends wiggle-walking across the dance floor, stealing glances from guys contemplating how to dump their current dates so they can head over to Gail Country. The seven hottest beach babes God ever created (well, that's what their bouncing booties say as they strut across the crowded room) find a cluster of round tables close to the bandstand.

"Goo bam," Sam says. I think.

"Huh?" I say just to be sure.

"Good band."

I nod. In here, speech, like resistance when dealing with the Borg on *Star Trek*, is futile.

Sam and I each order a bottle of Bud from the bartender, who happens to be another bud of mine, named, well, Bud.

"What's the maximum capacity of this room?" asks Sam, who, much like Ceepak, memorizes fire codes in her spare time.

I shrug. "Probably however many people are jammed in here right now."

Purple and pink lights flash on dancers waving their hands high above their heads. You can't really tell who's dancing with whom. It's one big wiggly, sweaty, writhing mass of barely clothed humanity. The guy in the light booth is switching colored lights in time to the beat, shooting spotlights at the disco balls left over from twenty summers ago.

And in waltzes Bruno Mazzilli, the baron of the boardwalk, looking like the cheesy fifty-year-old uncle crashing his niece's Sweet Sixteen party down in the rumpus room so he can scope out all the hot young bods. On his arm, if I'm not mistaken, is another friend of mine from high school—Marny Minsky. She's hard to miss. Has a head of sproingy blonde curls. Looks like she's smuggling rugby balls under her blouse.

The last time I saw Marny, she was crawling out of a wreck wearing some kind of Victoria's Secret swimsuit and stiletto-heel sandals. The minivan she'd been riding in had crashed into a rack full of rental bikes because the married guy who'd been plying her with champagne didn't want Ceepak and me to catch him cheating on his wife in the family soccermobile.

Marny looks young enough to be Bruno Mazzilli's daughter. I say this because Toni, one of Bruno's daughters, went to high school with Marny and me.

"Hey, Gail!" I can hear Marny shout—only because Steamed Broccoli just announced they're going to take a short break.

"Hey!" Gail shouts back.

"You go, girl!" Marny raises a plastic cup of something pink.

Gail and her gaggle of girlfriends all raise their plastic cups and give Marny another chorus of "whoo-hoos" (all the cups in our seaside bars are made out of plastic because you really don't want any of these inebriated people handling glass).

Mr. Mazzilli and Marny go over to Gail's table. The two bend and hug and air kiss. Mazzilli smiles. He admires the view. Both girls are in dive-suit-tight skirts that barely cover their butts.

Now Mazzilli whispers something to Marny, who giggles and whispers to Gail, who laughs and shakes her head.

"Come on," booms Bruno. "Live a little!"

"Not tonight."

"Okay. But we want a rain check!"

Mazzilli and Marny head off toward smoky glass doors labeled VIP, probably so they can canoodle in the dark.

"Bitch stood me up," the guy to my right mumbles. I notice he looks like a thirty-year-old nerd, only with big arm muscles bulging out of his shiny silk tee.

"Easy, Marvin," says Bud.

"Bitch. She owes me."

Bud swipes at the counter with his towel. "Really? For what?"

"I did her root canal," says Marvin. "For free."

"Free?"

"Well, I only took what her insurance paid."

Bud chuckles. "And of course you told the insurance company it was like two or three root canals, right?"

"So? I can't believe it, man. She told me she couldn't hang tonight because her grandmother was sick."

"Yeah," says Bud the bartender. "She used that one on me once, too. That's when you know it's over."

"It's true," I butt in because, well, it's happened to me, too. "When they invoke the sick grandmother, you're history."

"I usually says it's my little brother who's sick," adds Starky. "Either way, Danny's right. You need to move on, sir."

The nerdy guy, Marvin the dentist, gives us all this huffy "who asked any of you" look, slams a twenty on the bar, swivels off his stool, and stomps away.

"Was it something we said?" I joke to Bud.

"Probably." The bartender shakes his head. "Poor man. Gail Baker messed with his mind. Big time."

41

Bud thumps up a metal cooler lid and scoops up a jug full of ice cubes to make somebody a fruity colada.

"Hey, Joe," he hollers to a busboy who just backed in behind the bar with a fresh keg of beer on a handcart. "We need more ice."

"Sure, no problem," says busboy Joe as he turns around.

Only he's not a boy—more like a geezer. Craggy face, white stubble, stringy hair sticking up in wild clumps like he just came in from hurricane.

He looks exactly like he looked the last time I saw him.

Joe Ceepak.

My partner's asshole father.

8

I THOUGHT JOE CEEPAK WAS SUPPOSED TO BE IN JAIL UP IN OHIO.

Ohio.

The license plates on the red pickup that creamed Rita's rear bumper.

"What are you doing here?" I blurt out.

Mr. Ceepak glares at me. "Workin'."

He hunkers down to fiddle with some tubes and valves, hooks up the aluminum keg to the taps. Mr. Ceepak is, from my experience, a genius on anything related to beer. When I first met him, he told me his friends called him Joe Sixpack instead of Ceepak.

"So, how'd you get out of jail?" I ask it real loudly because, like I said, the man is a skeevey creep.

Mr. Ceepak stands up from the beer barrel and vise-grips the edge of the bar with both hands. He's squeezing so hard, the tendons rope up and down his arms. "I did my time, Officer Boyle," he says, biting back the bile he'd probably like to spew at me if it wouldn't cost him his crappy job. "I did my time."

"But sir," asks Sam, "do the terms of what I imagine to be your early release allow you to leave the state of Ohio for an extended period of time?"

He glares at Starky. "I gotta go get ice. How much you say you need, Bud?"

Bud stands frozen behind the bar like a human daiquiri.

"Huh?"

"Ice?"

"Oh. Bucket or two."

"Roger that," says Mr. Ceepak, simultaneously mimicking and mocking his son. "I'm on it."

He wheels the handcart down the back of the bar.

"Hey, Mr. Ceepak?" I call out.

He keeps moving.

"You driving a red pickup truck these days?"

He doesn't answer.

"You do your grocery shopping over at the Acme?"

Still no response. He lifts up the bar pass-through and heads off to the kitchen.

"Jeez-o man," I say to Bud, "you guys hired that scumbag?"

Bud holds up his hands. "Hey, wasn't my call, Danny Boy. I just work here"

"He did time, Bud. For murder. Well, they dealed him down to manslaughter."

"No way."

"Way," says Starky, who knows all about Mr. Ceepak and his monstrously heinous past.

"What can I tell you guys?" Bud starts wiping out beer mugs. "Mr. Johnson has a soft spot for ex-cons."

"Because they work cheap?" I say.

"Exactly."

Mr. Johnson is Keith Barent Johnson, another proud member of the Sea Haven Chamber of Commerce. He owns a slew of motels, rental homes, and Big Kahuna's Dance Club. I think Kahuna was his nickname in college.

I stand up. Slap enough cash on the bar to cover our tab. Stuff a few bills into Bud's tip cup.

"Come on, Sam."

Sam pops up off her stool. Neither one of us wants to be breathing the same air-conditioned air with old man Ceepak.

We head around to the rear of the building where the Big Kahuna staff park their cars.

I see Keith Barent Johnson's Cadillac. Hard to miss, what with the KBJ vanity license plates done up on New Jersey's "Shore to Please" specialty tags. I recognize Bud's Harley. And there, down by the Dumpster, is a 1980-something red Ford pickup truck.

"Bastard," I mumble, touching the streak of silver paint Old Man Ceepak scraped off his daughter-in-law's ride.

My partner, the good Ceepak, would probably secure a sample of this silver paint, take it the lab, and run it through a Fourier Transform Infrared Spectrometer like they do on that TV show, *Sherwin-Williams, CSI*. He'd compare it against the thousands of automotive paints in the computer data banks and match it to the paint on his Toyota.

Me? I go with my gut.

The jerk did it. He rammed into Rita's car on purpose. That's just how Joe Sixpack rolls.

I hear a door squeak open on the nightclub's loading dock.

I swear this place used to be a warehouse.

Joe Ceepak comes out dragging a black trash bag from the kitchen. It's leaking a stream of garbage juice as he lugs it down a short flight of steps. A sloshy mixture of Corona lime hulls, half-chewed ribs, smooshed baked potatoes, stale beer, and anything else on the menu folks didn't want to take home in a Styrofoam box.

"You messing with my wheels, Boyle?" he says when he reaches the Dumpster next to his truck. "You scratch it, I'll cut your nuts off with a blunt butter knife."

Now he eyeballs Samantha, who smoothes out her miniskirt in a futile attempt to make it magically cover her knees.

"So, who's your friend?"

Yep. He's his old nasty self.

I step between him and Sam.

"Earlier today, Mr. Ceepak, you left the scene of an accident," I say. "That's a violation of N.J.S.A. 39:4–129."

"What?"

"You broke the law. Look it up."

"You can't prove shit, smartass."

"Really? Watch us."

"Us? You still working with my retarded son?"

"Yes, sir. You still a pain in everybody's ass?"

He tosses up both hands. Grins. "It's what I do best, Boyle."

"So where are you staying while pursuing your new career in the exciting field of nightclub custodial sciences?" I gesture toward his leaky sack of garbage.

"Here and there, Boyle. Here and there."

"Could you be a little more specific, sir? We might need an address to put on your arrest warrant."

He rumbles up a phlegmy laugh. Grabs hold of the neck of his lumpy plastic bag. Starts to hoist it up off the asphalt.

"I gotta go back to work. Just tell Johnny I need to know where his mother's hiding." He tries to peer around me at Sam. "She let you diddle with those big ol' titties, Boyle?"

I channel my inner John Ceepak and refuse to rise to his bait.

Well, not completely.

"Fuck you, asswipe."

Mr. Ceepak finishes hoisting his fifty-pound sack of rancid garbage off the asphalt. Slings it sideways to heave it into the Dumpster.

The bag drizzles on me and Sam on its way up.

Mr. Ceepak lets rip with a rib-rattling laugh. "Guess she don't smell so sweet now, does she, Boyle? But, hell, I'd still fuck her. How about you?"

I step forward to deck him.

Sam grabs me by the back of my belt.

"He's not worth it," she whispers.

Yeah. That's what Ceepak would say, too. The real Ceepak. The one who's my friend.

"See you 'round, Danny Boy. Tell Johnny I'll be callin' on him. Can't wait to meet my goddamn daughter-in-law and her bastard son. See what kind of ass Johnny's old lady has on her."

I run Sam back to her place.

Date night is officially over.

"Thanks, Danny," Sam says when I walk her to her door.

"No problem."

"I'm sorry we're not . . ."

"Don't worry about it, okay?"

She touches her hair. It's sticky. "I smell like sour milk mixed with rancid vinegar and moldy cabbage."

"Yeah. It's the recipe for Big Kahuna's secret sauce."

She smiles.

"Good night, Danny. I really do love you."

There she goes again with the "L" word. I hear it but don't knee-jerk it back.

Then she kisses me. Big mistake. Our slimed lips taste worse than they smell.

9

FIRST THING SUNDAY MORNING, I'M AT BEACH BODS GYM,
because I know that's where Ceepak will be.

Since becoming a full-time cop, I've actually joined Beach Bods
and hit the gym whenever I can. At least once or twice a month.
Sometimes. If, you know, there's nothing good on TV. Or it's
raining.

Beach Bods is tucked into a strip mall on Ocean Avenue at Yel-
lowtail Street, where its neighbors are Teeny's Bikini's, the Paradise
Nail Spa (where nails go to get a facial or take a sauna, I guess),
Chunky's Cheese Steaks, Beachcomber Hair Salon, and The
Octopus's Garden florist shop.

I usually hit Chunky's after the gym. Figure I've earned it. I've
yet to sign up for the gym's "Holistic Health and Nutrition Class."
I'm not a big bok choy boy.

I pull into the parking lot. I can see people in gym clothes
jumping up and down on the other side of the plate glass windows.

Must be an aerobics class. I wouldn't know. Never took one. Ceepak comes out the front doors, toting his gym bag. His muscles look more pumped than usual because I guess they are.

"Hey!" I say.

"Good morning, Danny. Didn't expect to see you here so bright and early on a Sunday."

"Yeah. Me neither. Something's come up."

Ceepak cocks an eyebrow. He's all ears.

"It's your dad. He's back in town. I don't know how he got out of jail so early."

"Time off for good behavior, no doubt," Ceepak says as sarcastically as he can. "I understand the State of Ohio recently passed a Prison Reform Bill. Something to do with budget problems."

"He's working at Big Kahuna's."

"The nightclub?"

"Yeah. Sam and I saw him last night. Then we went out back to check out his car. Well, his truck. His *red* Ford pickup truck."

Ceepak whips the cell phone out of his civilian cargo shorts, which look a lot like his uniform cargo shorts only they're khaki instead of dark blue. He thumbs a speed dial number.

"Rita? John. As anticipated, my father has resurfaced. Here. In Sea Haven. Right. Danny did the leg work on this one." He covers the mouthpiece. "Rita says, 'Way to go, Danny Boy.'"

I blush.

"Honey?" Ceepak says this to the phone, not me. "Stay alert. It seems it was my father's truck that slammed into our Toyota yesterday. Danny and Samantha figured that out last night as well."

He covers the mouthpiece again.

I quickly say, "Tell her thanks."

He nods. "Danny says, 'Thanks.' Right. Indeed. He is rapidly growing into an excellent young detective."

I work my toe into the asphalt in the classic aw-shucks-'tweren't-nothin' move.

"I'm on my way home," says Ceepak. I notice his bicycle chained to a rack on the sidewalk in front of the gym. "No. We should stick to our plans. I refuse to give my father the satisfaction of thinking he can upset us or our routine. Roger that. Will do. Don't worry. It's all good."

Well, not really.

His father is an asshole. No way can that be considered remotely good.

"Love you, too."

Wow. Ceepak's saying it in public. Then again, he's married.

He closes the phone.

"Rita would like to invite you and Samantha to join us this afternoon for a round of miniature golf."

"I think Sam has to study."

"Commendable. T.J. as well."

"You guys sure you want me tagging along?"

"Certainly."

"Cool."

"For the golf. Not dinner afterwards."

I smile. "Where you taking her?"

"Stefano's."

"Really? Very romantic."

"So I have been told."

"By Rita?"

He nods. "Repeatedly."

"So, where do you guys want to play? Congo Falls? Dinosaur Gulch?"

"We thought we'd hit King Putt. That way, we could express our condolences to any members of the O'Malley family who might be working and share the news from the medical examiner."

"We got the preliminary report?"

"Roger that. As we initially suspected, Mrs. O'Malley died from a heart attack."

"Did the M.E. find anything, you know, hinky?"

"Negative. Dr. Kurth hypothesizes that Mrs. O'Malley had some sort of undiagnosed heart disease, perhaps an abnormal rhythm or a blockage in her coronary arteries, and her rising heart rate, brought on by the stress of the roller coaster ride, and its coincident inducement of a fight-or-flight rush of adrenaline, caused her myocardial infarction."

In other words, she scared herself to death because she had a bum ticker to begin with.

"It'd be good to see Skippy," I say. "I'm sure he'll be there. His dad makes him work Sunday to Sunday during the summer. Won't give him a day off. I hope he can go to his mom's funeral on Friday."

"I feel certain Mr. O'Malley will want all his children there."

And that's when another one of the O'Malley boys walks up the sidewalk.

He's with a friend.

A guy friend.

It's Peter O'Malley. The gay sheep of the family.

10

"HEY, PETER? PETER O'MALLEY?"

He stops. Sighs. Gives me this look. "Yes?"

"I'm Danny Boyle, friend of your brother."

"Which one? I am blessed with so many."

"Skip."

"Congratulations."

His friend—this macho, macho man with a shaved head, handlebar mustache, wearing a sleeveless leather vest—smirks at me. I peg Peter to be a year or two younger than Skippy. His mustachioed friend? Hard to tell. He has that ageless bad boy biker look.

"Now, if you'll excuse me," says Peter, "we want to take a body sculpt class."

"You have our condolences on your loss," says Ceepak, tucking his bike helmet under his arm.

"Yes," says Peter, "it's a very unfortunate turn of events. So many people wanted to wring my mother's neck. Now they'll never get the chance."

Biker Boy snickers. Jostles his hip to the left, which sends the chain attached to his wallet swinging.

"I take it you had issues with your mother?" Ceepak says to Peter.

"No, officer—she had issues with me."

"Come on, Peter," says his leather-loving friend. "Class is starting. You want to look buff in your funeral suit, don't you?"

They hold hands and head for the door.

"Maybe we could kiss in front of her coffin," says Peter, "give mommy dearest another heart attack!"

The glass doors whoosh shut behind them.

"Interesting," says Ceepak.

"Yeah," I say, as I watch Peter and his leathery friend through the plate glass windows. "So far, we're two for two."

"Indeed. The two O'Malley children we have spoken to both seem happy that their mother is dead."

"You sure about the M.E.'s report? Maybe Peter or Sean poisoned Mrs. O'Malley, gave her a drug that just made it look like she had a heart attack."

"Doubtful," says Ceepak. "And, as you recall, Peter was nowhere near the roller coaster yesterday morning."

"True. But maybe he used some kind of slow-acting poison that mimics a heart attack."

Ceepak gives me his double-eyebrows-up, extremely skeptical look. "Are you suggesting that, some time prior to ten A.M., Peter O'Malley administered a lethal dose of a drug perfectly timed to kill his mother during the inaugural run of the Rolling Thunder roller coaster?"

"Well, what if it was time-release, slow-acting, heart-attack-mimicking poison?"

Hey, if I'm going to stretch logic, I might as well stretch it till it snaps.

"Then, Danny, we should've asked the M.E. to do a tox screen for such a poison. As you know, tests for specific toxins must be requested or they won't be done. As a sidebar—I know of no known poison with all the properties you suggest it might possess."

"I guess I just don't like all these O'Malley's saying bad things about their dead mother."

"Danny?"

"Yeah?"

"I suspect they were saying these things long before she died."

Ceepak straps on his helmet, hops on his eighteen-speed bike, and heads for home.

I'm supposed to meet him and Rita at King Putt at three P.M.

Figures Ceepak would schedule an outdoor activity involving physical exertion for the hottest part of the day.

I decide to head into the gym. Hey, I paid my monthly membership fee so I figure I should step inside Beach Bods at least once during the month of May, which is almost over.

I show the girl behind the front desk my I.D. card.

"Are you interested in Chi Gung Yoga or the Total Body Sculpt class that just started?"

"Nah," I say. "I just thought I'd lift a few weights. Grunt a little."

She hands me a towel. "Enjoy your workout."

Yeah. Right. Like that's going to happen. I enjoy a cold beer. A hot slice of pizza. I do not enjoy voluntary artificial exertion.

I head over to the dumbbells and grab a pair of ten-pound weights to do a few bicep curls in front of the mirrored wall. I figure I could save my gym fees by going back to the Acme and lifting a few ten-pound sacks of sugar. Work my way up to the pet food aisle and those fifty-pound bags of kibble.

Behind me, in the mirror, I see Gail Baker over on a blue rubber mat where some people do stretches and stuff. She's wearing what looks like black Spandex underwear: a sports bra and sporty short shorts.

One of the Beach Bods trainers, a guy with a chin dimple goatee and Tibetan tattoo sleeves on both arms, has one hand on the small of Gail's back, the other on her extremely taut stomach, to coach her through a series of deep knee bends.

I stroll across the gym floor and pretend like I'm interested in the Smith machine, this piece of equipment that has a barbell fixed inside steel rails so you can slide the weights up and down to do your squats or bench presses without dropping everything on your head. I load it up with two twenty-pound disks so I can be closer to Gail.

You gaze at her incredible body, you want to look better naked.

While I'm slipping the weights onto the bar, I hear Gail tell her trainer, "Anyway, I can't slack off. Need to keep looking good."

"Then we'll work extra hard today."

"Thanks, Mike."

She does a few forward lunges.

Mike steps back, admires her form.

"Hey," he says, as Gail switches lunge legs, "if you're free this week, we should hang out."

"Maybe," says Gail. "Sounds like fun."

She stands up. Mike moves in and massages the top of her shoulders.

"I'd stretch you out afterwards. Give you a deep-tissue massage."

Gail laughs.

"So, when can we, you know, hook up?"

Gail does a flirty sideways twist so her breasts brush against muscle man's biceps.

"Like I said, I'm free any night or day this week. After that, I'm fully committed till July."

"Let me check my book. See if I can fit you in. Okay, on your back. Time for crunches."

I can just imagine these two having sex. Probably do three sets of ten reps. Probably have mirrors on the ceiling and all the walls. Probably wouldn't sell me a video of it.

I put in a good half hour. Okay, twenty minutes.

I do some lat pull-downs, seated rows, hamstring curls, and assisted chin-ups on this machine where you can set a counter-weight so you're only pulling up about twenty pounds of body weight but it looks like you're doing a manly-man chin-up, something I could never do in P.E. class, something Ceepak does whenever he has some spare time and sees a convenient hori-zontal bar.

Then, to work on my abs, I sit on one of those Swedish balls and try not to roll off it.

I'm toweling off some sweat when I see the dentist from the bar at Big Kahuna's swing open the front doors. He marches to the desk. Flashes the check-in girl his card.

She scans it. Scans it again.

"I'm sorry," she says. "It's being rejected."

"What?" The dentist strains to look over the desk and see what bad things the computer monitor is saying about him. "Look up Hausler. Dr. Marvin Hausler."

Computer keys clack.

"You haven't paid your dues in two months."

"What?" Now he reaches over, grabs the monitor and tries to swivel it around, only it's not on a lazy Susan type deal so it only budges an inch or two. "Let me see that."

I toss my towel in the wicker laundry basket and amble toward the counter.

My cop sense tells me we're about to have an incident.

"I really can't let you see the computer screen—"

"This is fucking unbelievable," fumes Hausler. "I come here every weekend."

"They updated the membership rolls late last night, told us to double-check everybody's cards today—"

"This is total fucking bullshit. I paid my fucking dues."

"If you'd like to put the charge on a credit card—"

"What? So you can double-bill me? Fucking forget it!"

I'm about to butt in when Gail comes out of the women's locker room in her street clothes, which, by the way, are just about as skimpy as her gym clothes. Up top she has on this tight little yellow-and-red Sugar Babies tee—looks like the vintage logo from a bag of Sugar Babies. I swear she bought it at a store for newborns, it's that small.

"Hey, Marvin," she says.

The dentist backs away from the counter. Stops acting like a spoiled brat.

"Hey," he says, his voice all silky and deep. Maybe he studies Luther Vandross CDs. "How's it going?"

"Great."

"Missed you last night."

"What?"

"The date we didn't have. How's your grandmother?"

"Huh? Oh—better. Thanks!"

"Good. Glad to hear it. Hey, I got Leno tickets for down in AC. Interested?" Dr. Marv is leaning one cocked arm against the counter now, putting on his suave 'n smooth moves.

"I don't know."

"We could take your grandmother with us. If she gets sick again, I could write her a prescription."

"That's sweet."

"Hey—I just want to be close to you."

I can't believe this. Dr. Marvin Hausler, DDS—whose face reminds me of the glasses-wearing chimp you'd see on a monkey calendar—is using recycled Carpenters' lyrics from 1971 to hit on Gail Baker? What do they teach these guys at dental school?

"I told you, Marv—I can't. Not anymore. Not right now."

"Why not?"

"Because, okay?"

"Because why?"

The dude sounds like he's two years old.

"Anyway," says Gail, flashing her dazzling white smile, which, I guess, Dr. Hausler had something to do with, "thanks for the invite. Have a great workout!"

Gail bounces out the door like a jiggling pack of Sugar Babies with only two candies left in the bag.

"Whoa. Wait up, Gail . . ."

Dr. Hausler storms off after her. Maybe he wants to give her a few flossing tips.

I turn toward the floor-to-ceiling windows and watch their sidewalk scene play out.

Gail, of course, keeps her cool. Keeps on smiling and looking hot as hell.

Dr. Hausler, on the other hand, is fuming. Waving his arms up and down like a sixth grader throwing a temper tantrum when he finds out his gorgeous teacher won't even consider dating him because, well, he's a kid and she isn't.

Rabid spittle is flying out of his mouth now.

I wonder why guys do this.

Do they really think girls will hop in the sack with them if they act like screaming meemies? That they'll suddenly say, *"You know, I find your loud threats and obnoxious antics strangely attractive. Let's go have sex."*

Ain't gonna happen.

Gail leans in and gives the dentist a quick peck on the cheek.

"Thank you," she says, I think. I need to take a class in lipreading.

"Fuck you," says Marvin—his lips are much easier to read. Especially because he keeps repeating himself: "Fuck you!" This time he adds "Bitch!"

Then he storms off to his sports car.

Gail bops up the sidewalk. I figure she has an appointment at that nail spa. Probably needs to get the white tips repainted so they keep looking good against her golden-brown tan.

Me?

I need to hit Chunky's Cheese Steaks.

I earned it.

"So long," I say to the girl behind the front desk, who's on her cell phone.

She waves so she doesn't have to interrupt her phone call.

"I know," she says to whoever she's chatting with, "the guy is, like, such a total jerk. No way would I ever let him drill me."

I smile.

A dirty mind is an eternal picnic.

A little before three, having taken Samantha a Chunky's Cheese Steak to help her plow through her law books, I head up Ocean Avenue to King Putt Mini Golf.

You can see the T-shaped pylon sign topped with a bright orange ball from half a mile away. At the base of the pole stands the Bob's Big Boy of Ancient Egyptian Golf: a six-foot-tall resin cartoon of the chubby Boy King himself. Instead of the classic staff of Ra, Tut totes a putting iron.

The miniature golf course itself is actually pretty awesome. Mr. O'Malley spent about a million bucks landscaping its curving hills, water hazards, "Sahara Desert" sand traps, fake palm trees, and carpeted putting greens. You can arc your ball over a sleeping camel's humps, try to shoot it through the Sphinx's legs, or see if you can jump it all the way across the bright blue (like Sno-Cone syrup) River Nile, which, in some spots, is two feet wide.

I pull into the parking lot. It's decorated with hieroglyphics on lampposts to help you remember where you parked. I see

Ceepak's silver Toyota over in the Owl section, so I look for a spot close by.

There are none.

They're all taken.

Including the slot right next to ol' dinged-up Silverado.

That's where Mr. Joseph "Sixpack" Ceepak has parked his red pickup truck.

11

I RACE ACROSS THE ASPHALT TO THE KING PUTT OFFICE—
this pink stucco building shaped like one of the pyramids: you get
your balls and putters in the base; the O'Malleys keep the books
and computers up in the peak.

A couple of kids, tears streaking down their cheeks, come running
out of the office, screaming, "Mommy! Daddy! Mommy! Daddy!"

I see parents near a minivan.

"Sea Haven Police," I say, even though I'm wearing baggy
shorts, sandals, and a Hawaiian shirt. "Please stay in the parking lot.
We have a situation inside."

Hey, if Mr. Ceepak is in there, we probably do.

When I enter the office, the first thing I see is Skippy O'Malley
behind the counter, panic in his pie-wide eyes, a terrified cat in his
arms. Skippy's in his official King Putt costume: a fake bronze
breastplate, striped skirt, and a Pharaoh hat.

The cat he's clutching to his chest—a tabby with pointy ears very similar to those on the carved Pharaoh cats propping up the brochure racks—is hissing angrily at Ceepak's dad, who is standing in front of the cash register, swinging a putter back and forth like he might shatter a display case on his next shot.

Ceepak and Rita have putters, too. They're standing to the right, in front of a Coke machine.

"You want me to call for backup?" I shout.

Ceepak—the good one—shakes his head. "No need, Danny."

Mr. Ceepak swivels around. Stares at me with glassy eyes. I have a feeling that this morning he swilled what he could out of all of Big Kahuna's empty beer bottles before he tossed them in the Dumpster.

"Boyle," he slurs. "Good name for you, kid, because you're a goddamn boil on my butt I can't get rid of no matter how much puss I squeeze out of it!"

Great. Not exactly the kind of description you want to hear so soon after wolfing down a Chunky's Cheese Steak with extra cheese.

Mr. Ceepak staggers back around and lurches toward his son, gripping his putter under the head so he can hold it like a ball-peen hammer.

Rita retreats half a step.

Ceepak does not. In fact, he nonchalantly hands Rita his putter. He doesn't need a weapon to face his sorry excuse for a father.

"Where is she, you sanctimonious sack of shit?"

"I'll ask you once more to refrain from using foul language."

"Fine. But first—you tell me where the hell your mother is hiding."

"As I stated previously," says Ceepak, striding forward, not at all afraid of the golf club quivering in his old man's hand, "she is where you will never find her."

"She has my fucking money! Three million dollars!"

"You are mistaken. Aunt Jennifer willed that money, in no uncertain terms, to Mom, and Mom alone."

"What's hers is mine."

"So you keep saying. However, according to the divorce papers—"

"We're Catholic, Johnny."

"While you were in prison, she had your marriage annulled by a church tribunal."

"She can't do that."

"She did." He hands his father a piece of paper.

Mr. Ceepak takes it. "What the fuck is this?"

"A restraining order."

"Huh?"

"It's a civil order that provides protection from harm by a family member or a psycho stalker," I chime in, because Sam chirped it to me the other night while she was cramming for her LSATs.

"You," Ceepak says to his father, "are not to have any further contact with me or my family, in person, by phone, at home, work or anywhere I or my wife and stepson happen to be."

"Fuck that—"

"Trust me, sir—if you violate this order, you will be incarcerated."

"Hey, he's violating it now!" This from Skippy. "You want me to cuff him? I have handcuffs."

He does? Did he save a pair as a souvenir when he was an auxiliary cop?

"My guns are at home but I have a wood back here." Skippy lets go of the cat, who jumps into a fuzzy doughnut-shaped bed as Skippy bends down to grab a driver with a humongous head, which, I guess is what Putt-Putt owners use for self-defense instead of the more traditional mom-and-pop grocery store baseball bat.

"Stand down, Mr. O'Malley," says Ceepak.

"Ten–four," says Skippy who seems to be enjoying playing cop-for-a-day.

Mr. Ceepak is staring at the sheet of paper his son just handed him. Trying to focus his bleary eyes. Moving his lips as he reads what is written there.

"How long you been planning this?"

"Ever since I heard from Lisa Porter Burt, the prosecuting attorney in Ohio. She informed me that you were angling for early release under the auspices of the new state law."

"Be prepared, huh?"

"Yes, sir."

"Fucking overgrown Boy Scout. This piece of paper is bullshit."

"I assure you, sir, it is not."

"Really? Okay, jarhead. How'd you find a goddamn judge on a Sunday morning?"

"This is what is known in New Jersey as an emergency restraining order. They may be obtained at any police station in the state."

Like the one where Ceepak and I work.

"Tomorrow, Judge Mindy Rasmussen will issue a temporary restraining order that will remain in effect for ten days or until our court hearing, whichever comes first. You, of course, will be invited to attend the hearing to tell your side of the story."

"Oh, I'll tell 'em, Johnny. I'll tell the world what a lousy excuse for a son you turned out to be. A goddamn disappointment. I'll tell that judge how you signed up for the fucking army instead of coming to work for me. Thought you were too good to be a roofer."

"Tell Judge Rasmussen anything you like. However, right now, you are in clear violation of the restraining order. If you do not vacate these premises immediately, it will be my duty as a duly sworn law enforcement officer to arrest you."

Ceepak's duty, my pleasure.

Mr. Ceepak stuffs his legal documents into his back pocket. "This ain't over, Johnny."

"Of that, I am quite certain, sir. However, I won't see you again until our court date. If I do, I will arrest you."

"Me, too," I toss in.

"Danny?" says Ceepak.

"Yeah?"

"Much as we all like you, you are not a family member."

"True. But if I see him near Rita or T.J. and you're not around . . ."

"Ah! Then you may indeed arrest him."

"Thought so."

Mr. Ceepak squints at us hard. Guess he doesn't like to see everybody in a room smiling except him.

"Fine. All I want is to find my wife. Work things out between us. But, no—you have to blow everything out of proportion, don't you, Johnny? Fine. I'll see you in court, son." He does a finger salute off his greasy forehead to Rita, tries to put a little of the ol' Joe Sixpack twinkle back in his foggy eyes. "Nice meeting you, ma'am. Who knew Johnny would grow up to marry a Polack beauty queen. I'm serious. I always thought he was a fucking faggot like his little brother."

And with that fatherly pearl of wisdom, Mr. Ceepak leaves the building.

"Sorry for the unanticipated intrusion," Ceepak says to Skip.

"That's okay. I love watching you work, sir. I'm hoping to re-enter the police academy in the fall."

Ceepak just nods. Because if he said something encouraging like, "good for you," he'd be lying. Plus, no way are they letting Skippy O'Malley back in. They caught him cheating. That's a "one strike and you're out" deal.

Mr. O'Malley, wearing a black suit, bursts into the office.

"Skippy?"

"Yes, sir?"

"Why the hell are there children crying in my parking lot?"

"We, uh, we . . ."

"I'm afraid that's our fault, Mr. O'Malley," says Ceepak.

O'Malley is a big, blustery man. He looks Ceepak up and down. Checks me out, too.

"You're the cops. The ones who . . ."

"Yes, sir," says Ceepak.

Mr. O'Malley nods. Puckers up his lips to fight down his feelings.

"Thank you. For all you did. For all you tried to do."

Behind the counter, I see Skippy hanging his head. Maybe he's sobbing again.

"I only wish we could have reached your wife sooner," says Ceepak.

"Don't beat yourself up, son. Dr. Kurth, the medical examiner, was kind enough to call me. Said Jackie suffered a massive coronary. Most likely died instantaneously. Didn't feel any pain."

Ceepak nods. He's heard the same thing.

"Skippy?"

"Sir?"

"Where's my other cell phone?"

Skippy turns and fumbles around on the top of a credenza, where there are buckets of colored balls and about a dozen cell phones sitting in charger bases.

He grabs one.

"Here you go, dad. Fully charged."

Mr. O'Malley takes it, hands Skippy another phone, which looks just like the one he just took. "Charge it. Died on me during mass."

"Yes, sir."

"Why weren't you there?"

"Church?"

"Yeah."

"I had to open at ten."

"Right. Good. I'll be upstairs in the office."

"Okay, Dad."

"And Skippy?"

"Yes, sir?"

"I thought I told you to take that damn cat to the shelter."

Skippy picks the cat up out of its bed. "I don't mind looking after him."

"Your brother Kevin is allergic. Mary, too."

"But Mom loved Gizmo."

"South Shore will find it a new home."

"I could keep him in my room."

"Skippy?"

"Yes, sir. I'll take him in first thing tomorrow."

"Aren't you working here tomorrow morning?"

"South Shore Animal Shelter opens at nine. I used to go out there sometimes with Mom, when she volunteered."

"Fine. Whatever. Just take care of it. I need you to start pulling your weight around here, son. When I tell you to do something, do it."

"Yes, sir."

Mr. O'Malley sighs and shakes his big Irish head.

Meanwhile, Skippy's freckled face goes red with embarrassment. He keeps hugging the cat. Stroking it.

Mr. O'Malley turns to face Ceepak and me.

"Officers. Thank you again. Skippy? I'll be upstairs. Order me a sandwich."

"The usual?"

"I don't care. Hell, surprise me."

Mr. O'Malley shakes his head again, mutters something about Jesus, Mary, and Joseph giving him strength, and heads up a spiral staircase to his office.

"I'll let the people in the parking lot know it's okay to come back in," I tell Skip, who looks totally bummed out.

"It's a kill shelter," he mumbles.

"What?"

"South Shore. If they can't find Gizmo a new home, they'll euthanize him. Put him to sleep. I've seen it happen. When I went out there with Mom—"

"He's a very attractive cat," says Ceepak, attempting to comfort Skip. "I feel confident he will find a new home. South Shore is where we found Barkley, our dog."

"My mom loved Gizmo."

Ceepak and I just nod because, well, we're guys and guys don't get all weepy about our pets in public because it's against the official (if unwritten) guy code.

All of a sudden, Rita pipes up: "We could take him."

"Come again?" says Ceepak.

"We could take the cat. We have the room."

"We do?"

"Sure. T.J.'s heading off to Annapolis in July. His room will be empty. Of course, a cat doesn't really need his own room . . . just a nice bed and some sunshine."

She reaches out her arms.

"Really?" says Skippy, his face brightening. "Are you sure, Mrs. Ceepak?"

"We've always wanted a cat, right, John?"

Ceepak clears his throat. "Well, dear, to tell the truth—"

"You can tell me later, honey."

"What about Barkley?"

"He's old. He'll be fine. We'll all be fine."

Skippy hands Rita the cat. "He likes when you scratch under her chin."

So Rita strokes the cat's chin. "Of course he does. Aren't you beautiful boy? Yes you are."

Rita Lapczynski once rescued a seagull with a broken wing from the middle of the road. She nursed it back to health and then set it free. Next, she and Ceepak rescued an old dog named Barkley who had been abandoned on the beach by a family that didn't like the stink of his farts anymore. Today, the Ceepak menagerie adds its first feline. I, of course, was the first stray human they took in. Rita's forever inviting me over for Sunday dinner or a cookout because my parents moved to Arizona ("it's a dry heat") as soon as my dad retired from the post office.

"Can I come visit him?" asks Skippy.

"Sure," says Rita who is holding the cat very close to Ceepak so he can pet it.

Ceepak does. Then he sneezes.

"My mom and I were the only ones in the family who loved Gizmo."

"You two were close, weren't you? You and your mom?" Rita says, oozing so much empathy, I wish she were my mom.

"Yeah."

"Well, you can come visit anytime you want."

"Thanks. Officer Ceepak?"

"Yes?" He sneezes again.

"You know why my mom had that heart attack yesterday?"

"Well, Skip, we suspect she had some sort of preexisting heart condition."

"Exactly. It was broken." Now he whispers. "By that bastard upstairs."

12

THAT "MOMMA'S BOY" STUFF CRAZY MARY KEPT YABBERING about on the roller coaster yesterday doesn't seem so crazy today.

I mean, I love my mom, but I wouldn't clip her toenails for her. I suspect Skippy might.

The Ceepaks and I postpone our golf date.

They need to go buy a litter box. And cat chow. And fur mice. Maybe a little catnip, too.

In the parking lot, I ask Ceepak what he thinks Skippy meant by that crack about his dad breaking his mother's heart.

"Not knowing, can't say," says Ceepak.

"It could be anything," says Rita, who never studied psychology but did work as a waitress for a dozen years, which makes her a pretty good judge of human nature. "He might have been mean to her about the cat. He may have helped estrange their sons. He may not have given her the time and attention she thought she deserved as his life partner."

Ceepak and I are both nodding. Like I said, Rita's good.

"And," she says with a heavy sigh, "he may have been cheating on her with another, most likely younger, woman."

Yeah. That'd break your heart after you had five kids together.

Ceepak sneezes again.

Rita is letting him hold the cat. She'll drive. I'm thinking they better stop off at the drug store and pick up a couple cartons of Claritin.

"See you tomorrow, partner," Ceepak says in between a set of double nose blows.

I'm definitely bringing a box of Kleenex to work tomorrow and doing all the driving.

Ceepak closes his eyes when he sneezes.

The week rolls on.

Ceepak and I both work Memorial Day Monday. Big crowds on the boardwalk. The ocean's too cold to go swimming, except for a few assorted Polar Bears, who always seem to be burly guys with forests of curly black hair on their backs. Sea Haven is running its annual Kite Festival on Oak Beach. Ken Erb is there in all his glory, showing off his new hand-painted silk Indonesian bird kite. It's twelve feet tall and sort of reminds me of one of the scary winged creatures from Harry Potter.

Tuesday, we write a couple speeding tickets. Help a kid with a flat tire on his bike.

Wednesday, Ceepak and I are off the duty roster, so Sam takes a day off from studying. We do the beach. I skimboard on the slick sand, she reads *Silent Counsel*, a legal thriller. Later, we head to the Sand Bar and scarf down clams on the half shell, clams casino, some shrimp jammers (shrimp stuffed with cheddar and deep fried), mozzarella sticks, and a bucket of beers. Then we go to my place and, well, do nothing because we're both too stuffed.

Thursday, Ceepak and I work the night shift.

We're cruising Shore Drive near Spruce Street. We're almost to the end of tree-named streets, about to enter the stretch of the island where the Sea Haven Street Naming Commission basically gave up and started using numbers instead of fish (further north) or picking up with second-tier trees, maybe Althorn, Bladdernut, and Chinaberry, for starters.

Ceepak and I are discussing the relative merits of the Philadelphia Phillies and the New York Mets and their chances of breaking our hearts again this summer, when, all of a sudden, this hot little sports car comes zipping around the corner of Tangerine Street and, tires squealing, roars down Shore Drive at fifty miles per hour.

The speed limit is fifteen.

"Lights and siren," I say, since I'm behind the wheel.

"Roger that," says Ceepak in the passenger seat. He flips the switches.

I stomp on the gas, take the shuddering Crown Vic straight up to eighty to close the gap between us and the little speed demon.

The sports car doesn't give us much of a run for our money. It pulls over to the curb. Our high-speed chase lasted two blocks, sucked down a quarter tank of SHPD gas.

Ceepak and I both get out of the cruiser.

The sports car window powers down.

"Hey, Danny."

It's Gail Baker. The hot waitress from The Rusty Scupper.

"Gail," I say, "I need you to step out of the vehicle."

"Sure." The door opens. She climbs out in her skinny jeans and snug Sugar Babies tee. "I was speeding, right?"

"Yeah."

"Sorry about that."

"Have you been drinking?"

"I had a glass of champagne, but that was, like, two or three hours ago."

"Why the big rush?" asks Ceepak, who has come around the front of Gail's car.

She shrugs. "Just need to get home. You want me to take a Breathalyzer test or something?"

Actually, we use an Alco Tester, but everybody still calls it a Breathalyzer. Now I notice something on her neck. An oval bruise.

A hickey?

"You okay?" I ask.

"Yeah. Thanks, Danny."

"Is that dentist still giving you grief?"

"Dr. Hausler?"

"I heard him at the gym Sunday morning."

"Don't worry. I can handle Marvin Hausler."

I turn to Ceepak. "You want to run an SFST?"

That's a Standardized Field Sobriety Test.

Ceepak nods and runs her through the three tests. He makes her follow a pen as he moves it back and forth to check her horizontal-gaze nystagmus—that being a weird word to describe the involuntary jerking of the eyeballs as they gaze side to side. When you're drunk, the nystagmus is more pronounced. So are a lot of things, come to think of it. Like how funny you think you are.

Next comes the walk and turn, followed by the one-leg stand with its accompanying balancing and counting routine.

Gail passes all three tests with flying colors.

So we write up a warning, citing her doing fifty in a fifteen zone. If she gets pulled over again for the same reason, then she'll get a ticket and a pretty hefty fine.

Gail says, "Thanks, guys." She folds up the warning and slides it down into the back pocket of her extremely tight jeans.

On Friday morning, Ceepak and I head over to Our Lady of the Seas Roman Catholic church for Mrs. O'Malley's funeral.

I'm inside because I knew the family.

Ceepak is out in the intersection directing traffic because, it seems, almost everybody on the island knew somebody in the family. I think Ceepak used to direct tank traffic rolling into Baghdad. I think this is worse.

I'm wearing my khaki pants and blue sports coat because I don't own a suit. Like I said, I'm twenty-five. Sam has a black dress that buttons up to her neck and covers her knees. The nuns I had in elementary school would be pleased. I keep expecting her to whip out a lacy veil to cover her head.

I, myself, haven't been to mass in a couple of years. My Saturday night activities seemed to impair my ability to wake up before noon on Sunday. Back in the day, I was an altar boy here. Some of the other guys in the altar boy corps were always daring me to swipe a few swigs from the communion wine when we filled the carafes before services.

No way. I had smelled that stuff. Franzia Sunset Blush. It came out of a box with a plastic tap. It stank like the sickly sweet juice at the bottom of a can of peaches. I think Franzia Sunset Blush is why I'm still a beer man and will forever pass on dipping my wafer into the wine chalice.

Sam and I take seats about six rows back. I remember to genuflect in the center aisle when we reach our pew. Hey, you can take the boy out of the Catholic church, but you can't take the Catholic out of the boy.

Mrs. O'Malley's coffin, draped in white, is sitting in front of the altar. Candles flicker. Soft organ music plays in the background. People are sniffling.

The front pews of the church resemble the front cars of the Rolling Thunder last Saturday, only Peter O'Malley was invited to this event. His boyfriend in the black leather vest and nipple rings, however, was not.

I see the nurse, dressed in a crisp white uniform, dabbing at the corners of Mary's mouth with a tissue she licks with her tongue, moistening it to wipe the dry white flecks off Mary's face. I almost hurl. My mom used to do that. Getting your face cleaned with a saliva-soaked Kleenex is worse than clipping curled toenails.

The O'Malleys are on the left-hand side of the church. In the front row on the right, I see another Irish clan. The red-headed woman with the aisle seat—who looks to be fifty-ish and angry—swirls around to address the white-haired lady sitting in the pew behind her.

"She was our sister before she was his goddamn wife!" The white-haired lady makes a quick sign of the cross, probably asking God to forgive the redneck for cursing inside his house.

Funerals are a little like weddings, only with sadder music and no kissing at the end. I'm guessing Sam and I are seated on the deceased's side of the church and that the folks in the front pews are Mrs. O'Malley's family.

Over on the widower's side, I see Mayor Sinclair, Bruno Mazzilli (with his wife and kids, not his girlfriend), Chief Baines, and most of the merchants on the island. Over here on the right, we've got Mrs. O'Malley's family, the neutral observers like me and Sam, and, sitting next to us, some folks in windbreakers with dog-and-cat patches on their sleeves from the South Shore Animal Shelter where Mrs. O'Malley must've been one of their top volunteers.

Bells jingle and Father Ed Steiner comes in. The altar boys carry a golden pot of holy water with a palm branch sprinkler sticking out. Father Steiner takes it and starts blessing the casket.

"In the name of the Father, and of the Son, and of the Holy Spirit . . ."

I don't get to hear much else.

Ceepak is tapping me on the shoulder.

He head-gestures for me to exit with him.

I turn to Sam. "I gotta go."

"Danny?" she whispers, in a way that lets me know I'm being extremely rude, ducking out early. Then she sees Ceepak. "Oh."

I step into the aisle. Remember to genuflect again. Follow Ceepak out into the blazingly bright sun.

"We have a situation," he says when we hit the sidewalk.

"What's up?"

"Someone dumped a dismembered body outside a home on Tangerine Street."

"Jeez."

"Danny?"

"Yeah?"

"It's Gail Baker. They found our warning ticket tucked inside the back pocket of her jeans."

13

HERE'S WHAT CEEPAK DIDN'T TELL ME RIGHT AWAY: GAIL'S jeans and lower body are stuffed inside a suitcase with her decapitated head.

Her torso and arms are in a second suitcase.

We're on Tangerine Street, a block and a half from where it dead-ends at the sand dunes.

My buddy Joey Thalken, who works with the Sea Haven Sanitation Department, is leaning against the back of his white garbage truck. Joey's the one who found the two rolling suitcases. He unzipped one to see why it was so heavy. Then he hurled.

I did the same thing the first time I saw a dead body. And mine hadn't been taken apart like a mannequin headed to storage.

"It's horrible, man," Joey says when Ceepak and I join him at the back of his truck. "I've never seen any . . . who could . . . what . . . did you see her, Danny?"

I nod.

"Sick. . . ." Joey barely spits out the word. "Some seriously sick dude did that, man."

Two of our guys, Dominic Santucci and Dylan Murray, have already crime-scene-taped the sand-and-pea-pebble parking pad in front of 145 Tangerine Street. The two suitcases—both about three feet tall—are sitting close to where Joe found them: leaning against a pressure-treated lumber enclosure built to corral six thirty-gallon garbage cans.

"You can't put out household items or bulk trash on Fridays," says Joey. "Just regular trash. No construction debris, no old furniture, no suitcases . . ."

No dismembered bodies.

"When did you discover the body?" asks Ceepak.

"An hour ago. Eleven. Hey, Danny?"

"Yeah?"

"Is it Gail? From the Scupper?"

My turn to nod.

"Jeez-o, man," says Joey.

Joe Thalken, being a male with a pulse, had, no doubt, spent a few lunch hours ogling Gail Baker's hot bod while wrestling with a leathery hamburger. Now he's seen it broken apart like a Barbie doll after a temper tantrum.

"Is there anyone we can call for you?" Ceepak asks.

"I'll be okay. Just need another minute."

"Should we contact the Sanitation Department, have them send someone over to relieve you?"

"No. I need to finish my route."

"No you don't, Joe," says Ceepak. "Not today."

"Yeah. I do."

Ceepak nods. He and I have worked with Joey T. on a couple of things in the past. We know he is a creature of habit, a Virgo who doesn't like varying his routine. The routine gives him comfort. Maybe today, the same-old same-old will help him cope with the most extraordinarily horrible thing he's ever seen in his life.

"Before you go back to work," says Ceepak, "we need you to swing by the house. Sit down with Officer Forbus. She'll take your statement."

"Should I do that now?"

"Probably smart," I say. "While it's, you know, fresh."

Bad choice of words. Joey puts a fist over his mouth. If his stomach wasn't already empty, he'd be tossing more cookies into the back of his truck.

"We'll ask Officer Forbus to come out," says Ceepak. "She'll escort you back to headquarters. Get you some water. Maybe a soft drink. Coca-Cola is excellent for a queasy stomach."

Joey looks up at Ceepak. "You ever . . . ?"

"All the time. I'd be worried if something like this didn't make me feel sick to my stomach."

"Thanks."

"Hang here."

Ceepak quickly radios Jen Forbus, who's on duty today and is probably our top cop for doing interviews. She used to run a blog or something. Anyway, she knows how to ask the right questions, get people to relax, put it all down on paper. She'll be on the scene in five. He asks her to get Denise Diego, our resident techie, to call Verizon. We need Gail Baker's cell phone records. They'll tell us who she talked to and where she was before some lunatic sliced her up into easy-to-pack pieces.

We move away from the garbage truck, study the taped-off crime scene.

That's when Sergeant Santucci struts over.

"Why are you here, Ceepak?"

"Chief Baines asked me to head up our end of the homicide investigation."

"Why? Murray and I caught the call."

"You'd have to ask Chief Baines."

"You really don't need to be here."

"The chief disagrees."

Santucci mutters. Two summers ago, Dominic Santucci was single-handedly responsible for about a hundred thousand dollars worth of damages when he shot up Mama Shucker's, a seafood shop about four blocks north of where we are now. Ever since, he's not really been one of the chief's favorites.

Now he waves a plastic bag under our noses. Inside is the warning ticket we issued Gail for speeding.

"I'm all over this thing. Already checked her pockets for ID. Found a wallet and this. Guess what?" He cracks his gum, pauses. "Her jeans weren't on her legs or her ass. They were stuffed in on top."

Ceepak's eye twitches. "How much of the crime scene did you disturb, Dom?"

Dominic Santucci and John Ceepak? Oil and water. Chalk and cheese. Mayonnaise and hot dogs. They just don't mix well.

"I did not disturb the crime scene. I ID'ed the body. What the hell have you two done?"

"Where is the wallet?"

"I stuffed it back in the pants for the CSI guys."

"And where are Ms. Baker's pants located?"

"Where I found 'em. Back in the suitcase on top of her legs and head."

Okay. I'm thinking about joining Joey T. over at the rolling puke wagon.

"It is absolutely critical that we keep this area clean," says Ceepak.

"We know that. Jesus, Ceepak. You think me and Murray are idiots?"

Ceepak doesn't answer. His eyes are focused on the gritty mix of sand and pebbles surrounding the suitcases. "The MCU unit will want to examine this area for tire treads, footprints."

The MCU is the New Jersey State Police Major Crimes Unit—detectives and CSI pros who assist state, county, and local authorities. The MCU has the kind of homicide investigation firepower a sleepy summer resort town like Sea Haven should never need.

I can see four miniature wheel tracks where the suitcases were rolled across the sand.

"No footprints," I mumble out loud.

"Roger that," says Ceepak, gesturing to the lines in the sand. "Note the parallel, striated furrows. Most likely the sand was raked."

"But not with a leaf rake," I add, because I think the grooves are too far apart, too deep.

"Good eye, Danny. Perhaps a gardening rake?"

Santucci snorts. "Jesus. You two. And what did they use to chop off her head? A Weed Whacker?"

I hear Dylan Murray's radio crackle with an unintelligible burst of words. Poor Murray. He's got the dubious distinction of being Dom Santucci's partner this shift. He takes the mic off his shoulder board. "We're at One forty-five Tangerine," he says. "Continue south on Ocean Avenue. Take the left after Spruce. Ten–four." He clips the mic back to his shoulder. "MCU. They're about a mile away."

"Thanks, Dylan," says Ceepak.

"Why you tellin' Ceepak about MCU?" snaps Santucci.

Dylan Murray shrugs. "I dunno."

I do. Everybody on the job in Sea Haven, including Chief Buzz Baines, knows Ceepak is our best guy at this kind of stuff. Everybody except Santucci.

A third SHPD cruiser crunches around the corner.

"What are Forbus and Bonanni doing here?" Santucci's seething now.

"I requested that they escort Mr. Thalken back to the house," says Ceepak. "Take his statement."

"Jen and Nikki? The girls?" Santucci sighs. Hikes up his pants. "This is a homicide, Ceepak."

"I'm well aware of the magnitude of the crime to be investigated, sergeant."

"But you call in Forbus and Bonanni, anyway? Jesus. I better bring 'em up to speed. Make sure they don't blow this thing."

He struts away.

"Jeez-o man," I mumble. "What a douche."

"Danny?"

"Yeah," I say when I hear the reprimand in his voice. "Our energies are better spent studying the crime scene."

"Correct. However, for what it's worth, I concur."

Wow. Ceepak just called Santucci a douche. Just took him more words than it took me.

Now he hunkers down and stares at the two suitcases.

"We'll need to canvass the neighborhood for witnesses."

"Yeah," I say. "No telling when the bags were dumped."

"Or why here."

Good point.

I check out the block. It looks like all the others on this part of the island. Vinyl-sided colonial homes with dormers for upstairs bedrooms. Sun-faded shades of gray, blue, yellow. A few scruffy-looking evergreen trees for barriers between lots. Not many cars parked in the street.

These are mostly rental properties. Three weeks from now, this place will be packed with minivans and SUVs loaded down with bicycle racks and luggage carriers. Today, all I see is a pickup truck way down the street near a house where they must be doing construction, because there's a twenty-yard Roll-Off Dumpster sitting in the driveway.

"Huh," I say.

"What?"

"See that long Dumpster? Why didn't our doer toss his suitcases down there? The walls are high enough to hide everything inside. You do a gut job on a house, there's all sorts of random junk that gets tossed in the Dumpster."

"Like old luggage."

"Exactly. We might not have found the body until somebody smelled it."

"Fascinating," says Ceepak.

I love it when he says that. Means I thought of something he hadn't thought of yet. Not that I'm keeping score.

"In some ways," says Ceepak, "it fits with what we see here. The wheel tracks clearly visible. But the footprints were obliterated with the garden rake."

"You think whoever did this wanted us to find the body?"

"It's a possibility."

"Why? Is he sending some kind of message? Do you think the mob did this?"

Ceepak answers my question with one of his own: "How well did you know the victim, Danny?"

"We, you know, talked."

"Were you ever romantically involved?"

"With Gail Baker? Nah. She was way out of my league. Although . . ."

"What?"

"She used to go out with Skippy O'Malley. Maybe I had a shot and didn't even know it."

"Any known enemies?"

"Gail? No. More like broken hearts. She was a serial dater. She'd hang with a guy for a while, then move on."

I remember the dentist.

"We should talk to Marvin Hausler."

"Who is he?"

"Dentist. I think he and Gail were hot and heavy for a

weekend he'll never get over; she got over it by Monday. He's been kind of stalking her."

"Come again?"

"Last weekend at the gym, he threw this big fit. And, at Big Kahuna's Saturday night, he called her a bitch because she stood him up."

Ceepak's been jotting down notes in the spiral pad he keeps in the left hip pocket of his cargo pants. "Definitely worth a go-see," he says.

"She also seemed to be flirting with this dude at the gym."

"Dude?"

"One of the trainers. Last weekend, they were teasing each other. Talking about hooking up. But that was four or five days ago. By now, he could want to kill her for dumping him. Gail Baker went through guys the way I go through potato chips."

"We should compile a list of these young men."

"We could check with Bud, the bartender at Big Kahuna's. He knows all the local dirt."

Ceepak keeps staring at the two suitcases.

"What do you see?" I ask.

"Two things. On the handle, the remnant of a luggage tag."

I see it, too. One of those sticker deals they wrap on when you check your bag. The flappy part is torn off.

"If there is any scanable information on what's left, we might be able to decipher what flight the bag was checked on."

"And who was on that flight," I add.

"Precisely."

"Would the killer use his own suitcases?"

"If he or she acted in haste, hadn't premeditated the mutilation, he or she might."

"What's the other thing?"

"Next to the torn tags."

I see orange yarn pom-poms. One on each handle.

"That's what my mom does," I say. "So she can spot her suitcase on the baggage carousel."

"Does your father do the same thing?"

"Nah. Only women do that."

"Such has been my experience as well."

So . . .

That's why Ceepak was doing the "he or she" thing.

Maybe Gail didn't run into a jealous old boyfriend. Maybe she bumped into somebody's girlfriend who couldn't stand the competition.

14

THE MCU PEOPLE ARRIVE.

The boss is a new guy named Bill Botzong who took over when Dr. Sandra McDaniels retired after working her last case in Atlantic City.

She'd seen enough, she told Ceepak. Except her grandkids; them she wanted to see more.

"Has anything been moved?" Botzong asks.

Ceepak has to explain Santucci's rummaging through the luggage looking for ID and then his repacking of said luggage.

"This Santucci still here?" asks Botzong.

"Across the street," says Ceepak. "Knocking on doors."

"Good," says Botzong, who looks like a chemistry teacher I had in high school, only he's wearing the navy blue CSI shirt plus aviator glasses and a Star Trek Bluetooth device in his ear. On weekends, I'm guessing, he goes to comic book conventions. "Hey, Carolyn?" he calls out to one of his crew.

"Yeah?"

"Put in a call to that forensic anthropologist in PA. The guy who analyzes knife and saw marks. I want to know what our guy used to decapitate our victim and sever her limbs. Serrated kitchen knife or Ginzu, hacksaw or chainsaw? I want make, model, and manufacturer's suggested retail price."

"On it."

"Carolyn Miller," says Botzong as Miller walks away. "Good people. Getting her doctorate in forensic geology. She'll be all over the ground here. If there's a footprint or a wad of chewing gum or a pebble from a parking lot on the other side of the island, she'll find it."

"We noted that the sand has been raked to mask footprints," says Ceepak.

"Yeah. But the rake man didn't know I was bringing Carolyn. You walk on water, she'll tell me your shoe size."

"We're going to work this side of the street," says Ceepak. "Canvass for witnesses. We've initiated retrieval of the victim's phone records and have requested a search warrant for her apartment. We'll send over a team. Lock it down for your guys."

"You the lead on this thing for SHPD?"

"Ten–four."

"Good. Sandy McDaniels told me I should hire you to come work for us. Interested?"

"Not right now."

"Think about it. You work with us, you get one of these." He points to his Bluetooth device. Now he gestures toward the crime scene. "When we know anything, you'll know it, too."

"Appreciate that."

"Hey, George—we need to wrangle a truck to get these suit-cases back to the lab as soon as Susan's done taking pictures. Something with refrigeration. Get on the horn, see if a grocery store or a water-ice shop or Ben and Jerry's or the local Boar's Head meat distributor can help us out here—"

—-—

While the CSI guys comb the crime scene and pack up their grue-some luggage, Ceepak and I head up the block toward the beach.

We ring doorbells, knock on doors. Tangerine Street is a ghost town. The lights aren't on and nobody's home. We move to the next block, the one closest to the beach. In Sea Haven, the closer your home is to the pristine sandy beaches, the higher the price tag. The homes in this block are big and boxy and built on stilts so they won't get flooded when the next hurricane hits.

"Rentals," I say to Ceepak as we walk away from our tenth empty home. These mansions are a lot like Sea Haven—they fill up after the Fourth of July and empty out after Labor Day.

Finally, at number 3 Tangerine Street, we find a human being. And a dog.

We actually hear from the dog first, because the instant we ding the dong, there's snarling and growling on the other side of the door.

"Puck? Sit!"

Puck is not sitting. His paws are still trying to scrape through the door.

"Puck? Heel!"

Okay, I'm not a dog owner, but I know "heel" is not the cor-rect command in this situation, unless, of course, the screaming woman is giving tips on what part of our bodies the mutt should aim for first.

I see Ceepak unsnapping the right thigh pocket on his cargo pants. That's where he keeps the Snausages.

The door creaks open. About two inches.

The snarling beast is a little yappy lap dog. One of those white fluff balls that looks like a dust mop without the pole.

Towering over him is a woman in a bathrobe. Her hair is bun-dled up in a towel turban. She has seaweed smeared all over her face. We'll call her Mrs. Shrek.

"May I give your dog a treat?" asks Ceepak. He always asks first. In these pricey neighborhoods, you never know when the mutts might be on a holistic, wheat-free, ultra-low-carb, all-raw, mercury-free, vegan doggy diet.

"What is it?" the woman asks.

Told you.

"A new product called Snawsomes. Peanut butter and apple flavor. My dog loves them."

"Sorry. Puck is only allowed Banana Pupcakes. Our maid bakes them."

Puck drops to all fours and is content to grumble at us. Or his owner. I think he sniffed out the Snawsomes and is miffed that he has to go organic.

"Maria was giving me a seaweed facial," she says, gesturing toward her green mask. Guess that's why it looks like she fell asleep over a bowl of split-pea soup. "Are you two here on official business?"

"Yes, ma'am. I'm Officer Ceepak. This is my partner, Officer Boyle."

"Valerie D'Ambrosio."

"Ms. D'Ambrosio, the Sea Haven Police Department is investigating an incident here on Tangerine Street."

"Did someone call in a complaint? Because it wasn't me."

"Did you hear or see anything unusual last night."

She hesitates. "No. But, as I told the other officer, I sleep with ear plugs."

"What other officer?"

"I forget. Italian name. Santa Lucci."

"Santucci?"

"Yes. Do you know him?"

"Yes, ma'am."

I glance over my shoulder. See Santucci and Murray working the opposite side of the street. I wonder how they got here before us.

The woman in the door crack shifts her weight. Ceepak and I see way too much thigh. It's spray-tanned and scary. Think congealed beef gravy.

"You know, come to think of it, Puck might've heard something—very late. Three or four in the morning."

"How's that?"

"He started barking up a storm. I didn't get out of bed, of course. My doctor has me on Ambien. Makes me groggy."

"Do you know the people who live up the street at 145 Tangerine?"

"No."

Ceepak fishes a business card out of his shirt pocket. "If you think of anything else, please give us a call."

We walk away from the house.

"So how did Santucci get down here before us?" I ask.

"Not knowing, can't say."

"Sounds like the dog is our only witness."

"So far, Danny. So far."

We have one more house to check out on this side of the street, so we hike down the asphalt. There are no sidewalks on Tangerine, just the pavement, then the sandy edge of the pavement, and then more sand, speckled with weed patches.

We pass a small breezeway between number 3 and number 1 Tangerine Street, definitely the most expensive house on the block. These ones on the beach corner usually sell for a couple million dollars. Then the new owner tears the old house down and builds a modern-art masterpiece of sharp angles with multiple sun decks for one or two million more. Up the breezeway, I see an outdoor shower, so the renters, or owners, can wash the sand and salt out of their hair when they come up from the beach.

"Looks like someone is staying here," says Ceepak, indicating a recyclables bin at the corner. In the Rubbermaid barrel, I see dark green champagne bottles, vodka bottles, scotch bottles, and one of those squat cognac bottles you see in magazines but figured nobody ever actually drank out of because liquid gold would be cheaper.

We march up the concrete walkway past some shrubs, the kind that look like pine-coated curly fries. When we get to the porch we see something the neighbors probably can't see or we'd get all sorts of complaints: lewd garden gnome sculptures, including a nude Mama and Papa Smurf testing out the springs in their ceramic Smurf bed and a naughty gnome flashing her boobies. There's another gnome, wearing nothing but his red pointy hat, perched at the edge of the porch. He's poised to pee on the rose bushes.

We ring the doorbell.

Knock on the door.

Ring again.

Knock again.

So unless the porno statues start talking, we've got nothing.

"We need to talk to Samantha's mother," says Ceepak. "See if she knows who rents out this house. Who the current occupants might be."

Sam's mom, Mrs. Starky, knows everything about everybody— a fact that creeps me out on a regular basis.

Santucci and Murray stroll across the street from number 2 Tangerine.

"You guys get anything?" asks Santucci.

"One dog who heard something at three A.M.," I answer.

"Next door? The rug rat, right? Puck. Thing barks like a maniac. Yip-yip-yip."

"How'd you get there before us?"

"The early bird gets the worm, Boyle. We got bubkis on the south side." Santucci looks at his watch. "Three o'clock on the dot. I'm heading home. Guess you guys can't, huh, Ceepak? Guess that comes with being 'in charge' of shit. Enjoy. Come on, Murray. Let's roll. The Yankees are playing tonight."

Santucci swaggers up the street toward their parked patrol car.

Murray hangs back. "You guys need anything? I'm good tonight if you want an extra pair of legs."

"Appreciate that, Dylan," says Ceepak. "Danny and I might run down some of Ms. Baker's known acquaintances this evening. Not much more we can do until the M.E. completes the autopsy and MCU shares what they learn from the forensics."

Dylan nods. "You need anything, give me a shout."

"Murray?" Santucci screams. "Come on. I don't want to miss the first pitch."

Which isn't for, like, four hours.

Murray, shaking his head, takes off to join Santucci.

"Where next?" I ask Ceepak, because the Mets aren't playing so I got nothing to hurry home for.

"Your bartender friend. It might be our most efficient means of piecing together a more complete picture of Ms. Baker's romantic entanglements."

"Yeah. Bud knows more than even Mrs. Starky."

15

WE SWING BY THE HOUSE SINCE IT'S ON THE WAY TO BIG
Kahuna's.

I need to hit the locker room and get out of my funeral clothes.
Ceepak wants to check in with Denise Diego, see how she's
coming with Gail Baker's cell phone records.

As we walk up the front steps, Mayor Hugh Sinclair is walking
down. For a change, his sunglasses are on his nose instead of dangling around his neck on a Croakie.

"Hot one," he says to Ceepak, his face crinkling into a squint.

"Yes, sir."

"Say, guys, I was just talking to Chief Baines. Couple things ..."

Here we go.

"Now, I know you two don't need to be reminded of this, but
let's not blow this thing out of proportion. The young girl ran into
somebody she shouldn't have. They meet in a seaside bar, she had
one too many kamikazes, one thing leads to another ..."

"Was there something else?" says Ceepak, who never likes to make any murder the victim's fault.

"Yeah. Let's not bother the neighbors up and down the street where you found the suitcases. For all we know, the bags were just dumped there because, well, for no reason whatsoever. Some out-of-towner, he picks up the beach babe in a bar, hacks her to pieces in the parking lot, stuffs her into a couple empty suitcases, then drives around town looking for a quiet street, and he just happens to pick Tangerine. So let's not punish the folks on that street for something none of them had anything to do with."

Ceepak takes off his own sunglasses so he can peer with confusion at Mayor Sinclair. "So far, we have made contact with only one resident on Tangerine Street. A Mrs. D'Ambrosio."

"Did she tell you anything?"

"We took her statement."

Ceepak's not going to lie but he's not going to tell Mr. Bright-Yellow-Polo-Shirt everything we know, either.

"We need to be inside," he says.

"Right. One more thing, guys: We need to treat this like the heart attack thing on the roller coaster. Keep it on the Q.T. School's out in three weeks. Let's not scare off any potential tourists by blabbing about it to the mainstream media."

"We do not discuss any ongoing investigation with the media. That's why we have a public affairs officer. Danny?"

I give the mayor a two-finger salute off the bill of my cop hat, or where the bill would have been if I were wearing my uniform, which I'm not because I had to waste time on the steps with the mayor.

I do a quick change in the locker room, say hi to everybody hanging out around the coffee pot, and then Ceepak and I check in with Denise Diego in our tech center.

She's removed all the *Lord of the Rings* figurines from her workstation and replaced them with *Dark Knight* paraphernalia. I just hope she doesn't start doing that Joker lipstick thing. She eats so many nacho cheese Doritos, she already has an orange ring around her lips.

"How's it going?" Ceepak asks.

"Excellent. Just had to wait for the M.E. to officially declare Ms. Baker dead, which happened moments ago. Verizon's pulling everything now. Should have it in a couple of hours."

"Well done. Thank you, Denise."

"No problemo. 'I like this job! I like it!'"

Ceepak stares. I chuckle. It's a line from the Batman movie.

———

We're officially off the clock, but we stay on the job.

It's the Ceepakian way.

Around 5 P.M., we pull into the parking lot of Big Kahuna's Dance Club. The place doesn't really start hopping until around nine, so we have our pick of spots. Except the handicap ones near the front door. Ceepak would never take one of those even if we are the only car in the parking lot. That would be cheating.

The second we enter the nightclub I smell spilt beer, wet carpet, and stale perfume. The place smells like a hangover feels. We see Bud behind the bar slicing lime wedges for people to jam into their Coronas. Next he'll probably do the oranges for bottles of Blue Moon. I hope no new beer starts a fad with kiwi fruit any time soon.

"Hey, Bud," I say.

"Danny boy, what's up?"

"Nothin'."

Okay, this is what guys say even when they walk into a bar before it's officially open while wearing a full police uniform—gun, cuffs, baton, and walkie-talkie included—accompanied by a six-two tower of power, also in uniform

"We need to ask you a couple of questions," I say since any Bar Zone is in my area of forensic expertise. "This is my partner, Officer John Ceepak."

Bud wipes his limey hands on his apron so he can shake with Ceepak without making him smell like a Mojito.

"Dude," he says as he and Ceepak shake. "Heard all about you. You guys need a beverage? Coke? Fruit juice? I figure you can't do a beer and a shot."

"Roger that," says Ceepak. "Water would be nice."

"Danny?"

"I'm cool."

Bud fumbles around under the counter looking for a clean glass. Has trouble finding one. Why do I think Mr. Joe Ceepak is not only the world's worst father but maybe its worst dishwasher, too?

"Hey, Officer Ceepak—can I ask you a question before you guys ask yours?"

"Certainly."

"Is Danny really as good with that pistol as everybody says?"

"Indeed. In fact, he recently set a new record at the range."

I shrug modestly. "It was an indoor firing range. No wind to compensate for."

Ceepak grins. "I suppose that's why *The Police Marksman* magazine wants to interview you."

"You're the cop who will not tell a lie, right?" Bud says to Ceepak.

"Right."

"So that means Danny really did it! Awesome!"

He shoots water into a semiclean cocktail glass from the bar's fountain gun.

"Is my father here?" Ceepak asks out of the blue.

"Your father?"

"Your new busboy," I help out.

"Oh. Right. Duh. Danny told me he was your old man." He lets it hang there. Stares at Ceepak. Nods a little. I can tell Bud's trying to figure out how Dudley Do-Right could have Sir Skeevelot for a father. "Anyway, Joe's cool. You know. Does his job. Tells everybody to call him Joe Sixpack, and, since it's a bar, they do."

"Is he here?"

"Nah. Won't clock in until six."

"Any sense of when he might be moving on?"

"Nope. Says he has some family business to take care of."

Now Ceepak just nods and stares.

So I jump in. "Bud, we need to ask you about Gail Baker."

"Sure. Why?"

"Someone killed her."

Bud's too stunned to even say "No way."

"I had lunch at the Scupper on Tuesday," he mumbles. "She was just in here. Couple nights ago."

"Was she with anybody?"

"Yeah. Mike. Mike Charzuk."

"Who's he?" I ask.

"Trainer at the gym. Has a chin goatee like Springsteen. You know—the tiny triangle." He points to his chin to give us the visual.

"Yeah," I say. "I saw them goofing around together last weekend at the gym. She said she was free to hook up with him this week."

"Lucky bastard," mumbles Bud. Then he remembers that Gail is dead, throws up both hands. "No disrespect."

"What about the dentist?" asks Ceepak.

"Marvin Hausler? Yeah—you guys should definitely check him out. Total psycho killer qu'est que c'est material."

Ceepak and I quote Springsteen; Bud goes with Talking Heads.

"What makes you say that?" asks Ceepak.

"Dr. Marvin was also in here on Tuesday—I think because all well drinks are two for one on Twofer Tuesday. Anyway, he sees

Gail and Mike doing their aerobics routine out on the dance floor, almost went postal on us. Your pops helped out. Hauled Hausler to the door, tossed him into the parking lot, scared the living shit out of the little dude."

Great. Busboy Ceepak is doubling as a bouncer.

"Anyone else we should be aware of?" asks Ceepak.

"You mean other guys?"

Ceepak nods. Bud thinks.

"No. Not really. Last weekend, she came in with a bunch of her girlfriends. Didn't see her much over the winter or spring."

Ceepak's cell phone chirps. The business line.

"This is Ceepak. Go." He covers the mouthpiece so he can mouth, "MCU, Bill Botzong."

I nod. It's the state police. Maybe they found something.

"Roger that," says Ceepak. "Agreed. Very unusual. We'll look into it. No. We should have her phone records soon. Right."

He closes up his phone.

"Thank you for your time," he says to Bud. "If we have further questions. . . ."

"I'll be here."

"Danny?" Ceepak head gestures toward the door.

"What's up?"

"The State CSI crew has transported the two suitcases back to their lab in Hamilton."

"And?"

"In examining the contents, they came upon all of Ms. Baker's bloody clothes—jeans, undergarments, socks, shoes—everything except a shirt."

"Well, she was definitely wearing a shirt when we wrote her up last night."

Ceepak nods. He remembers it, too: Tight. Snug. Four sizes too small. Mustard-yellow with cranberry lettering: Sugar Babies. Just like the candy wrapper.

"We need to talk to Santucci," says Ceepak.

We sure do.

Maybe when he went on his treasure hunt for Gail's ID, he decided to take home a souvenir T-shirt.

16

I GIVE SAMANTHA STARKY A QUICK CALL TO LET HER KNOW
our unofficial standing Friday night date is officially cancelled.

Our murder investigation "To Do" list just keeps getting longer.

Go to the dentist (we have a 5:45 appointment).

Talk to Santucci about a missing T-Shirt.

Track down Gail Baker's phone records.

Wait for the medical examiner and Major Crimes Unit to tell
us what they've learned from the forensic evidence—especially
those torn luggage tags.

Swing by The Rusty Scupper, see if any of Gail Baker's work-
mates can clue us in to who may have wanted to hurt their star
waitress.

Go back to that Naughty Gnome Museum on Tangerine
Street, knock on the door, see if Papa or Mama Smurf are home.

We're cruising south on Ocean Avenue toward the Sea Haven

Smile Center, which is what Dr. Marvin Hausler calls his dental office in a strip mall at the corner of Jacaranda Street. We're at Fig, five blocks north.

"Isn't that where Mrs. Starky works?" asks Ceepak as we stop at a traffic light near All-A-Shore Realty.

"Yeah."

"Let's pull in. See if she can tell us anything about the owners of that corner house on Tangerine Street."

"Even though Mayor Sinclair told us to leave the innocent citizens alone?" I say, just snarky enough for Ceepak to know I'm kidding.

"All the more reason to investigate further," he says.

Yeah. My man has a very well-tuned BS detector. It buzzes like crazy every time we're near our mayor, a city council member, or politicians in general. With that many booze bottles in the recycling bin, Ceepak is figuring somebody might have been there last night. So, for him, it's worth a quick chat with Mrs. Starky.

For me? Not so much.

Let's just say Sam's mom isn't crazy about Danny Boyle and her only daughter being romantically linked, especially the assorted sleepover dates. I don't think Mrs. Starky would ever cut off my head and stuff it into a suitcase, but she may have other Lorena Bobbitt–style ideas in mind, if you catch my drift.

But duty calls.

So we park out front and head inside.

The office of All-A-Shore Realty always smells damp and moldy—like yesterday's bath towel that never got dry because you kind of clumped it on the rack on top of some other wet towels. There are ugly black amoeba splotches crawling across the ceiling tiles near the air-conditioning vents. I always think I'm gonna come down with Legionnaires' disease when I drop by Mrs. Starky's workplace.

"Hi, Danny," says Janet Costello, the girl behind the front

counter. She answers the phones while stuffing the plastic "Welcome to Sea Haven" bags every renter receives when they pick up their keys. They're crammed with coupons for all sorts of stuff like 15% off fudge at Pudgy's Fudgery, $1 off any pie at Pizza My Heart, and a free dental exam at the Sea Haven Smile Center (two X-rays included). Janet and I have been pals since high school.

"Is Mrs. Starky available?" I ask.

Janet grimaces. Guess she knows what's coming.

"Hang on." She presses a button on a phone with fifteen blinking lights. "Mrs. Starky? Danny Boyle and another police officer are here to see you. Yes, ma'am."

Janet gently returns the phone to its cradle.

"She'll be right out." Now she looks ill.

"Appreciate it," says Ceepak.

"Excuse me. I need to, um."

"Take your break?" suggests Ceepak.

"Yeah!" Janet Costello dashes up the hall.

But not quickly enough. Mrs. Starky steps out of a door.

"Where do you think you're going?"

"Bathroom?"

"Make it fast."

"Yes, ma'am."

Janet hurries to the last door on the left. Goes in. Pulls the door shut. I hear her lock it.

"I was just on the phone with my daughter," Mrs. Starky says to me. "You remember her, Daniel?"

"Of course."

"Well, she tells me you broke another date. I told her she was lucky."

Ceepak steps up: "Officer Boyle and I are working on a murder investigation and have had to temporarily put our personal lives on hold."

"You do that a lot, don't you?"

"Yes, ma'am. I suppose we do."

"Which is why, if you don't mind a little free advice, the two of you should grow up; stop playing cowboy all day."

My fingers tickle the handgrip of my Glock.

Not really. Just in my mind. And my dreams.

Mrs. Starky looks like she sounds. Dyed hair that streams down to her too-low-for-her-age neckline. Her bangs hit her eyelashes because I suspect her hair curtains are designed to cover scars from the assorted facelifts that pulled her puffy cheeks back to her ears.

Years ago, my mother told me the spookiest thing: the girl you are dating will become her mother when you marry her.

I think I want to join Janet Costello in the toilet.

"We need some information," says Ceepak, totally unruffled by Mrs. Starky.

"Me, too," she says, turning to me again. "Are you ever going to get serious, Mr. Boyle? Because Samantha could do a whole lot better. I tell her she should date the boys at law school. Go on-line. Do Match dot com." She turns to Ceepak. "No disrespect to your wife, Officer Ceepak, but who in their right mind would marry a cop?"

My turn: "Well, if somebody didn't marry us, where would all the little cops come from?"

Mrs. Starky just sighs. I think I proved her point for her.

"What kind of information do you need?" she says to Ceepak.

"We'd like to talk to the owner of number One Tangerine Street."

I see her nose twitch a little, which means it wants to twitch a lot but her plastic surgeon made the skin too tight in the last nose job.

"Why?"

"They may have been witnesses to a murder."

"The waitress?" The way she says it, she wanted to say, "The whore?"

"Yes, ma'am. Gail Baker."

She turns to me again. "Friend of yours, Daniel?"

"Yeah. Sort of."

Hey, I know just about everybody on the island; I grew up here.

"Figures. Does Samantha know about this one?"

"What? That she's dead?"

I'm hoping that knocks the horsey tooth smile off her painted face, but it doesn't. Instead, she goes for the low blow.

"That seems to happen to a lot of your ex-girlfriends, doesn't it, Danny?"

"Mrs. Starky?" This from Ceepak. "We came here for information. If you have issues with your daughter's romantic relationships, may I suggest that you discuss that matter privately with the concerned parties at a more appropriate time?"

That's how Ceepak says, "Shut up, you old windbag."

The nose tries to twitch again. Just one nostril.

"What do you need to know?"

"Evidence on the scene indicates that number One Tangerine Street, unlike most of the other homes on the street, is currently occupied and, therefore, may present our best opportunity for locating a witness."

"We handle number One Tangerine," she says.

"Is it a rental property?"

"During the high season. The owners typically use it themselves through the end of June."

"So the owners would be the ones using it now?"

"That's right."

"Can you tell us how to contact them?"

"Do you have a warrant?"

"I beg your pardon?"

"A search warrant? Some sort of official document compelling me to release confidential information?"

"No, but—"

"I'm sorry. I have privacy issues to consider."

I put my hands on my gun belt, let the leather crinkle. "You did hear us say we're investigating a murder, right?"

"Protecting my client's privacy is my primary concern. I'm sorry you wasted your time stopping by. And, Danny?"

"Yes, ma'am?"

"The next time a girl tells you that she loves you, at least pretend you heard her say it. Spare her mother the teary phone calls."

I know the receptionist at Dr. Hausler's office, too.

"He'll be right with you guys," she says—with a smile, naturally.

The Smile Center is the same sort of drop-ceiling box of an office as All-A-Shore Realty. Only here the walls and fake flowers are pink. Like gums, I guess. There's this huge black-and-white photograph behind the receptionist desk of two models with dazzlingly bright smiles.

"Officers?" Dr. Hausler comes into the waiting area in his lime green smock.

"Dr. Marvin Hausler?" says Ceepak in that scary way you never want to hear a law enforcement officer say your name.

"That's right. What's this all about?"

"Gail Baker."

"What about her?"

"We understand you two dated."

"Is that against the law?" The monkey-faced schmuck in the smock thinks he just made a funny, so he triumphantly pushes his glasses up on his nose.

"No, sir," says Ceepak. "However, Ms. Baker was recently murdered."

"What?"

I help the dentist out: "Somebody killed her."

Dr. Hausler blinks a lot. "Stephanie?"

"Yes, sir?"

"Perhaps you should go home."

Stephanie grabs her stuff, jams it into her pocketbook, and scoots out the door.

"Am I a suspect?" Dr. Hausler asks when the receptionist is gone.

"Where were you last night, Dr. Hausler?" says Ceepak.

"I am a suspect, aren't I? Why? Because I called her a bitch and a tease?"

"Last night?"

"I had a date."

"With whom?"

"This girl."

"What girl?"

Hausler unsnaps the collar of his smock. "Her name was Amber."

Ceepak and I each puzzle up an eyebrow.

"She works for an escort service. Elegant Encounters." Dr. Hausler fumbles in his pants—the back pockets, thank God. Pulls out a wallet. "Here. This is the credit card receipt. They put the girl's name on the receipt, but I think it might be an alias or a stage name."

Well, duh.

"When did your 'date' begin?" asks Ceepak.

"Eight o'clock."

"And when did it end?"

I'm guessing eight-oh-two.

"She left at three or four in the morning."

"Why the long night?"

Dr. Hausler blushes.

"We ended up in a barter situation."

"Come again?"

"Her tooth was hurting her. Number fifteen on the upper

right. The pulp chamber had seriously deteriorated and she desperately needed a root canal. So, we came here."

Why do I think Dr. Hausler gave Amber all the nitrous oxide she wanted?

"The procedure took quite some time . . . and then . . . well . . . as I stated, it was a barter situation."

"Do you have a phone number for this Elegant Encounters agency?" asks Ceepak.

Dr. Hausler dips back into the wallet. Pulls out a black-and-pink business card. Or, it could be one of those club cards they punch every time you buy something, like at the coffee shop; get enough hole punches, you get a freebie.

"Elegant Encounters provides a very useful service," Hausler goes on while Ceepak jots down the information from the card. "They cater to professional and upscale gentlemen seeking companionship—men whose lifestyles may not allow them the opportunity to meet quality people in conventional ways."

I figure in his spare time Dr. Hausler memorizes the portal pages to porn sites.

"Do you know of any other men who were dating Ms. Baker?" Ceepak asks.

"Pick up the phone book."

"Can you be a little more specific?"

"Look for a rich man. Probably someone older. A lot older. Very wealthy."

"Why do you say that?"

"Gail liked her bling. The shinier and flashier the better. On our last date, I gave her this diamond pendant necklace. Cost five thousand dollars at the Tiffany store over in Red Bank. Came in the little blue box with the bow, the whole megillah. You know what Gail said when I gave it to her?"

We play along. Shake our heads.

"She told me it was cute. That's when I noticed her diamond

earrings. They probably cost four times as much as my chintzy necklace!"

The happy couple in the black-and-white photo behind the counter is still smiling. Dr. Hausler, not so much.

"We'll attempt to corroborate your story with the escort service," says Ceepak, "and we may need to speak with you again."

"I'm not going anywhere."

The way he says it, it sounds like he's commenting on the state of his life, not his travel plans.

Ceepak's cell chirps. The personal line.

He answers it.

"Hello."

I hear a voice leaking out, and it doesn't sound like Rita or his stepson, T.J. I know both their squawks.

"How did you get this phone number? I see. No. It's not a problem, Skip. I'm glad you called. That's right. We are currently investigating her death. And, may I offer you my condolences. If memory serves, you and Gail dated a few years back."

Yep. Back when Skippy was a part-timer with a cell phone stuck to his ear when he should've been directing traffic.

"We're on our way."

He closes up the cell phone.

"Dr. Hausler, thank you for your time."

"Sure. I . . . I . . ." He fumbles for words. "I'm sorry someone did what they did to Gail. She was so full of life. Now she's dead."

He probably should've fumbled a little longer.

Ceepak nods grimly. Gestures toward the door.

We head out, hit the parking lot.

"What's up?" I ask.

"Skip O'Malley. He, like Dr. Hausler, thinks Gail Baker may have been dating a wealthier, older man."

"Really? Who?"

"His father."

17

KING PUTT MINI GOLF IS STARTING TO GET CROWDED.

This is where the families with kids come after they boogie-board on the beach all day, before they go out for the fifth pizza of the week. More will come after dinner, before ice cream.

We park off to the side of the big pink pyramid, right beside the King Putt pickup truck. The door panel is painted with a bubble-nosed cartoon of the boy king in his Pharaoh hat—a green golf ball where the emerald scarab usually goes.

As we hike across the parking lot I can see a sunburned boy in a baggy T-shirt and shorts lining up his shot on hole number eleven: The Sphinx. I want to tell him to forget about aiming for the tunnel between the lion's paws, go for the bank shot; carom your ball off the curb to the right. But he's nine and I'm supposed to be more mature. Just ask Mrs. Starky.

"T.J. and his buddies are coming here tomorrow morning," says Ceepak. "A farewell to Sea Haven party. Rita's organizing it.

I hope we don't have to miss the entire affair. I imagine we will be rather busy."

Hi diddly dee. The cop's life for me. Duty calls, the family suffers.

Ceepak's stepson will be shipping off to Annapolis in a couple of weeks to start what they call "Plebe Summer." Apparently, it's the naval academy's version of boot camp. T.J. will not get to see any family or have any liberty or shore leave (or whatever they call hanging out with your buddies) until Plebe Parents' Weekend in August.

"Is Dave Tranotti gonna be at the big send-off?"

"Roger that."

"Cool."

Tranotti is a little older than T.J. and is already a midshipman at Canoe U., which is what some people call the naval academy. Tranotti, another local, is the one who put the bug in T.J.'s ear about applying for an appointment to Annapolis. Some guys grow up this close to the ocean, they want to play with boats for the rest of their lives. BIG boats.

Ceepak taps his top shirt pocket. "I need to pay for the boys." He pulls out a folded-over check to make sure it's there, stuffs it back in.

Skippy comes out of the office pyramid in a windbreaker that covers the top half of his pleated Egyptian chariot driver skirt. I see the Pharaoh hat stuffed in the pocket.

"Thanks for coming over, you guys," he says, sounding kind of nervous. "I have a fifteen-minute break. Maybe we could talk across the street? One of those benches?"

He points to the Pig's Commitment, a restaurant where pork and pancakes are the main attractions. There are a couple of benches out front for people waiting for tables during the morning rush. It's 6 P.M., so they're empty.

That means I get to see Mrs. Starky's horse-tooth smile again.

There's an ad for All-A-Shore Realty on the back of the bench.

"Uh, Mr. O'Malley?" someone calls behind us.

It's a guy in green coveralls holding a Weed Whacker.

"What is it, Fred?"

Fred lifts the Weed Whacker a little higher. "I ran out of gas."

"Then refill it."

"Okay." We can see Fred thinking. It appears to be hard work. "Should I, like, go down to the gas station?"

Skippy gives us a perturbed "do-you-see-what-I-have-to-work-with" sigh.

"There's a gas can in the shed!" He gestures toward another pyramid, about fifteen feet tall, situated behind some fake palm trees on the far side of the bright blue River Nile snaking through the course. I see there are two handles on the front of the triangular structure. Clever. A hidden tool shed.

"Okay. Thanks, boss. When I refill the gas, should I keep whacking the weeds?"

"Yes—but only in the parking lot and around the fences. Not where people are playing!"

"You got it, Skipper!"

Fred salutes and bops off to gas up.

Skipper shakes his head. Sighs again. We go across the street.

"I found this when I was taking out the trash this morning. I try to pull out any recyclable paper. My dad just stuffs everything into one big can."

He shows us a sheet of paper with something printed on it. It's stained brown and dripping at the bottom.

"Sorry," says Skip. "Dad wadded it up and crammed it into an almost empty cup of coffee."

Ceepak reaches into his cargo pants pockets, pulls out a pair of forceps so he can examine what appears to be a digital photo printout.

It's a picture of Skippy's father, his arm draped around Gail

Baker's bikini'd waist at the Rusty Scupper. I recognize the red-and-white-checked tablecloths in the background. He's holding a bottle of beer. She's got her waitress pad. Both Gail and Mr. O'Malley are laughing, like they just shared a joke with whoever is behind the camera.

"He was trying to get rid of it," says Skippy. "When I heard Gail had been killed . . ." He chokes up for second. "Twice in one week. The bastard . . ."

"Come again?"

"Nothing."

Ceepak takes a small paper bag out of the below-the-knee pocket on the left leg of his cargo pants. Slips the crinkled picture into the evidence bag.

"Is this your only evidence of a relationship between your father and Ms. Baker?"

"Yeah. I mean, so far. I could, you know, look around. Check his phone records."

"That won't be necessary," says Ceepak. "And thank you for bringing this evidence to our attention."

"Is my father a suspect in Gail's murder, now?"

"He will be on our radar."

"You guys might want to talk to Aunt Frances. My mom's sister. Frances Ryan. She's still in town. I bet she'd know if my mom thought Dad was cheating on her with Gail or some other girl. They talked about everything."

I remember Aunt Frances from the funeral, snapping at the white-haired woman in the pew behind her, *"She was our sister before she was his goddamn wife!"*

Why do I have a feeling that Aunt Frances thinks about as much of Paddy O'Malley as Mrs. Starky thinks of me?

"Do you know where she is staying?" asks Ceepak.

"Over at the Atkinsons' motel. The Mussel Beach."

"And she'll be there tomorrow?"

Skip nods. "Yeah. All day. I'm taking her up to Newark Airport first thing Sunday morning."

"Thank you, Skip."

"I guess I still have a little detective in me."

"Indeed," says Ceepak. "I'm just sorry that your private investigation has, perhaps, exposed some ugly truths about your family."

"That's okay. My dad and I aren't that close. But I guess you know what that's like."

Ceepak gives Skip one of his confused-bird looks. His big jarhead tilts ever so slightly to the right. He does this when somebody says something he wasn't expecting—or something extremely rude.

"Well, I better get back to work," says Skippy.

"Us, too," says Ceepak.

"Right. Okay. Thanks for swinging by."

"Thanks for sharing your evidence with us."

Skippy thrusts out his hand. Ceepak takes it. Gives it a good shake.

Skippy beams.

Man—he so wants to prove to us that he could be a good cop. Well, he wants to prove it to Ceepak. I'm just always standing next to the big man in blue.

"Oh, one more thing, Skip," says Ceepak, reaching into his shirt pocket, pulling out that folded-over check. "My stepson and his friends will be visiting your golf course tomorrow morning. I believe they will be a party of six."

"Don't worry about it," says Skippy. "It's on the house."

"No. I insist on paying."

"And I insist on not taking your money."

"Skippy?"

"Sir?"

"I believe the Chiefs of Police Code of Ethics says it best: 'I will enforce the law courteously and appropriately without fear or

favor, malice or ill will, never employing unnecessary force or vio-
lence and . . . never accepting gratuities.'"

Skippy nods.

"It's forty-eight bucks for six of them," he says, sounding like
one of the nuns back in grade school just read him the riot act,
only this time it was Sister Ceepak.

Ceepak writes him a check. Skippy takes it, heads back to his
pyramid to hand kids their balls. Sorry. Whenever I think about
Skippy's job, I can't not go there.

The radios squeal on our belts.

"Unit A-twelve? Unit A-twelve?

"I got it," I say, grabbing my mobile unit off my belt. "This is
Officer Boyle."

"Be advised, Lieutenant William Botzong, the acting unit super-
visor of the MCU detectives, would like to talk to youse two."

Our new dispatcher. Dorian Rence. She tries to talk like an
episode of *Law and Order*, but every now and then, a Joiseyism
slips in.

"Be best to field the call on a land line," says Ceepak.

"We'll head back to the house," I say into my radio and get a
head nod from Ceepak for saying the right thing. "We can be there
in five."

"Ten–four," says Dorian. "I will advise Detective Botzong as to
your disposition and whereabouts."

"Thanks." I clip the radio back to my belt.

"Let's roll," says Ceepak. "Sounds like Detective Botzong has
new information to share."

Yeah. With "us twose."

18

"I'M GOING THROUGH THE CALL DATA NOW," SAYS DENISE Diego when Ceepak and I hit the house. "Should have something to show you guys in ten, twenty minutes."

She's at the vending machine. Refilling her Doritos stash. Fueling up on Red Bull.

"Thanks," says Ceepak. "Would you like a soft drink, Danny?"

"Sure."

We grab a couple of cold Cokes.

"So what do you think of Skippy's evidence?" I ask.

"Extremely circumstantial," says Ceepak. "I would imagine that many of the male patrons of The Rusty Scupper have asked Ms. Baker to pose with them. I am given to understand that the same sort of snapshots are often taken at Hooters."

True. I have two of those and one of Gail. I keep them hidden in a shoebox up in my closet.

"Skippy used to date Gail," I say.

"Indeed. I recall he was quite infatuated with her."

Yeah. That's who he was gabbing with when he was a summer cop and Ceepak yanked the phone out of his ear.

"So, why does he want us to think his father was having an affair with Gail Baker?" I ask.

"Because he and his father have 'issues.' I fear he is attempting to take advantage of Ms. Baker's death for his own purposes."

Wow. Not cool, Skip. Not cool.

I follow Ceepak into the dispatcher room where Mrs. Rence sits at a wraparound desk cluttered with computer monitors, punch-button consoles, and three-ring binders filled with police codes and emergency protocols.

"Welcome back, boys," she says when she sees us. "Detective Botzong will call at eighteen fifteen hours."

I smile. Mrs. Rence, who is what they call an empty nester, took this civilian job when her last kid shipped off to college. She's only been with us a couple of months but has already learned how to use the military time clock. I think Ceepak gave her lessons.

"Shall I put the call in the conference room when it comes through?" she asks.

"Roger that," says Ceepak. "And Dorian?"

"Yes, John?"

"We call it the interview room."

"Really?"

"Ten–four."

"Sorry. Too many years working for the electric company."

"It's all good," says Ceepak.

Mrs. Rence (we all call her that because, well, she looks like someone's mom) opens a little wire-bound notebook. Jots down "Interview Room" under a list of other terms: Dee Wee (driving while intoxicated), the house (the stationhouse, where we are now), Loo (slang for "Lieutenant" that cops actually like).

116

"Dorian," says Ceepak, "do you know how we can get in touch with Sergeant Dominic Santucci?"

"He clocked out at fifteen hundred hours," she reports. "He'll probably be working his side job tonight."

Side job? I thought he was going home to catch the Yankees.

Mrs. Rence flips through a purple binder where she has everything organized inside plastic flaps. I think she might be a scrapbooker on weekends.

"Here's his card. 'Italian Stallion Security.' This business number here is really just his cell phone."

Ceepak jots the number down.

"Thank you, Dorian. And thank you for not only learning your job so quickly but for doing it so well."

"You trying to butter me up so I'll bring in another loaf of pumpkin bread?"

"Yes, ma'am."

She laughs. "I've got work to do here. So ten-whatever, youse two."

We set up shop in the interview room, which is really just a room with a long table, a one-way mirror, a couple of chairs and a speakerphone. It's also where we store the Christmas lights in the off-season, which, in certain parts of New Jersey, means you take 'em down at Easter, put 'em back up after Halloween.

The phone burps. Ceepak punches the speaker button.

"This is Ceepak."

"I have Detective Botzong for you. Please hold."

We do. We sit and stare at the phone like it's a dog we expect to roll over or something.

"Ceepak?"

"Yes, sir?"

"Bill Botzong. Sorry to keep you waiting."

"No problem."

"We have a lot to talk about. My team's moving fast. You guys pick up anything at your end?"

"We've talked to the few neighbors currently in residence on Tangerine Street."

"And?"

"All we have so far is a dog barking at three A.M."

"Could coincide with the body dump," says Botzong. "The M.E.'s initial time-of-death estimate is one A.M. Friday. Our guy kills Ms. Baker, cuts her up, stuffs her into the suitcases, goes looking for a spot to drop the bags. He picks, for whatever reason, Tangerine Street. Gets there about three in the morning. The dog hears the pickup truck—"

"Your sure it was a pickup?"

"Carolyn Miller is. Probably a Dodge Ram, she says. See, a guy working a rake, he has to stop raking at some point. This guy, he did it all the way back to the running board on the side of his truck, or so we suppose. Carolyn found tire tracks in the sandy edge of the street where he couldn't rake because he was too busy driving away."

"Do you have a model number?"

"BFGoodrich G-Force T/A KDW 205/50ZR 15s. They got this unidirectional racing stripe–style tread design and an increased interior groove offset for snow and sand traction."

Wow. Ms. Miller is good.

"Any of Ms. Baker's known acquaintances pickup truck jockeys?"

"Negative," says Ceepak. "So far, we have talked to Dr. Marvin Hausler, a local dentist, who had been overheard on several occasions making derogatory remarks about Ms. Baker. He and she had been romantically involved for a brief period of time. The dentist, while harboring deep-seated resentment toward the victim, has an alibi."

"You buy it?"

"Yes. It is a rather embarrassing admission, one I do not think he would offer were it not true. He told us he was with a hired call girl from an escort service on Thursday night into Friday morning."

"Yeah," says Botzong. "They don't usually go with that one unless it's true."

"We have some other leads," I toss in, just because I feel like we're letting the team down. They've got a time-of-death estimate and Carolyn Miller on the tires; we've got nothing except a yippy dog, a disgruntled dentist who drills hookers for free, and a digital cheesecake photo of Mr. O'Malley posing with Gail "Bikini Babe" Baker.

"We are also attempting to contact Officer Santucci, one of the initial responders to the crime scene," says Ceepak. "He is currently off the clock. We'll talk to him about the missing T-shirt."

"Good," says Botzong. "But it may not have been in the bag when he went rummaging through it searching for ID. Analysis of her jeans and undergarments suggest Ms. Baker was naked when she was dismembered. The bloodstains on the fabric are passive transfers. Pool pattern. The clothes were most likely placed into the suitcases on top of the severed limbs. They soaked up blood like a sponge would."

"They were not spattered?"

"Correct. Therefore, the clothes were not present during the dismemberment process, which . . ."

There's a pause as Detective Botzong shuffles through some papers.

". . . was most likely done with a Lenox twelve-inch, thirty-two-teeth-per-inch, bi-metal hacksaw blade with their Tuff Tooth design. Virtually unbreakable. A ten-pack costs fifteen dollars and twenty cents at Home Depot."

"So," says Ceepak, "the missing T-shirt may still be at the scene of the crime."

"Right. Or in the doer's memory box. He might be one of these psycho souvenir takers."

Ceepak and I give each other a quick glance. We've dealt with one of those before; he was playing Whack A Mole up and down the island with buried body parts.

"We're also talking to Continental Airlines," says Botzong."

"About the partial baggage tags?" asks Ceepak.

"You saw those, huh?"

"Yes. During our initial survey of the crime scene."

"You're good, Ceepak. Anyway, we have half a bar code and half a number. Not much to work with, but the airline's seeing what they can dig out of their computers."

That might be our lucky break. The tags could tell us whose suitcases we're dealing with. We know they're not brand-new; somebody used them on a trip. Most likely, our killer checked them on a Continental flight because you only have suitcases with remnants of baggage stickers if the bags belong to you.

"Cause of death?" asks Ceepak.

"Blunt force impact. Somebody clobbered her in the back of her head repeatedly. Something hard and small. Maybe a hammer."

I sip my Coke. Hope it will settle my stomach.

"There's some good news," says Botzong. "Dr. Kurth assures us Ms. Baker was not sexually molested."

Ceepak nods. "Good to know. Any trace of the killer on her body?"

"Nothing. No hair, no lint, no prints. I'm thinking he was wearing Saran Wrap. Knew what he was doing. However, we did find some interesting evidence in Miss Baker's hair and under her nails."

Ceepak flips over a page in his notebook. "Go on."

"Shampoo and soap. My team tells me the shampoo is Johnson's No More Tears No More Tangles Plus Conditioner for Straight Hair."

The whole name goes into Ceepak's book.

"Doesn't help us much," says Botzong. "They sell the stuff everywhere. Likewise with the soap. Irish Spring Original, what they call their Ulster Fragrance."

That seems strange. Irish Spring is typically a guy soap, although the ads used to have this lovely Irish lass saying, *"Manly yes, but I like it, too."* I never met a real woman who did.

"She was probably holding the soap when our doer came at her from behind," Botzong continues.

"How so?" says Ceepak.

"She really dug her nails into it. Gouged the bar. We found the soap burrowed up under all four fingernails on her right hand."

"So, your hypothesis is that the assailant broke into her home and surprised her while she was showering?"

"No," says Botzong. "We inventoried her home when we went through it. She used Pantene and Dove. I'm figuring she knew the guy who did this. Went to his place. Maybe she wanted to clean up before or after they did what they went there to do."

"He probably dismembered her in the shower as well," says Ceepak. "He would be able to wash away the evidence."

"Right. We find the shower, we'll find blood, I guarantee it," says Botzong. "You can't scrub it away completely. We get in there with Luminol and a UV light, we'll find residue." He pauses. "Of course, the scenario doesn't make much sense."

"Because Dr. Kurth estimates the time of death to be one A.M. Friday?" says Ceepak.

"Exactly. Maybe she'd take a shower that late, but shampoo? I don't know. Her hair was long, down past her shoulders. Wouldn't dry right away. And who hits the sack with sopping wet hair, especially if it's not your own bed or pillow?"

"Good question," says Ceepak.

There's a knock at the door. Denise Diego. She waves a sheaf of papers to let us know she's found something.

"Detective Botzong?" says Ceepak.

"Yeah?"

"We have just been joined on this end by Officer Denise Diego, who has been running down Gail Baker's cell phone records. We, of course, have not had time to analyze or filter her findings."

"That's okay. Give it to me raw."

Ceepak motions for Diego to come into the room. Gestures toward the speakerphone. The floor is hers.

"Okay. There's a lot of data in the dump. Ms. Baker worked her cell to the max. Calls. Texts. E-mails. On my first pass, I concentrated on her final twenty-four hours."

"Good call," says Botzong on the voice box.

"Thank you, sir."

"What'd you find?"

"Couple things. First—she made dozens of calls to the same number, an M. Minsky, here in Sea Haven."

"That's Marny," I say. "One of her best friends."

Another item goes on the To Do list.

"What else, Officer Diego?" says Ceepak.

"A couple of calls to Mike Charzuk."

"The trainer at the gym," I say.

"What time?" Botzong asks.

"The last one was eleven forty-five P.M. Thursday."

"When did we issue Ms. Baker the warning ticket, Danny?" asks Ceepak.

I try to remember what I wrote down. "Like, eleven."

"So, she most likely contacted the personal trainer immediately afterward."

"Why would she do that?" asks Botzong. "Why call her calisthenics coach?

"They were, you know, talking about hooking up," I say. "Maybe they finally did."

"Someone else for you guys to talk to."

"Roger that," says Ceepak. "He is definitely on the list."

And moving up. If he talked to her that late, the hookup may have ended with a hammer and hacksaw in the shower.

"Anything else?" asks Ceepak.

"That's it until right after midnight. Twelve-oh-five A.M. she sent a short text message."

"Short?"

"Not much data in the transfer. That was the last time she used her phone."

"To whom did she text?"

Diego runs her finger down two different sheets of paper, looking for a match.

"Area code 609. Another local number. Mr. Patrick O'Malley."

19

OKAY.

Maybe Skippy is a better detective than we gave him credit for.

"Does that last number appear elsewhere in the phone records?" Ceepak asks.

"Yeah," says Officer Diego. "Several times. Earlier in the month. Almost once a day through last Saturday morning, then nothing until last night."

"You know this Patrick O'Malley?" asks Botzong.

"Roger that," says Ceepak. "One of Sea Haven's most prominent businessmen. His wife died last Saturday from a heart attack during the inaugural ride of Mr. O'Malley's new roller coaster."

"Yeah, I read about that. You think maybe the heart attack might've been caused by something besides an adrenaline rush?"

"We had no reason to think so previously."

Yeah. But maybe now we do. Maybe the wife was giving Mr. O'Malley too much grief about his girlfriend Gail.

"Twice in one week . . ." I mumble.

"What's that?" says Botzong on the speakerphone.

"Danny?" This from Ceepak.

"It's what Mr. O'Malley's son said. 'Twice in one week.'"

"Implying," says Ceepak, "that his father was implicated in Ms. Baker's death as well as that of his wife."

"Guess you guys better go have a chat with this Mr. O'Malley. See if he has any receipts from Home Depot for hacksaw blades."

As soon as we're off the conference call, Ceepak gives Diego a new assignment: search the public real estate records and find out who owns number One Tangerine Street.

Good. Means we're not going back to All-A-Shore Realty to talk to Mrs. Starky. I won't be verbally castrated again until the next time Sam invites me over for Sunday dinner.

While Officer Diego clacks her keyboard and scours historical real estate transactions, Ceepak and I hit the road and head north on Beach Lane.

Time to talk to Skippy's poppa—if we can find him at the Rolling Thunder. Meanwhile, Dylan Murray, who stayed on the clock after Santucci punched out, is on the street with his partner, Ron Edison, tracking down Mike Charzuk, Gail's personal trainer and the second-to-last person she called. Mrs. Rence is also helping out, calling Santucci's cell phone. Repeatedly.

"He must have it off," she reported in her last radio transmission. "No answer and no busy signal."

"Keep trying."

We're moving past the Sea Spray Hotel when Dylan Murray radios in.

"Unit A-twelve, this is Baker-six."

Ceepak's at the wheel, so I take the call.

"This is A-twelve, go ahead."

"We're with Mr. Charzuk at Beach Bods gym. He has one more client scheduled. How shall we proceed?"

I glance over to Ceepak.

"Have them ask Mr. Charzuk to join us at the house at twenty hundred hours."

"Dylan," I say into the mic, "we'd like to talk to him in an hour—at eight."

"At the house?"

"Right."

"We'll offer him a ride."

"Thanks. Let us know if he turns down your invitation."

"You got it. Out."

It's nearly seven now. I sense Ceepak's plan. We spend the next hour with the last guy to communicate with Gail, then head back to the house to chat with the second-to-last guy. There's a pecking order to these things.

We pull into a municipal parking lot butting up to the boardwalk and have our pick of spaces, because, like I said, our seaside resort stays pretty sleepy until the end of June. We hike up a ramp that will have us hitting the boards pretty close to Pier Four, home to the brand-new Rolling Thunder. The tarry scent of creosote is almost strong enough to overpower the food odors sputtering out of the open-air concession stands. Almost. Italian sausage sandwiches with onions and peppers put up a pretty good stink fight.

"Looks like they are testing the electricals," says Ceepak.

On the horizon, we're treated to a disco inferno of flashing colored lights. They must have all the bulbs on the Rolling Thunder synched up to a high-tech computer. They flicker, blink, strobe, and streak like chaser lights up and down the humps of the wooden scaffolding. Then they blast through a rainbow of color bursts. It's pretty awesome. Probably even more amazing when you're slightly buzzed. Trust me. My high school buddies and I could sit and stare at a blinking Ferris wheel for hours after chugging a few brewskis and smoking something I'd have to arrest myself for smoking these days.

"Hello, Samantha." Ceepak sees her first.

"Hi, guys! You still on the clock?"

"Roger that."

"Hey, Sam," I say, kind of sheepishly, because a) her mother royally reamed me out a couple of hours ago, and b) she's with a group of six or seven other kids her own age. I say that because Samantha Starky is four years younger than me. The crowd looks like her college buddies.

"How's it going, Danny?"

I shrug. "We're, you know, following up on a couple things."

"Cool."

"Is this *the* Danny?" asks one of her girlfriends.

"Yep. Oh, shoot—I forgot. You've never met any of my friends from school, have you, Danny?"

Okay. I think that was a dig.

Three girls and two guys are clustered around Sam now, nibbling on fried candy bars, sizing me up. A third guy who just paid for his fried Twinkie joins them. He's wearing a Rutgers Law School sweatshirt and shorts. Go Scarlet Knights.

"You're Danny?" The way he says it, I think he was expecting someone bigger, more intimidating. "We've heard so much about you."

"What is that thing, Richard?" Sam asks Sweatshirt Man with a flirty little giggle.

"Twinkie," Richard says with a mouth full of sponge cake and cream. "I thinkie."

The college kids laugh. They're into witty word play. Me and Ceepak? Fuhgeddaboutit.

"Meet Richard Heimsack and the rest of my study group," explains Sam. "We've all been working so hard, we wanted to blow off a little steam."

"Thanks for letting us borrow Sam tonight," says Heimsack, his mouth full of creamy mush. "She sure knows how to show a guy a good time. On the boardwalk, I mean."

He winks. I think that was another funny. Richard Heimsack must be the class clown in Tort Reform 101. With a last name like that, he better be.

Ceepak flips up his wrist, checks his G-Shock watch. "Danny?"

Yeah. I agree. Time for us to say buh-bye.

"We need to hit it," I say to Sam.

"Right."

"I'll call you tomorrow."

"Okay. Stay safe, you guys."

"Roger that," says Ceepak.

We march across the boardwalk toward the thunderbolt neon lights spelling out Rolling Thunder.

"Sorry about that," I say to Ceepak.

"About what?"

"Sam and her friends. Slowing us down."

"Not to worry." We keep walking. Out of the corner of my eye, I catch Ceepak pursing his lips, trying hard to think of what to say. "Danny . . . this job . . . it can put enormous strain on one's personal life and relationships."

"Yeah. I know."

It's a wrecking ball.

The Rolling Thunder isn't open for business; they're just testing out the lights, running empty trains around the track, greasing the rails. We go under the blinking entryway sign and head for the ticket booth.

We bump into our second surprise guest of the night: Sergeant Dominic Santucci, all decked out in black boots, black cargo pants and a black commando-style shirt. There's a radio clipped to his belt. It's black, too.

"Dom?" says Ceepak.

"Ceepak."

"What are you doing here?"

Santucci gestures with his head toward the ticket booth. "Running security for Mr. O'Malley."

"But the ride isn't even open."

"Doesn't matter. Mr. O'Malley asked me to escort him around town tonight."

"May I ask why?"

"He pays, I show up. Badda bing, badda boom."

"We need to talk to Mr. O'Malley."

"About what?"

"A matter related to our ongoing investigation."

"What? The dead chick in the suitcases?"

"Is Mr. O'Malley here?"

"Well, duh, Ceepak. What kind of security operation you think I run? Get hired to guard a guy and not guard him? Jesus."

"Let me be more specific. Where is Mr. O'Malley?"

"He and his son, Kevin, are walking the track. Making sure everything's copacetic for the big opening tomorrow."

"When will he be back down?"

"Five, ten minutes I figure."

"We need to ask him a few questions."

"Hang on." Santucci unclips his radio. "Mr. O'Malley? This is Security One, over."

We wait. Santucci chews his gum. Loudly.

"What the hell is it, Dom?" comes a snarl out of his radio.

"Couple of my buddies from the Sea Haven PD just dropped by. Say they want to talk to you."

"About what?"

Santucci turns to Ceepak. "What about?"

"The murder of Gail Baker."

Santucci chews his cud a little more slowly. Fewer pops. He brings the radio back to his mouth.

"That girl I was telling you about. Over."

"Mr. Santucci?" says a new voice on the radio. "This is Kevin O'Malley."

Santucci's back stiffens. I get the feeling Kevin is in charge of hiring security guards for O'Malley Enterprises. "Yes, sir?"

"Kindly inform the officers that we'll be down in five minutes."

"Will do. Over and out." Santucci clips the radio back to his belt. It's black, too. "They'll be down in five."

Right. We were paying attention.

"We'd also like to ask *you* a few questions, Dom," says Ceepak.

"Me? What about?"

"Did you remove an article of clothing from the suitcases?"

"What?"

"When you went searching for ID in Ms. Baker's clothing, did you take anything out of the two bags?"

"Are you freaking kidding me? You think I grabbed a souvenir or something?"

"Did you?"

"Fuck you, Ceepak. Okay? I'm off the job, so I can say it. Fuck. You."

"How long have you been employed by Mr. O'Malley?"

"None of your fucking business."

"What sort of things has he asked you to do in the past?"

"Keep annoying assholes like you out of his face, you jar-headed jag-off."

"Did you know about Mr. O'Malley's relationship with the deceased?"

"What, his wife?"

"Gail Baker."

Santucci's eyes slide back and forth a couple of times. He swipes at his mouth with his hand. "If he had a relationship with her, he didn't tell me."

"Does he pay you extra to lie for him?"

"What?"

"You do it pretty well," says Ceepak. "However your eye movements and hand gestures betray you, Dom. Avoiding eye contact. Touching your face."

Santucci gives us his donkey laugh, but it comes out sounding stilted. "You watch too much fucking TV, Ceepak."

"Dom?" Kevin O'Malley and his father emerge out of the darkness behind the ticket booth. "What's going on?"

"Mr. O'Malley, I'm Officer John Ceepak. This is my partner Danny Boyle."

"We know who you are," says Kevin.

"We need to ask your father a few questions."

"About what?" says the older Mr. O'Malley, stepping forward. It's a warm June night, but he's wearing a seersucker suit and white buck shoes. He was wearing the same outfit last Saturday. Must be his official uniform.

"Your relationship with Gail Baker."

"Don't say a word, Dad," advises Kevin. "Lou Rambowski is on the way."

Ceepak's eye twitches. Every cop in Sea Haven (and most of New Jersey) knows and despises the lawyer Louis "I Never Lose" Rambowski, ever since he helped a punk up in Newark get a free pass by making the jury believe it was a dead cop's own fault he got shot in the back of his head.

"Very well," says Ceepak, "we'll escort Mr. O'Malley to police headquarters and—"

"I know how to find headquarters," says Santucci. "I'll drive Mr. O'Malley."

"When will your lawyer arrive?" asks Ceepak.

"Late," says Kevin. "He's driving down from Montclair."

"How about we do this first thing tomorrow morning?" suggests Mr. O'Malley.

"We'd prefer discussing this matter this evening."

"Sure you would," says Kevin. "When my dad's lawyer's burned out after a three-hour drive."

"Look, fellas," says Big Paddy. "I'm not going anywhere. I've got a goddamn roller coaster to open tomorrow. I just buried my wife . . ." His voice catches. "I am not a flight risk."

"Fine," says Ceepak. "How early might you and your lawyer be available?"

"What time is the opening, Kev?"

"Ten."

"Will eight work for you, Officer Ceepak?" asks Mr. O'Malley, turning on his Irish charm.

"Seven is better."

"Jesus, Mary, and Joseph," he grumbles. "We'll bring the god-damn donuts. Come on, Dominic. Drive me home. This has been one helluva lousy day."

20

"I WONDER IF THE PERSONAL TRAINER LAWYERED UP, TOO," I say as we cruise back toward the house.

"It would be his right, Danny, and, even when innocent, an advisable move."

Ceepak. The guy not only plays by the rules, he thinks they're there for a reason besides making me wake up way too early on a Saturday morning.

"Before we talk to Mr. Charzuk," says Ceepak, "let's swing by Tangerine Street. See if the residents of number one are home tonight."

I'm at the wheel, so I keep us headed south on Beach Lane when we hit Cherry, the street where the municipal buildings and station-house are all clustered together. We roll through a forest of alphabetical tree-named streets and come to the corner of Tangerine.

The lights are not on in number one.

"Let's go knock on the door," says Ceepak.

Sure. Maybe they go to bed early. Like right after watching Jeopardy at 7 P.M.

We head up the steps to the porch.

"The statues are gone," I mumble.

Ceepak pulls the Maglite off his utility belt, flicks it on. Swings the beam across the shrubbery clumped around the small landing. Guess he's looking for tiny footprints. Maybe the gnomes all magically came to life last night and scurried away.

There's a burst of static on my radio.

"This is Diego for Ceepak and Boyle," comes a crackle out of the speaker.

I tug the thing off my belt.

"This is Boyle. Go ahead."

"Hey, Danny. Found what you guys were looking for. That house on Tangerine? Number one, right?"

"Right."

"Okay, it's owned by a corporation called Stromboli Enterprises."

"You're kidding me, right? Stromboli?"

"Hang on. Let's put a smile on that face."

She's quoting *The Dark Knight* again.

"There's more. This is why it took me, like, longer than five seconds to do a real estate title search. I had to dig through a sack of S-Corp crap to find some names. Here we go: Bruno Mazzilli is the CEO of Stromboli. Keith Barent Johnson is the chief operating officer. Hey, doesn't Mazzilli, like, own all the boardwalks?"

"Yeah. Thanks, Denise."

"And Johnson's a big cheese, too, am I right?"

"Affirmative," I say with a sigh.

"Thought so. You guys need anything else tonight?"

Ceepak motions for me to hand him my radio.

"Denise? We are going to need a subpoena," says Ceepak. "For Mr. O'Malley's phone records. The number corresponding to the one you ID'd on Gail Baker's bill."

"Yeah. Figured as much. It's already in the works."

"How long has this Stromboli Enterprises been the owner of number One Tangerine Street?"

"Um . . . four years. It's listed as an asset of the corporation. They have a couple of cars, too. Mustang convertibles. Sounds like a good place to work. Lots of perks. Probably free food."

"Thank you. Go home, Denise. Grab some shut-eye. I have a feeling we'll be running you ragged tomorrow as well."

"Saturday?"

"Yes. I'm afraid so."

"Cool. There's nothing on TV except baseball and infomercials about Snuggies. Hey, as soon as the O'Malley paperwork comes back from the judge, I'll let you know."

"Roger that." Ceepak hands me back the radio. "We are quite fortunate to have Ms. Diego on our team."

I nod, kind of absent-mindedly, because the hamster wheel in my head is spinning. Well, it's creaking like a rusty bicycle chain. I don't feed my hamsters enough sugar water.

"What's on your mind, Danny?" says Ceepak, making me think my mental gym equipment is squeaking out my ears.

"Mr. Mazzilli, the CEO of this shell company—Stromboli Enterprises—he was with Marny Minsky last Saturday at Big Kahuna's, which just happens to be owned by Stromboli's COO, Keith Barent Johnson."

Ceepak nods. He can sense I am attempting to make a logical deduction. I'm kind of new at it so it's slow going. He's patient. He'll wait.

"Gail Baker was also at the club, with a group of girlfriends. Gail and Marny were all air-kissy. Mazzilli saw the two of them in their mini-dresses, hugging like that, and he looked like, well, he looked . . ."

I'm trying to think of a grownup word for "horny."

". . . lascivious! The two girls were in really short, really tight skirts. Showing lots of thigh."

"What did you see Danny?"

I want to say "too much" but resist the urge.

"I saw Mr. Mazzilli whisper something naughty to Marny, who then whispered to Gail. She laughed. Shook her head. Mr. Mazzilli said, 'Live a little.' Gail said, 'Not tonight.' Mazzilli said he wanted a 'rain check.'"

"What do you suppose Mr. Mazzilli whispered to Ms. Minsky?"

"I dunno. Something lewd. I think he wanted, you know, both girls. A three-way. And Gail didn't seem upset by the suggestion. She just didn't want to do it that night."

"Have you seen Ms. Minsky since Saturday, Danny?"

"No. We should check with Bud. See if she's been back to the club."

"Agreed. Ms. Minsky and Ms. Baker were close?"

"Yeah. Looked like it."

And Mazzilli wanted to see them closer. Probably here. Number one Tangerine. The pornographic garden statues were supposed to help the girls get in the mood for a little frisky fun.

"I think this is Mr. Mazzilli's love shack," I blurt out. "I think he and Mr. Johnson bring their girlfriends, their mistresses, their goomahs here instead of The Smuggler's Cove."

The Cove is our local Motel No-Tell. You can get hourly rates on the room even if, like most guys, you only need three minutes.

"So," says Ceepak, picking up on my logic thread, flimsy as it is, "you hypothesize that, at a later date, perhaps Thursday night, Mr. Mazzilli once again made his proposal to the two young ladies."

"And don't forget, we have the Mazzilli–O'Malley connection."

"Indeed. They are partners on the roller coaster."

"Maybe, if Gail and Mr. O'Malley were texting each other, having an affair like Skippy suggested, Mazzilli knew about it. Wanted to be partners on that, too. Maybe he wanted a four-way."

My stomach lurches up into my mouth at the thought of two flabby middle-aged men—undoubtedly with muffin tops around their bellies—rolling in the hay with taut and tawny Gail and Marny.

But I soldier on.

"Maybe the four of them came here. One thing leads to another, Gail ends up dead, and Marny, afraid she's next, hightails it out of town."

"Interesting," says Ceepak.

"It's just a hunch," I say. "A wild idea."

Ceepak nods. He knew that's what it was.

"We need to search this house!"

"What would be searching for?" Ceepak asks.

"Evidence!"

"Danny, the Fourth Amendment requires that searches be specific and reasonable."

I think Ceepak should run for president—he's an expert on constitutional law, too.

"As you know," he continues in his calm, professorial tone, the one he uses whenever I make a bone-headed suggestion, "a judge will only approve our request for a warrant if we are specific as to the items we are searching for and prove that probable cause exists that the specific item will be located in a specific place at the time the warrant would be executed."

"Unless it's in plain view," I toss in. "Then we don't need a warrant to seize it."

"Only if we are legally in the location at the time the item is seen."

Bummer.

Ceepak glances at his watch. He knows Gail's personal trainer will be at the house in half an hour. "What do you suggest, Danny?"

"Let's look around a little. We've got time. See if we can see anything out in the open."

"Such as?"

"I dunno. Gail's missing Sugar Babies T-shirt?"

"Very well. Let's take a quick look around."

"Can we look through the windows?"

"Negative."

Yeah. I guess it's not considered plain view if you climb up on each other's shoulders to sneak a peek.

So we head down the porch steps and stroll through the manicured pebble lawn.

"Let's circle around back," I say.

Ceepak nods.

I'm hoping there's a clothesline where Mr. Mazzilli might've hung his blood-soaked cabana outfit.

We head up the alleyway of concrete pavers that runs between Mr. Mazzilli's place and the neighbor's. The sun's low in the west, sinking down on the bay side of the island, so its fading beams are blocked by Mrs. D'Ambrosio's two-story house next door and the PVC fence on the borderline between the properties. It's kind of dark. Hard to see where we're walking. I knee something wobbly. Glass bottles jingle.

"Sorry."

Seems I accidentally bumped into that booze bottle recyclables barrel that somebody dragged back here—probably when they came over to hide the lewd lawn ornaments.

The rattling bottles and cans startle Puck. We hear yippy barks on the other side of the fence.

"Interesting," says Ceepak.

Yeah. This walkway must pass a window where Puck likes to snooze. Was somebody else back here very early this morning? Is that what made him start barking up a storm at three A.M. when every dog I've ever met is usually sound asleep on the living room couch or curled up in their master's favorite chair?

Ceepak flicks on his Maglite and spotlights the outdoor shower built up against the fence that I noticed earlier.

It's really just the Jersey Shore equivalent of an outhouse, even behind the most expensive home on the block. Typically, you have your white-washed tongue-and-groove walls, an elevated cedar deck for a floor, and a drain that dumps water on the sandy soil that'll drink anything it can get, even if it's soapy.

Ceepak swings his light down to the bottom of the propped-open door. There's a cinder block acting as a doorstop, maybe so the inside will dry out, keep down the mildew and toe fungus grunge.

We move closer.

Peer through the open door.

In plain view we both plainly see two things: a bottle of No More Tears No More Tangles Plus Conditioner for Straight Hair and a green bar of Irish Spring soap.

Time to call Bill Botzong and the state CSI crew.

I think we just found where the shampoo and soap residue came from.

21

TWO NJ STATE POLICE GUYS SHOW UP TO LOCK DOWN THE shower stall.

"Botzong's up in Hamilton," says the one named Reynolds (but we can call him "Spuddie"). He and his partner, a guy named Malone (no known nickname), have unrolled enough Crime Scene Do Not Cross tape to wrap a dozen yellow mummies.

"We're gonna preemptively lock down the house," adds Spuddie. "You guys working on warrants?"

"Roger that," says Ceepak, who is crouching in front of the open shower door, playing his light against the wall of the stall. I notice that, every now and then, it hits a splotch of white that doesn't quite match the surrounding white wall.

Like somebody painted over a stain they didn't want us to see.

A bloodstain.

"We should have no problem obtaining warrants for the shower," says Ceepak. "But we might have to push the judge to gain access to the house."

"Big shots own the place?" asks Malone, gesturing at the boxy McMansion.

Ceepak nods. "Two of the town's leading citizens."

"Your judge one of 'em?"

"No." Ceepak gets up from his crouch. "How long do you estimate that it will it take Detective Botzong to arrive?"

"It's a long haul from Hamilton," says Spuddie. "Maybe fifty, sixty miles. I'm guessing Bill and his crew will show up around eight thirty, nine o'clock."

"Danny, you and I should head back to the house, talk to Mike Charzuk. We'll circle back in forty-five minutes, catch up with Detective Botzong."

"Cool," I say.

The two state cops glare at me. The Staties always shave the sides of their heads and wear their hats so the crimped brim practically touches the tip of their noses. They also wear riding pants and black boots like they're working for a dictator in some tiny country where the women have to wear sacks over their heads. They're very scary military-looking dudes. More so than Ceepak—who really was military.

So I add, "Ten–four." They seem to like that better.

"No one in or out," Ceepak says to Spuddie and Malone, giving them a two-finger salute off the tip of his cap.

"Roger that," says Spuddie, saluting back.

"We're on it," adds Malone.

"Appreciate it," I say.

They glare at me again. Probably wonder how I ever became a cop. Yeah. I wonder that sometimes, too. I used to round up shopping carts in the parking lot at Wal-Mart. Then I met Ceepak and life's been one big roller coaster ride ever since.

Mike Charzuk is waiting for us in the lobby of the stationhouse, on the other side of the short railing that separates the police from those we're sworn to protect. Makes us feel safer.

Charzuk is not alone. Peter O'Malley, the gay son, is sitting next to the personal trainer in one of our scoop-bottomed plastic seats.

Does this mean Charzuk is gay, too?

If so, why were he and Gail talking about hooking up?

Am I looking at another potential three-way here? The two-guys-one-girl kind I never actually wanted to include in my personal fantasy files?

"Mr. Charzuk?" says Ceepak.

"Yes, sir," says Charzuk, standing up. Smoothing out his sweatpants.

"I'm just here as a friend," says Peter O'Malley.

"I was kind of nervous about coming alone," says Mike.

Ceepak nods. "Understandable. We just want to ask you a few questions. Is Mr. O'Malley your lawyer?"

"No. Just . . . a friend."

O'Malley blinks—silently daring us to ask "what kind of friend?" But we don't.

"I work for Peter's landscaping company," Charzuk explains, "when I'm not at the gym."

Oh. That kind of friend.

"Would you like a lawyer present while we talk to you?" asks Ceepak.

"Do I need one?"

"That is entirely your call. If you cannot afford one—"

"No. That's okay. I want to help you guys catch whoever did this to Gail."

"May I come with Mike?" asks Peter O'Malley.

"Are you a lawyer?" asks Ceepak.

"No."

"Then you will need to wait out here."

We sit down in the interview room. Charzuk has a bottle of water.

I grabbed a cup of bad coffee because this figures to be a long night. The coffee has been on the Bunn burner so long, it smells like gym sock soup.

Ceepak? He's on whatever natural fuel Zen masters tap into. I think he could go seventy-two hours without sleep and stay totally alert. I think he had to over in Iraq.

"Were you and Ms. Baker romantically involved?" Wow. First question out of the box. Ceepak's on a tight schedule.

"Is that important?"

"Yes."

"Now and then."

"How about this week?" I ask.

He shakes his head.

"Really?" I press on. "Then why were you two talking about hooking up last Sunday at the gym?"

"Huh?"

"I overheard your conversation."

"You work out?" He sounds surprised. I guess he caught a glimpse of my physique. "At Beach Bods?"

"Yeah."

"Sorry. I didn't recognize you."

"She told you she was free for the week."

"That's right."

"You offered to give her a 'deep tissue' massage afterwards."

Charzuk sits back in his chair. Rubs his tattooed arms like he's cold. "You heard all that?"

"Yeah."

I think I'm freaking him out.

"Look, we weren't romantically involved. We just liked to, you know, help each other out from time to time. Physically."

I nod like I know how that goes.

Yeah. Right.

Ceepak's eyebrows, however, are arched halfway up his forehead.

This whole friends-with-benefits, sex buddy stuff is new to him. I think it became an American tradition while he was overseas serving his country instead of back here making booty calls.

"Gail really couldn't afford to get, you know, serious about me or any guy her own age."

"Pardon?" says Ceepak.

"She . . . her money . . . to earn a living . . . the tips at The Rusty Scupper aren't great . . . she wasn't a prostitute or anything. . . ."

"But?" Ceepak says for him.

"She was more like a geisha girl. Made rich men happy. They, you know, said thanks. Gave her stuff."

The bling the dentist told us about.

"They paid for her clothes, her gym dues and training sessions. All she had to do was, well, keep looking amazingly hot."

"Who are these wealthy men?" asks Ceepak.

"She never named names. Called them her sugar daddies."

Making her a sugar baby. The tiny T-Shirt was either her little joke or her Hooters-style uniform.

"Where would she rendezvous with these gentlemen?"

"I'm not sure. I know it wasn't a cheesy hotel like the Smuggler's Cove or anything. They had really classy parties all the time. Champagne. All the lobster and prime rib she could eat, which wasn't much, because she had to keep the weight off to keep her men happy."

"Did she ever talk about a house on Tangerine Street?"

"No. I think it was some place on the beach, though. She'd call it the Sugar Shack or the Beach Boys Clubhouse."

"Thursday night, right before she was murdered, Ms. Baker called you."

"That was right before?" He takes a long drink out of his water bottle.

"Do you remember the content of your conversation?"

"Some. Sure. Yeah. She'd been to the party house. Said she had wanted to just hang and chill with her 'sorority sisters' but one of the 'gentlemen' at the house wanted to, you know, get busy with her. But this guy wasn't *her* guy."

"They had assignments?" I ask.

"You could call it that. Each girl had their main man. Marny might know more."

"Ms. Minsky?"

"Right. She's the one who got Gail into the whole scene. Recruited her. Told her she'd have some laughs, meet some amazingly rich men. Gail even got to hang with the mayor."

"Mr. Sinclair?"

"Yeah. He was at the house a bunch of times. She met some state senators, too and could get you tickets to any concert or game or anything. Gail's old guy had some urgent family business to deal with this week so that's why she told me on Sunday that maybe we could hook up while he dealt with whatever. But, like I said, it didn't pan out."

"Why the late night call on Thursday?"

"She was in a jam, didn't know what to do. I guess this drunk jerk at the house grabbed her and sucked on her neck so hard he gave her a hickey, like they were in high school."

I remember seeing the neck hickey.

"She booked, hopped in her car, went speeding out of there, like fifty in a fifteen zone."

Remember that, too.

"A couple of cops pulled her over. Gave her a warning."

Ceepak and I are both nodding now.

"She thought the guy who'd been groping her might cause trouble. Kick her out of the club. And that would mean losing everything!"

He pauses. Realizes that, in the end, Gail lost a whole lot more.

"Anyway, I told her she should call her guy. Tell *him* what this other guy had tried to do. I figured her sugar daddy would protect his . . ."

He wants to say property.

"...investment. Gail thought that was a great idea. Said she was going to text him right away. I reminded her it was nearly midnight. She told me she didn't care."

It all lines up with what we already know.

Big Paddy O'Malley had to be Gail Baker's sugar daddy.

That's who she texted after she called Charzuk.

"She'd gone to that house to celebrate," he adds, shaking his head.

"Celebrate what?"

"I think this is why she didn't want to fool around with me anymore. She had convinced herself she had a shot at actually marrying her guy. 'Becoming the next Mrs. Moneybags,' is what she said when we went out dancing Tuesday night. I guess her guy had just dumped his wife—something they all say but never really do."

"How well do you know Peter O'Malley?" says Ceepak.

"He's my boss. He designs the landscapes, hires me and a couple other guys to do the installations. The heavy lifting."

"And how does Peter O'Malley feel about his father?" asks Ceepak.

"Big Paddy?"

"Right."

"They're not very close."

"Would Peter be happy to see his father go to jail?"

"I don't know. You'd have to ask him."

"I'm interested in your opinion."

"Well, I know he doesn't like his old man, but he doesn't hate him like he hated his mother. I think she tried to send him to a camp in Texas to cure him of being gay or something."

"Did Peter O'Malley in any way coach you on what to tell us tonight?"

"Peter? Why would he do that?"

"Did he?"

"No. I just didn't want to come down here alone. I called a couple people. Peter was the only one willing to come with me."

"Commendable," says Ceepak. "He must be a very good boss."

"Yeah."

Ceepak stands up. "You'll be in town for the foreseeable future?"

"Yes, sir."

"We may need to talk to you again."

Now I stand, and Mike Charzuk takes the hint. We're done. He's free to go. He can stand, too.

"I hope you guys catch whoever killed Gail," he says, sliding his chair under the table.

"Rest assured, Mr. Charzuk," says Ceepak. "We will."

Yeah, even if it was one of the town's big dogs.

Like Big Paddy or—even bigger—our mayor.

22

"I WISH PETER O'MALLEY WASN'T CONNECTED TO MIKE Charzuk," says Ceepak as we roll south, heading back to number One Tangerine.

"You think O'Malley is pushing Charzuk to say bad stuff about Big Paddy?"

"Mr. Charzuk insists that such is not the case. So, I will take him at his word."

I'm driving. Ceepak's thinking.

I can always tell. He gets this faraway look in his squinty eyes, like he's back in the turret up top on an armored personnel carrier over in Iraq, hunting unseen enemies.

"Let's stop at Three Tangerine first, Danny," he says after a long moment of tire-humming silence.

"Mrs. D'Ambrosio and Puck?"

Ceepak nods. "According to Mr. Charzuk, very powerful men, including Mayor Sinclair, were occasional guests at the so-called Sugar Shack."

"Mayor Sinclair's married," I say. "Three kids."

"I suspect most of the men fit that same profile."

Yeah. They're all cheaters—putting them in direct violation of Ceepak's honor code.

"Danny, do you remember what Mayor Sinclair said to us on the steps of the stationhouse?"

I'm ready to answer, "Have a sunny, funderful day," because that's what the doofus says every time he gets half a chance. But Ceepak fills in the blanks for me:

"'Let's not bother the neighbors too much up and down Tangerine Street.'"

"Right! Probably because they'd seen him hanging out where maybe he shouldn't have been hanging out."

And I mean that last bit literally.

"Let's go bother the next-door neighbor," says Ceepak, a glint in his eye. I think it's the glint he got when he scoped out a sniper nobody else had seen up in a Baghdad bell tower.

Mrs. D'Ambrosio greets us at her front door in the same bathrobe she was wearing earlier, even though it's almost ten o'clock at night. She's cradling Puck in her arms.

"What's with all the police next door?" she asks.

"The State Police Office of Forensics Sciences is investigating what we believe to be a crime scene."

"At the frat house?"

"Ma'am?"

"Sorry. That's what I call it. Some nights, it's like that movie *Gorilla House* over there."

I think she means *Animal House*.

"Loud parties?" says Ceepak.

"Let's say boisterous. A lot of high-pitched squeals and giggles from the girls. Very young girls."

"Have you ever filed a complaint?"

"No. Officer Santa Lucci told me it would be a bad idea."

"You mean Sergeant Santucci of the Sea Haven Police Department?"

"Is he really a cop?"

"Yes, ma'am."

"Huh. He told me he was. Wasn't in uniform, though. Didn't have a badge except this thing that said 'Security.' My kid has one just like it, only his says 'Deputy.'"

"When did you talk to Officer Santucci?"

"Two weeks ago. When I first moved in. He told me I was early, that the season didn't really start till the fourth of July. He was dressed all in black so I didn't argue."

He must've been working his side job—Italian Stallion Security.

"Anyway, he told me the 'festivities' next door at number one would die down at the end of the month, that the house would be rented out to tenants on a week-to-week basis. But, until such time, the police weren't interested in hearing from me about anything going on next door because some very important people with even more important friends owned the property. So, if I did complain, well . . . I'm not sure . . . but it sounded like I might be the one who'd end up getting arrested because, as Mr. Santa Lucci pointed out, this house has several code violations."

"Did he mention what those might be?"

"No. He didn't have to. I understood what he meant: if I made trouble for the boys next door, they'd make worse trouble for me. I know they know the mayor."

"You've seen him next door?"

"Once. Came in a SUV with tinted windows. Puck and I peeked through the curtains. Saw him go inside. Probably up to the third-floor deck. That's where they have the hot tub. And you should see the girls running around over there in their skimpy bikinis. It's like an invasion of Playboy Bunnies—only Playboy Bunnies wear more clothes."

"What about last night?" says Ceepak. "Did Officer Santucci come over here again?"

"He didn't have to. I got the message the first time."

"Ms. D'Ambrosio?"

"Yes?"

"You are free to call the Sea Haven Police Department any time you have a complaint or problem of any sort."

"Really? What about Officer Santa Lucci?"

"I would not worry about him."

"Really?"

"Yes, ma'am. I'd be surprised if he's on the force much longer."

We hike next door and join the cluster of State CSI guys outside the shower stall.

"You guys nailed it," says Detective Botzong. "This is definitely our crime scene."

"Danny played a hunch," says Ceepak, giving me all the credit like he does every time I stumble into doing something smart.

"Good hunch, Boyle." Botzong shows us a bar of Irish Spring in a Baggie. "See the fingernail marks?"

"They're rather deep," says Ceepak.

"Yeah. She really gouged it. I figure she tightened her grip on the bar when our doer burst in and surprised her. That's why we found the soap residue so far up under her nails."

"And the shampoo?"

"It's a match."

"So if she was taking a shower out here—"

"It would explain why we didn't find blood splattered on her clothing."

"She was naked when she was assaulted."

"Exactly. The perp folds up her clothes, stuffs them in the

suitcases on top of her severed limbs, maybe keeps the T-shirt for a trophy."

Ceepak gestures toward the walls. "Did you find blood in here?"

"Yeah. Carolyn Miller scraped off one of those white globs. The guy tried to paint over the evidence. Stupid idea. Carolyn's in the van, running a preliminary scan with our portable spectrometer. See if we can ID the paint. Run it through the database. Excuse me. You guys ready with the video?"

"All set," says a CSI guy toting a Sony digital camera.

"We're about to do the Luminol," says Botzong.

Luminol is used to detect trace amounts of blood left at crime scenes because it reacts with the iron found in hemoglobin (the oxygen-toting compound in the blood) in a process called chemiluminescence, which sounds like something they'd say in a TV commercial for cosmetics when it's actually the same thing that makes firefly butts and light sticks glow. The glow show won't last forever, so the MCU guys will roll video to record the splotches that will show up with a bluish-green luminescence.

"Spray that wall where Carolyn scraped the sample," Botzong says to another tech.

The guy does.

The wall is splattered with glowing blue-green dots.

"Do the other wall."

The guy sprays again. More dots glow. It's almost like somebody flicked a wet paintbrush drenched in blood against the wall.

The Luminol goes on all four walls. All four walls put on a polka-dot lightning bug show.

Ceepak hunkers down. Strokes his chin. Stares into the shower stall.

"It doesn't make sense," he mumbles.

"Agreed," says Botzong, who hunkers down beside Ceepak.

They look like two guys playing touch football about to scratch out a play in the dirt.

"Typically," says Ceepak, "the blood would splatter in a pattern dictated by the movement of the weapon."

I nod because I studied this in cop school. A guy whacks somebody in the head, pulls the hammer back, swings for the head again, pulls it back. Every time he pulls it back, he sends up a stream of blood droplets off the hammer head that splatter on the ceiling or wall or whatever.

But these splatter patterns are on all four walls.

"Maybe he worked his way around her?" suggests Botzong.

"Or maybe she was thrashing," says Ceepak.

Botzong nods. "The blood gets in her hair. We get this paintbrush-type pattern."

"Was there much blood in her hair?"

"Nope. This does not compute."

"Was there any other evidence in the shower?"

"A couple of hairs. Long ones. We think they belong to the girl. We dusted for prints. The door. The spigots. Nothing."

Ceepak cocks up an eyebrow. "Not even from the victim?"

Botzong shakes his head. "The doer might have wiped things down when he was done."

"Doing so would have smeared the blood splatter patterns. We'd be seeing streaks and smudges, not droplets."

"Yeah. We need to get into the house. Look around. How goes the warrant?"

"Slow," says Ceepak. "Unfortunately, some high-level locals were involved in the activities that took place in this home."

"How high up are we talking here?"

"We've got the mayor and a couple of state senators," I toss in. "Plus the guy who owns most of the boardwalk amusements. And the head of the chamber of commerce."

"What exactly were they all doing here?" asks Botzong.

"Having sex with young women who were not their wives,"
says Ceepak, so matter-of-factly, it sounds like they came here to
have their teeth cleaned.

He flicks up his wrist. Checks his watch.

"Danny, I think we need to split up. Transport me back to the
house. I will contact Chief Baines. Stress the urgency of obtaining
the warrant to search the house. Work the phones if need be. Call
Judge Rasmussen."

"What do you want me to do?" I ask.

"See if you can locate your friend Marny Minsky. She was most
likely here last night. Perhaps she can fill in some gaps for us."

"I'll check out Big Kahuna's. Some of the other hot spots."

"Warrant or not," says Detective Botzong, "we're locking this
house down. No one's going in until we do."

"Can we do that?" I ask.

"One of the perks of the job," says Botzong. "We can restrict
entry while waiting for a warrant."

I turn to Ceepak, my Legal Eagle. He nods. It's all good.

A pimped-out ride with one of those subwoofers the size of a
washing machine crawls up Tangerine Street. It also has a muffler
that's been monkeyed with so it'll sound like a bass guitar with a
bad case of gas. The combination makes the ground shake enough
to put us on the Richter scale.

The rolling boom box comes to the end of the street.

Sean O'Malley is behind the wheel. Even in silhouette, I recognize his dorky cab–driver hat. He sees us seeing him. Gives us a
wiggly finger wave.

Ceepak strides across the pebble lawn. I'm right behind him.
Ceepak gives Sean the universal kindly-roll-down-your-window-
sir signal. O'Malley complies. Now the throbbing bass line has
lyrics. Bad ones about ho's and niggaz.

"Evening, officers."

"Turn it down."

"Yo—is cranking tunes against the law?"

"Yes. In fact, two of them: The hours between ten P.M. and swven a.m. are designated as quiet hours throughout the residential areas of Sea Haven Township. Also, it is against local noise ordinances for a car stereo to be heard from a distance of fifty feet away. I heard you over at the shower stall, which is sixty feet away."

Ceepak counted his lawn strides. Awesome.

Sean turns down the crunk junk.

"May I ask what you're doing here, Mr. O'Malley?"

"Just chillin'."

"May I suggest you do it somewhere else?"

Sean leans across the passenger seat, tries to look around Ceepak's bulky body, which is blocking his view. "What's with all the po-po's?"

"Kindly move along."

"Whas goin' down?"

I step forward because I speak white-boy rap: "Roll out. Bail."

That means beat it.

"Aw-ite. Aw-ite." Sean rolls up his window. I glance into his back seat.

"Ceepak?" I say as I give him a sideways head bob.

Sean O'Malley's transporting a pair of porno gnomes. The copulating Smurfs we saw on the porch last night are bouncing around on his back seat. Sean pulls a U-turn at the dead end where the street butts up against the dunes, crunches across some seashells.

"Should we stop him?" I ask.

"We can't," says Ceepak. "There's no law against transporting lawn ornaments."

"Maybe he stole them."

"No theft has been reported."

"So, what's he doing with them in his car?"

"Perhaps he is in charge of tidying up for his father or his father's friends."

"Bill?" It's Carolyn Miller—the CSI genius who pegged the tire treads. She's coming out of the state team's mobile lab.

"What've you got?" says Botzong.

"I don't think that white gunk is paint," she says.

"Come again?"

"It's shoe polish. White shoe polish."

When I hear that, all I can think of is Big Paddy O'Malley's seersucker suit.

And, of course, his white buck shoes.

23

"YOU KNOW, MR. O'MALLEY WEARS WHITE SHOES ALL THE time," I say. "It's like his official costume. The way Springsteen and the E Street Band always wear black."

Behind the wheel, Ceepak nods.

"So he probably has gallons of white shoe polish to paint over blood stains."

"But why would Mr. O'Malley want to kill Ms. Baker?" Ceepak asks. "They seemed to have had an understanding in regards to their sexual liaisons."

"I dunno. Maybe, once Mrs. O'Malley had her heart attack, Gail started pressuring him to get married, like Charzuk said."

"You need to find Ms. Minsky, Danny. She might know if Gail Baker was, indeed, pressuring Mr. O'Malley. It might give him sufficient motive."

We hit the house.

Chief Baines is there.

"John? We need to talk."

"Indeed we do. Sergeant Dominic Santucci has been threatening citizens with official retribution if they instigate any form of complaint against one of his security firm's clients."

"Santucci? I wanted to talk about this house on Tangerine Street."

"Santucci's involved with that as well."

"Well, Mayor Sinclair—"

"Has been a visitor to what can best be described as a sex den for Sea Haven's wealthiest citizens."

The guys clocking in for the late shift are moving through the lobby a little more slowly than usual. You mention a "sex den," they'll do that.

"Married men consorting with girls young enough to be their daughters—"

Ceepak, of course, is simply stating what he knows to be the truth, because that's what Ceepak always does.

"Not here," says the chief. "In my office."

They disappear behind a door and I head into the locker room to change into my civvies. I'm more or less working undercover tonight. I need to blend in. Might even need to wear a backwards baseball cap.

First stop is Big Kahuna's.

I slip Phil the doorman ten bucks and get my hand stamped.

It's about 11:30 on a Friday night. The place is packed with locals blowing off steam, blowing their paychecks. Bud is behind the bar, popping tops off plastic long-neck bottles of beer. My pal Cliff Skeete is seated at the sound controls. There's no live band tonight, so Cliff is picking up some extra cash spinning tunes on his, believe or not, computer. Turntables are so last millennium.

I make my way across the dance floor. Cliff has his headphones draped around his neck and is bopping to the prefabricated electronic beat of the Underdog Project's "Girls Of Summer." As far as I can tell, the lyrics are all about girls walking in the sand with honey-coated complexions and cinnamon tans. Plus a lot of yeah-uh-yeah-yeahs.

"Yo, Cliff!"

"Danny boy!"

"You got any Springsteen in your iTunes library?"

"How old-school you gonna get on me, brurva?"

We knock knuckles. "You seen Marny?" I ask.

"Minsky?"

"Yeah."

"Not tonight, bro. Who you with?"

"Nobody. I'm kind of on the job."

"For real? This is what cops do? Go clubbin'?"

"Only when we have to. How you been holdin' up since the remote?" I ask Cliff, who lets his supercool mackdaddy face droop, but only for a second.

"Hangin' in."

"Cool. Catch you later," I say, because I see Sean O'Malley at the bar.

He's with a girl, not a garden gnome. A different girl, not the Argentine firecracker from last weekend. This girl is short, brunette, and built. I figure she's a girl of summer—got a honey-coated complexion and a cinnamon tan.

Wow.

The disco music and its breakfast cereal lyrics have brain-washed me.

"Yo, Sean," I holler. He went to school with my little brother so he has to answer when I "yo" him. It's an unwritten rule.

"Danny Boy Boyle." He's bouncing in place to the beat. Has his Irish cap turned sideways on his head. "Twice in one night. Wassup, brurva? This music is bumpin'!"

I lean in so I can whisper without his date hearing me, although she has that obliviously blurry look most hotties get whenever I draw near.

"Where's Daisy?" I ask.

"Who?"

"The girl you were with last weekend."

"She be history. This is my new dime." He gestures toward the brunette, who's still staring off into space. "She is so fly!"

Meaning she's a ten and very appealing. She also looks totally smashed.

"So, Sean, how come you drive around town with Smurfs in your backseat?"

"Aw, that just be a favor I do fo' a friend."

"What friend?"

"Bruno."

"Mazzilli?"

"King of the boardwalk, biatch."

"So you work for Mr. Mazzilli?"

"When he axe me I do."

"Sean?"

"Yo?"

"You grew up in Sea Haven. Went to Catholic School. How come you talk like that?"

"Like what?"

"An uneducated idiot."

Sean's eyes get all beady. "Don't you have a bad guy to catch or something, Danny Boy?" He's totally dropped the gangsta rap.

"Yeah. I just hope it isn't you."

"What's the problem here, Boyle?"

I turn around.

Dominic Santucci.

"Who said there was a problem?"

When I started on the job, Santucci used to scare me. Mostly because he was riding my butt all the time. Now? I think he's kind of pathetic. Besides, I was there when he shot up the lobster tanks at Mama Shucker's Raw Bar. He may carry a lethal weapon, but if you're his target, not to worry. He couldn't hit a bull's-eye the size of a manhole cover.

"Mr. O'Malley here is still in mourning over the loss of his mother," says Santucci.

"Yeah," I say as Sean and his new squeeze, ignoring Santucci and me, suck each other's faces. "My bad. 'Scuse me."

I walk away from the bar.

Santucci follows me.

"You on the job?" he asks.

"Yeah. You on your other job?"

"Yeah. And guess what? Right now, I'm pulling down more per hour than you'll make all night."

"Who you running security for, now? Bruno Mazzilli?"

"Confidential."

"What's Mazzilli so worried about?" I ask. "He's got you running interference and Sean O'Malley cleaning up his front porch. Who picks up his dry cleaning? You?"

"Word to the wise? Keep your nose out of this thing. People with money—they can rock your world if you mess with theirs. They can reach out and touch anybody they want to. No matter who they are or where they live—even if it's Paradise Valley in Arizona."

"What? Now you're threatening my parents?"

"I'm not threatening nobody, Boyle. I'm just sayin'." He snaps his gum three times hard. Swaggers away.

I let him.

Ceepak and the chief will deal with Santucci. In fact, I wouldn't be surprised if they were filling out the Italian Stallion's walking papers right now. Santucci's side job is about to become his only job—if he doesn't go to jail first for helping to hacksaw Gail Baker, something I could see him doing if it paid enough.

I head back to the dance floor.

I see Bruno Mazzilli dancing (and I use that term loosely) with a raven-haired hottie who isn't Marny Minsky in a wig. Guess all the sugar daddies are in the market for new girlfriends.

And then I see Samantha Starky.

She looks a little wobbly, which is how she usually looks after sipping one weak drink. Low tolerance for alcohol. She's kind of hanging on to her law school study buddy Richard for support, hands linked around his neck. It's not a slow song but Richard's swiveling his hips like maybe he wishes it were.

"Danny?"

She sees me. Unclasps her hands. Stumbles out of her dance sway.

"What are you doing here?" she slurs. I move in. Steady her by the elbow. "I thought you had to work?"

"Yeah."

"Oh!" Her hand goes up to her mouth. Her eyes bug open wide. "Is this work?"

"Yeah."

I glance over at Richard.

"Uh, hi," he says, smiling nervously. Stuffing his hands in his pockets. Maybe he's heard how good I am with my gun.

"How many drinks did you buy her?" I ask.

"Just two. Maybe three."

I shake my head. One is Sam's limit. Doesn't matter what it is. Beer, wine, rum. One drink and Samantha Starky is plotzed.

"Can you take me home?" Sam asks, hanging on to the front of my shirt. "I'm drunk."

"Yeah."

"Thanks, pal," says Richard. "I owe you one."

I just nod. Dude doesn't dig taking on responsibility, like watching out for the girl he boozed up so he'd have a shot at her pants.

"Come on." I prop a hand under Sam's arm. Guide her toward the exit. All the while, I'm scanning the crowd. Looking for Marny. Sam is an unexpected delay of game, but she needs to go home and sleep it off. I guide her toward the DJ booth.

"Hey, Cliff?"

"Yo?"

"I'm taking Sam home. If Marny comes in . . ."

"I'll give you a shout. Text you."

"Thanks. Appreciate it."

We're walking to the door when the damn song about the girls of summer finally quits rhyming "sand" and "tan."

"We need to talk," Sam mumbles when the music dies.

"Okay."

"About us." It comes out "ush."

"Fine." We make it to the bouncer stand.

"Richard is very nice guy, Danny. My mom likes him a lot."

I'm sure she does—mainly because he isn't me.

"And I like you . . ." Sam is babbling. "I'm just not sure if I like *us* anymore . . . I'm so young . . . you know . . . don't know what I want to do . . . who I even am . . ."

Her Oprah moment carries us out the door to the parking lot.

"My Jeep's over this way."

I walk. Sam stumbles. If I wasn't holding her up, she'd definitely be falling down.

I'm wishing I hadn't parked in the rear. Behind the Dumpster. Near Mr. Ceepak's pickup truck, which, unfortunately isn't a Dodge Ram so we can't lock him up as a suspect in the murder of Gail Baker.

"Danny, seriously, I don't think you're ever gonna be my Mister Right. More like Mister Right Now. I'm twenty-one, you're twenty-five."

We make it to my Jeep.

And I realize there's somebody already sitting in the passenger seat.

She's wearing really short cutoff jeans and a bulging tube top. Has a springy Brillo pad of curly blonde hair.

"Hey," she says with a nervous titter.

"Danny? Who the hell is this?" Sam is sounding more and more like her mom.

"Marny," I say. "Marny Minsky."

24

"SHE A FRIEND OF YOURS?" SAM DEMANDS.

Inside my Jeep, Marny's eyes go all Bambi-in-the-headlights on me.

"You gotta help me, Danny!" she says, her voice soft and shaky. "I need you!"

That doesn't help.

"Who is this person?" says Sam.

If Sam were still a cop, I'd tell her.

But she isn't.

"A friend," is all I say.

Sam's been sizing Marny up. Checking out her barely legal top and shorts combo. Diapers cover more.

"When were you going to tell me?" she asks.

"What?"

"That you already had a hot new girlfriend even before I drank two Mojitos and one Cosmo just so I could be brave enough to break up with you because I really used to like you and now I think I'm starting to like Richard and, anyway, my mother is right about you—why buy a cow when the horse is free?"

Yeah. Sam's drunk. She usually doesn't mangle her metaphors.

"Problems over there, officer?"

Great. Mr. Ceepak just showed up. He's leaning against his pickup and sneering at me.

"Came out to catch a smoke. Didn't know there'd be a floor show."

"You're that horrible man," says Samantha, trying to point, teetering sideways on her heels. "Mr. Sixpack! Joe Sixpack."

Mr. Ceepak's eyes crawl all over Sam's body as he sucks down a deep drag on his cigarette. "That's what my friends call me, sweetheart. You wanna be my friend? I know I'd sure like to be yours."

"Gross!" Sam totters backward. I simultaneously break her fall and butt-bounce the passenger side door shut behind me so Mr. Ceepak doesn't see Marny and start hitting on her, too.

"Hang on, Sam," I mumble.

"Leggo. You're grosser than him. You got a girlfriend with gigantic boobs that look fake. Are they fake?"

Mr. Ceepak is laughing a wheezy laugh as wet as the slurped end of a milkshake.

"Don't they need you inside?" I say.

"I'm on my break. Hey, Officer Boyle—has Johnny come to his senses yet?"

"You mean is he going to tell you where his mother is?"

"Yeah."

"Why? Has hell frozen over?"

"Cute, Boyle. I forgot—you're the funny one."

"Hey, Ceepak!" It's Bud the bartender, yelling out the back door. "College kid just puked all over the dance floor."

My turn to smile. "Duty calls."

Mr. Ceepak grinds his cigarette butt out under his boot toe.

"Tell soldier boy he hasn't heard the last from me."

"Right. But if he *sees* you, you're going straight to jail. That restraining order stuff—it really works. Especially if the person you're supposed to stay away from is a cop."

"Fuck you, Boyle." Mr. Ceepak strolls back to the club.

I grab the cell phone off my belt. I could call the house; organize police protection for Marny while I drive Sam home.

But then Santucci might find out where she is from one of his friends. He has a few. Well, Officer Mark Malloy. That's one. There might be another. One of the guys still bitter about John Ceepak cracking so many big cases while they write speeding tickets in school zones.

So I call a friend of mine's taxi company to haul Sam home.

When she's safely inside the cab, I climb into my Jeep.

"Is everything okay?" Marny asks.

"Yeah."

"Who was that girl?"

"That's Samantha Starky. My ex-girlfriend."

"I'm sorry."

"Don't be. It wasn't your fault."

"My boobs aren't fake."

"Okay." Good to know.

Marny relaxes slightly. I think because my jacket got all bollixed up when I buckled my seat belt and she saw the pistol strapped to my chest.

"So, how you doin', Marny?"

"Terrible. I haven't slept since they killed Gail."

"They?"

She nods. Her kinky hair bounces like a golden Slinky convention.

"The guys who rent the house on Tangerine Street?" I ask.

"You know about that?"

"Yeah. I'm a cop now, remember?"

"That's why I followed you here. I waited in the parking lot at the police station until you came out. I was afraid to go in on account of Dominic."

"Officer Santucci?"

"He runs security for Mr. Mazzilli and Mr. O'Malley at the house."

"Did you drive over here?" I ask.

"Yeah." She gestures toward the sporty red Miata parked in the space to next to me.

"Does Santucci know your car?"

She puts two dainty fingers over her "uh-oh-SpaghettiOs" expression.

"He might," she says in a frightened whisper.

"Okay," I say. "We need to get you out of here."

I crank the ignition.

"Can we go to your place?" she asks. "I think they're watching mine."

Again with the "they."

"Yeah," I say. "No problem."

I pilot my vehicle through the parking lot, head around the side of the building.

Santucci comes out a side door.

I reach over, put my hand on top of Marny's coiled hair, shove her down below the dashboard.

"Stay down for a second, okay?"

"Okay. And Danny?"

"Yeah?"

"Thanks."

I don't say anything because Santucci is staring straight at me now.

I put on a big smile.

Santucci looks hyped up. Maybe Mr. Ceepak caught a glimpse of Marny and went inside to tell the guy who had offered to buy him a beer if he spotted the curly-haired girl in the photograph he was shoving under everybody's nose.

"Boyle?" Santucci shouts. "Pull over!"

I give Santucci a two-finger salute off the brim of my invisible cop cap and keep on driving. He angrily signals for me to "pull over to the side of the road, sir." I ignore him. Right now, I'm the cop. Santucci's just the douche bag making more money than me.

I don't think he saw Marny.

As I pull out of the parking lot, I glance up to my rearview mirror and see him stomping toward the Dumpster and Marny's red-hot Miata.

Time for Ms. Minsky to be put in protective custody.

My apartment building used to be a motel until the owners realized they wouldn't have to clean the toilets if they turned it into rental units.

They filled in the swimming pool in the central courtyard, unplugged the vacancy sign, got rid of the ice maker, and sold all their sheets and towels in a yard sale.

Inside my unit, it still looks like a motel. You open the door, you see the bed. You also see ugly maple paneling. Beyond the bed, I have a tiny kitchenette with a mini fridge and one of those two-cup coffee makers. They sold it to me at that yard sale. I do have a brand-new plasma-screen TV that takes up most of one wall (HBO is no longer free). I set up a lumpy recliner against the wall on the opposite side of the room. It's where I watch football and where I'll be sleeping tonight.

"You need the bathroom or anything?" I say to Marny.

"Thanks, Danny. Do I look awful?"

That would be impossible. Marny is built like the proverbial brick house. However, I note goosebumps on her thighs just below her cutoffs and, not that I'm looking, two Purdue pop-up indicators signaling extreme chilliness.

"You look cold," I say.

"Yeah."

"There's a robe hanging on the back of the bathroom door. I washed it two days ago." I raise my right arm. "Scout's honor."

She smiles. "Thanks, Danny."

"Go grab it. I'm going to call my partner."

"Is he a cop?"

"Yes, but he's one of the good guys."

Actually, he's the goodiest guy of all.

———

"I think you made the right call, Danny," says Ceepak.

I'm on my cell phone. Marny's still in the bathroom. I hear the shower running.

"Thanks," I say. "She's extremely creeped out by Santucci and, well, other cops."

"To be expected."

"But, we knew each other in high school . . . so she . . ."

"As I stated Danny, you made a very prudent decision. FYI, Chief Baines will soon request that Officer Santucci resign his position with the force. If he refuses, the chief will file the necessary paperwork to initiate the termination process."

"Cool. So, what should I do with Marny?"

"Talk to her if she feels like talking tonight. Let her sleep. Then transport her to the Bagel Lagoon at six hundred hours."

Ceepak lives in an apartment above the bagel restaurant.

"Rita and T.J. will look after her until you and I bring this matter to a satisfactory conclusion."

Great. I wonder when that might happen.

"How go the warrants?" I ask.

"Officer Diego and I are going through Mr. O'Malley's phone records now . . ."

I glance at the Sony Dream Machine on my bedside table, a holdover from the apartment's days as a motel room, and only fifty cents at the yard sale. It's after midnight.

". . . Judge Rasmussen assures us we'll have what we need to search inside the Tangerine Street home by nine thirty A.M."

"You might tell Rita that Marny needs clothes."

There is a moment of silence. "Come again?"

Great. Now Ceepak thinks I have a naked female witness in my bedroom.

"I mean, she has clothes, but, well, they're kind of grungy and, uh, not enough."

"I see. Any idea as to size?"

"Petite. Except . . . you know . . . up top."

"Roger that," says Ceepak without a hint of adolescent mammary fascination. That's my department. "Rita will know how to handle it."

"Thanks. Oh—I saw your dad again tonight. At the club."

"Did he ask after me?"

"Yeah."

"How thoughtful." And that, my friends, is Ceepak being sarcastic.

The bathroom door pops open with a push and a warble. It always does that after a shower; the steam warps the wood. Marny comes out in my bathrobe, which goes down to her toes; her hair is wrapped up in my Mussel Beach Motel towel, which I borrowed from my friend Becca's place and mean to take back. Tomorrow.

She's carrying her shorts and shirt, not to mention her bra and panties.

All she has on under my robe are her flip-flops.

"See you in six hours," I say to Ceepak.

I close up my cell.

"Who was that?" Marny asks.

"John Ceepak. My partner."

"Hey—is he the guy who was with you when you ran me and that doctor dude off the road?"

"Yeah."

"That was hysterical! When we wrecked into all those bikes."

Yeah. A regular laugh riot. If you forget the part about how I thought I was going to die.

"That's kind of when it started," she mumbles.

She goes to bed, sits on the edge. I take the recliner.

"He was my first, you know, older married guy."

I nod. Let her talk.

"I got Gail into it."

"How?"

"I told her about this great group of rich guys I'd been hanging with. One of them bought me the Miata and it wasn't even my birthday."

"Mr. Mazzilli?"

Marny shakes her head. "Mr. Johnson. He was my first. The first one to take me to the house on Tangerine Street."

"What goes on there?"

She gives me a look. "You know . . ."

"Yeah. So, Gail Baker was with Mr. O'Malley?"

"For about three months."

"When Mrs. O'Malley died, did she want to marry him?"

"I hope not. He's, you know . . . old."

"And rich."

"True. But we didn't need to marry them for their money. They had wives for that."

Okay. It makes sense. Sort of.

"But," says Marny, "I think Gail told too many people about what was going on. She even wore that silly T-Shirt."

"The one with 'Sugar Babies' on it?"

"Yeah. We were supposed to be, you know, discreet. Classy. She was kind of broadcasting it. I know she told her personal trainer. That is so against the rules."

"There are rules?"

"Sure. Like, we can never call our guy. Text messages only. And we never went anywhere our man might be with his wife and family. We weren't supposed to rub any noses the wrong way in it, you know?"

"Sure," I say, because I've known Marny long enough to know what she's trying to say even when she says it wrong.

"That's why they killed her like that, left her in a public place. To warn the rest of us." She shivers. "I think I need to leave town, Danny. They'll come after me next."

"Why?"

"Because Gail and I were close and Mr. Mazzilli wanted us to do this, you know, thing with him and Gail said no and that really torqued Bruno off so if he had them do that to her they'll do something worse to me because I laughed."

"What?"

"He wanted a three-way. Grabbed Gail. Squeezed her ass. Sucked on her neck. She pushed away and said, 'Sorry, there's no way two girls can share three inches.'"

I smile.

"Yeah," says Marny. "That's what I did, too. Only I laughed. And Mr. Mazzilli heard me."

"He can't get you here," I say. "Grab some sleep. First thing in the morning, I'm taking you to my partner's place. You're in protective custody now, okay?"

"Okay." She pulls back my blankets. Fluffs up a pillow. Turns to me and says, very shyly, like we're cousins on a camp-out, "You want half the bed?"

"Nah. I'm not really sleeping tonight. I'm on guard duty. Gotta keep one eye open at all times."

I give her a wink and sit in my chair.

She pulls up the covers. Yawns.

"Remember Ms. Fabricius's math class?"

"Marny?"

"Yeah?"

"Go to sleep."

"Okay."

She yawns one more time, flops sideways, and, I swear, conks out on command.

I take off my holster. Lay the Glock in my lap.

I'll wake it up if I need it.

25

"WOULD YOU LIKE MORE WATER?" ASKS CEEPAK.

Marny shakes her head. The blonde coils bounce. "No, thank you."

It's a little after six in the morning and we're sitting in a booth as far from the windows as we can get at the Bagel Lagoon. The Coglianese brothers open their place early every day; bakers always do. Marny has barely touched her cinnamon-raisin with a schmear of cream cheese. She is wearing my navy blue POLICE windbreaker like a vinyl sack but is still shivering, and not because she's cold.

Rita's at the counter talking to Joe and Jim about Marny and how important it is for them to forget they ever saw her.

The brothers nod. They dig Ceepak and Rita, their upstairs neighbors. They also look juiced about keeping a secret, playing cops with us.

Me? I'm a little tired from snoozing in the chair with one eye open all night, but I'm happy Marny is safe. She looks more wiped out than me. Pooped. Still, Ceepak needs to ask her a few questions.

"Was Mayor Sinclair ever present at the house?"

"Yeah. A couple times. He liked the hot tub. I was with him one night. Bruno asked me to, you know, show him a good time. This was back when Bruno, Mr. Mazzilli, wanted to buy that burned-down pier for the roller coaster him and Mr. O'Malley wanted to build."

Ceepak nods. Guess he understands New Jersey politics. Guess we all do. You grease the wheel. Let people dip their beaks. That's why you see so many of our elected officials perp-walking into court with handcuffs on their wrists and raincoats over their heads.

"Tell us about Mr. O'Malley."

"He was kind of bossy at the house," says Marny. "Told me I was getting chubby this one time when my face was bloated after a heavy night of partying. He could also be very generous. Gave Gail a ton of money to buy better clothes. He had a thing for lingerie, too. I think he runs a tab at Victoria's Secret. And, he bought her, like, a ten-pack of personal training sessions she couldn't afford so she wouldn't get fat."

"Were Mr. O'Malley and the mayor close?"

"How do you mean?"

"When the mayor dropped by the house on Tangerine Street, was Mr. O'Malley with him?"

"I don't think so. No. It was Bruno and Mr. Johnson and the guy who owns the newspaper. He was there. Said I could make a ton of money modeling swimsuits for local stores like Teeny's Bikinis and offered to give me an audition."

Yeah. Right. A private audition, I'm sure.

"Did you ever see the mayor with Mr. O'Malley?"

"No. But Gail might've. You could ask—"

She realizes what she almost said.

Her eyes tear up.

"I'm sorry."

Ceepak reaches across the table. Gently puts his gigantic hand on top of Marny's tiny one. "Ms. Minsky—what happened is not your fault."

"I got her into this. . . ."

"Perhaps. But you did not kill her."

"Who did?"

"We can't say for certain. Not yet. However, Danny and I intend to find out."

"We better get busy," I say, standing up. It's time for us to hit the house, put on our uniforms, climb into a police car, and go nab the bad guys. Once we, of course, figure out who that might be.

Rita comes to the table with a white paper bag.

"I got us some cold cuts," she says to Marny. "We can make sandwiches later—after you wake up from your nap. I put fresh sheets on our bed. Oh, and I found a pair of jeans that'll probably fit. Plus, I've got all sorts of blouses and shirts and stuff. If you need anything else, T.J., that's our son, he'll run out and buy it before he heads off to this going-away party a couple of his buddies are throwing for him."

"Where's he going?" asks Marny, sounding like the twenty-four year old kid she actually is.

"Annapolis!" says Rita, beaming over at Ceepak who beams back. "He's going to be an officer."

"And a gentleman," I add because I like that movie.

"Awesome," says Marny, momentarily brightening.

"You'll be safe upstairs in our home," says Ceepak.

"You sure will," says Rita. "So relax. Finish your breakfast. Oh, I got you some chocolate milk."

"Danny?" Ceepak gestures that it's time for us to go.

I toss my once-bitten bagel in the trash, follow him to the counter.

"Thank you, gentlemen," he says to the Coglianese brothers.

"Fuhgeddaboutit," says Joe, the one in charge of stirring the bobbing bagels in a boiling vat with a giant wooden canoe paddle. "Anybody tries to go upstairs what shouldn't, they got to get past me and my paddle!"

Ceepak and I head out to the parking lot and hop into my Jeep.

"How come you had so many questions for Marny about the mayor?" I ask when we're both seatbelted in.

"In examining Mr. O'Malley's phone records, Denise Diego ID'ed a phone call to Mayor Sinclair's home phone number at three fifteen yesterday morning."

"Right after the dog barked?"

"Affirmative. And, using GPS coordinates triangulated from cell towers, we were able to pinpoint the location where Mr. O'Malley made the phone call."

"Where?" I ask even though I don't really have to.

"One forty-five Tangerine Street. The house where we found the two suitcases."

Seven o'clock on the dot, we enter the King Putt pyramid.

Skippy, looking very sleepy, is already on the job and has to undo the lock at the bottom of the front door to let us in. Fortunately, he doesn't have to wear his chariot skirt and breastplate until the miniature golf course opens around ten.

"Hi, you guys," he says, sounding kind of glum. "Dad and Kevin are upstairs with the lawyer."

That would be their oily shyster Louis "I Never Lose" Rambowski. I wondered why the floor felt so slippery.

Skippy trudges back behind the counter to buff the shiny heads of a hundred putters and inventory his balls.

There I go again.

"They brought you guys doughnuts," says Skippy.

"Very considerate," says Ceepak.

We climb the spiral staircase to the office.

When we hit the top of the steps, I see Mr. O'Malley seated in a plush rolling chair, feet up on his desk a dozen box of "Donut Connection" glazed and sprinkled treats near his shoes.

Bad idea.

Not the donuts, the shoes.

He's wearing those white bucks again, and I'm thinking he buys Shine Rite Shoe Polish in bottles the size of milk jugs. He sees us come in, pulls down his dogs, sits up straight.

"Officers," he says. "Good morning." He gestures toward the open pastry box. "Hungry?"

"Not really," says Ceepak.

"I ate a late dinner," I add.

We sit down in the two visitor chairs fronting the desk.

"This is my father's lawyer," says Kevin O'Malley, pacing around the back of the desk, pointing to a bald man in a very natty suit leaning against a credenza, both arms crossed over his barrel chest. "Louis Rambowski."

The lawyer looks like he has his bald head buffed on a regular basis. Maybe Skippy lent him a putter rag. Or maybe Mr. O'Malley has one of those stand-up shoe polishers for his white bucks and Rambowski bent over to use it this morning.

Now he stands up from his casual leaning pose. Smoothes out his lapels.

"Officers," he starts in, using his silky smooth courtroom voice, "let me just say that my client has every intention of cooperating with your investigation." He smiles. The way crocodiles do. "In fact, it is in Mr. O'Malley's best interest to help you in any way possible because, when you locate and apprehend the true perpetrator, he will be completely exonerated."

He gestures that we may proceed.

So Ceepak does.

"Mr. O'Malley, why would the deceased, Ms. Gail Brewer make . . ." He glances at his notepad. "Fifteen separate phone calls to you in the week prior to her death?"

"Who says she did?" asks barrister Rambowski.

"Verizon," I say as snottily as I can and still be a cop.

"I'll answer that," says Mr. O'Malley, smiling magnanimously.

"She needed business advice. Ms. Baker, who was employed as a low-paid waitress at a restaurant called The Rusty Scupper, had bigger ambitions. In fact, she dreamed of opening her own restaurant some day."

"She came to Dad seeking business advice," says Kevin.

"And," says the lawyer, "a business loan."

All three of them are smiling like first graders in the Christmas pageant who memorized all their lines and recited them without making one single mistake or pooping their pants.

"As you may know," Rambowski continues, "Mr. O'Malley is quite active with the Junior Achievement Program at the local high school, a program that teaches economics and entrepreneurship and that nurtures the business leaders of tomorrow."

"That's where Dad first met Ms. Baker," says Kevin, who, I have a feeling, is the one who concocted this lame script. "When she was in high school."

Ceepak does not seem impressed. "Why did Ms. Baker send you a text message just after midnight on the day of her death?"

The lawyer raises a hand to object. "Is that what your phone records indicate?"

Well, duh.

"Twelve-oh-five A.M.," says Ceepak. "What did she text you about?"

"I don't recall," Mr. O'Malley says with just the hint of a smug smile.

"You don't remember?"

"I don't recall."

"Perhaps you should check your phone. Reread her message."

"Excuse me," says the lawyer, "do you have a warrant to search my client's cell phone or just his usage records?"

"The records."

"Then why are you badgering him about showing you the actual phone?" Louis looks like he knows he's going to win again.

"I'm sorry," says Mr. O'Malley. "I get a million texts every day. I can't recall the content of each and every one."

"That is why," says Ceepak, "I'm suggesting that you open your phone and reread the text at this time."

"When you get a warrant, perhaps he will," says the lawyer, puffing out his bulldog chest. "Next question."

Ceepak flips forward in his notebook.

"Why, Mr. O'Malley, did you call Mayor Sinclair at three fifteen A.M. yesterday?"

"What?" Kevin and his dad say it at the same time. Looks like they don't have a prerecorded answer for this one.

"I'm sorry," says Ceepak, "perhaps my question was unclear."

So he repeats it. Using the exact same words.

"I did no such thing!" says Mr. O'Malley.

"The phone company's records indicate otherwise."

"Impossible."

"The same phone that received the text message from Ms. Baker at twelve-oh-five A.M. was also used to call Mayor Hugh Sinclair's home phone number at three-fifteen A.M. Now, according to the medical examiner, Ms. Baker was killed at approximately one A.M. That would give you plenty of time to receive her text, arrange a meeting, kill her, dispose of the body, and then call the mayor."

"Is that an accusation, officer?" asks Rambowski.

"It is, currently, a hypothesis."

Mr. O'Malley turns to Kevin. "Look into this. The phone thing."

"Yes, sir."

Ceepak flips forward another page.

"Why did you take Ms. Baker to the house on Tangerine Street?"

"I'm sorry," says Rambowski with a chuckle. "You'll need to be more specific. . . ."

"Number One Tangerine. A home owned by Stromboli

Enterprises, a holding company headed, Mr. O'Malley, by your business partner Bruno Mazzilli."

"Excuse me," says the lawyer, "do you have any proof that my client was ever present at said location?"

"Yes," says Ceepak. "We have a witness."

"Who?" snaps Kevin.

"Someone who was there at the same time as your father and Ms. Baker."

"Who?"

"We are not at liberty to divulge the witness's name."

"That's it," says Rambo the lawyer, "we're done here. Take your donuts and go. This ends our voluntary participation in your witch hunt."

Up comes Mr. O'Malley's hand to silence his attorney. "Hang on, Louie. Did you say number One Tangerine, officer?"

Ceepak nods.

"I remember now."

Kevin's shaking his head. Looks like Dad is about to go rogue. Cook up his own lies.

"I took Ms. Baker there to meet Bruno, that is, Mr. Mazzilli. She needed financing and Stromboli Enterprises is always looking for interesting new ventures, especially anything involving seasonal eating establishments. I thought the two of them should meet."

Right. It was a Junior Achievement field trip. To the hot tub.

Ceepak flips forward another page in his book.

"Mr. O'Malley, why did your late wife fly to Buffalo, New York, two years ago?"

"What?"

"Why did she fly to Buffalo, New York?"

"You're out of bounds officer," says Rambowski.

"Mr. O'Malley?" says Ceepak, ignoring the lawyer.

"Buffalo is where Jackie's sister lives. She, I don't remember . . ."

Jackie might've gone there two years ago . . . just to visit. Was it around the holidays?"

Ceepak nods. "November."

"Okay," says Mr. O'Malley. "Two years ago. Yeah. She did Thanksgiving at her sister's place. Took Mary with her. I took the boys to Morgan's Surf and Turf."

"How is any of this relevant?" asks the lawyer.

My turn to arch an eyebrow because I don't know where Ceepak's going with this.

He turns to me. "Sorry, Danny. I failed to mention this new piece of evidence earlier. I'm afraid I was too intently focused on securing the safety of our star witness."

I shrug. Whatever. I'm cool.

"What the hell are you trying to pull here?" demands Rambowski. "Surprise evidence? Secret star witnesses? You watch too much TV, Officer."

"Perhaps so," says Ceepak. "However, be that as it may, earlier this morning, Continental Airlines was able to extrapolate enough information from the luggage tag remnants the State Police Major Crimes Unit removed from the handles of the two rolling suitcases containing Ms. Baker's dismembered body."

"And?"

"Those were your late wife's suitcases, Mr. O'Malley."

26

THE POMPOMS.

Ceepak was right. The suitcases belonged to a woman. Mrs. O'Malley.

Things aren't looking so hot for her husband right about now. The victim texted him at midnight. Somebody used white shoe polish to paint over the blood splotches in the shower stall and Mr. O'Malley is the only adult male I know who actually wears white shoes that aren't sneakers. Then he calls the mayor from the scene of the crime. And the suitcases Gail Baker's body parts are stuffed into belong to his wife.

I'm ready for Ceepak to read the roller coaster mogul his Miranda rights.

Instead, he looks at his watch.

"What time is your grand opening?" he asks.

"Hmm?" says Mr. O'Malley, who looks like he's in a state of shock.

"We're going ten to ten," says Kevin. "We're keeping it simple this time. Just a tie-in with W-A-V-Y. They'll do an all-day live remote broadcast, but down on the ground, not in the cars. That's our only planned publicity, but Dad should be there for the kickoff."

Sounds like Kevin is expecting Ceepak to slap on the cuffs, too.

"When do you anticipate being free again, Mr. O'Malley?" asks Ceepak.

It's an interesting choice of words. I'm tempted to blurt, "Never" because life plus twenty-four-years was the sentence handed down to the last sick dude who killed and dismembered a Jersey girl a couple of years back.

"I'm sorry, what was the question?" says Mr. O'Malley, his eyes looking as vacant as the Mussel Beach Motel in March.

"When will you be able to continue answering our questions?"

"If you have more questions, ask them now," says the tough-guy shyster, trying to force Ceepak's hand.

"Unfortunately, we have not yet been able to search the house at number One Tangerine. Judge Rasmussen, however, will be issuing a search warrant within the next two hours. Further questioning of Mr. O'Malley will be contingent on what we find inside the residence."

The lawyer tosses up both arms. The shoulder pads in his spiffy suit bunch up around his neck. "This is preposterous! You can't keep my client on tenterhooks!"

Ceepak ignores Rambowski, focuses on the pages of his spiral-bound note pad. I need to buy some of those. Might stop me from making faces at dipstick attorneys in Italian silk suits that cost more than I'll make all month when they use words like "tenterhooks," which sounds like something REI might sell to campers so they can hang up their pup tents.

"I do have one more question," says Ceepak.

"What?" demands the lawyer, his hands shooting to his hips.

"Why, Mr. O'Malley, do you wear white buck shoes?"

"What?" says his lawyer. "How can my client's choice of shoes have any bearing on—"

Up comes Mr. O'Malley's silencing hand again.

"Why," he says slowly, "did Colonel Sanders wear a string bow tie or Orville Reddenbacher those glasses? It's all about branding. Folks see my white bucks and seersucker suit, they know it's me from a mile away. I want to dress like it's summer three hundred sixty-five days a year because summer is what my business is all about."

Ceepak nods. Makes sense to him. Maybe he belonged to Junior Achievement back in Ohio. Doubtful, but possible. John Ceepak has lived his life trying to do the right thing, which is seldom the thing that will also make you rich.

"What brand shoe polish do you use?" Ceepak asks when he's done nodding.

"What?"

"Is there a particular brand of white shoe polish you prefer?"

Mr. O'Malley looks to his son. "Kevin?"

"Kiwi. The liquid polish. It's best for scuffs."

"Kevin gets it for me."

"They carry it at the Acme, CVS. It's a rather common brand."

"Thank you," says Ceepak as he dutifully jots down Kiwi on a fresh sheet in his tidy notebook. "Do you polish your own shoes?"

"Huh?" says Mr. O'Malley.

The lawyer laughs a little. "This isn't the army, officer. My client can't be reprimanded for not spit-polishing his shoes."

"I think Jackie had the maid take care of it," says Mr. O'Malley, his voice distant. "She always told me to leave a pair outside my bedroom door first thing in the morning. Guess I'm going to have to take over running the household, too."

"I'll help," says Kevin.

"Thanks, son. I really miss your mother . . . all that she did for me . . . for the family."

Everybody's in sympathetic-nod mode.

Except me.

I think Mr. O'Malley killed my friend Gail. Sliced her up like a butcher working through a side of beef. I really don't care who's going to polish his shoes or run his home. Heck, he may not have to worry about it, either; I have a feeling he'll soon be rooming at the New Jersey State Prison in Trenton. They don't wear white bucks. Goes against their brand image as "inmates."

Ceepak stands up, somewhat abruptly. "We'll talk with you gentlemen again at noon. Please present yourselves at police headquarters on Cherry Street at that time."

Rambowski takes a step forward and it looks like he wants to go chest to chest with Ceepak. Good luck with that, pal.

"Do you have plans to incarcerate my client at that time?"

"If evidence recovered inside number One Tangerine indicates that Mr. O'Malley should be put into custody, rest assured we shall do so."

I catch Mr. O'Malley shooting Kevin a look.

"And," I say, "just so you don't waste your time sending over Sean or a cleaning crew, the State Police already have the house locked down tight."

"Excuse me, officer," says Rambowski, "are you in any way implying that my clients would tamper with potential evidence?"

"Yeah. I guess so."

Hey, you work with Ceepak long enough, you end up telling the truth on a regular basis.

Ceepak and I roll out of the King Putt parking lot. He's behind the wheel.

"He did it, right?" I say.

"So it would seem," says Ceepak in that way he has of letting me know he really hasn't made up his mind.

"What? You don't think he did?"

186

"If he did, I am somewhat surprised at his stupidity and sloppiness."

True. Most criminals leave you a trail of breadcrumbs to track. This guy's dropping whole loaves—those round pumpernickel ones the size of armadillos.

"Well, who else?" I say. "Mazzilli? That's what Marny thinks. Mazzilli and the mob."

"It is too early to reach a definitive conclusion, Danny. We haven't even searched inside the house, the one place where all the current suspects intersect."

Ceepak takes an unexpected left turn on Ocean Avenue.

"Where we heading?" I ask.

"North. Mayor Sinclair's house. It's early. I don't think he goes to his office until ten or eleven."

Probably later if he had a busy night in a hot tub somewhere.

We pull into the mayor's driveway.

He lives north of the center of town, up where the homes are more like compounds behind stockade fences and evergreen walls. I see his son Ben's motorcycle leaning up against some boxwood shrubs. Looks like he parked it there after scootering home drunk. No big surprise. We've been writing the kid up ever since I was an auxiliary cop working the Tilt A Whirl case with Ceepak, and Ben Sinclair terrorized an entire video arcade.

We go ring the doorbell.

After about the fourth ding-dong-ding, Mayor Sinclair shuffles to the foyer in pajamas. His crimped hair is sticking out at all sorts of jagged angles. Maybe he went punk overnight, the better to communicate with his wayward son. Then I see a pair of bright red Crocs on his feet and a scrolled "HS" embroidered on his chest. He sleeps preppy, too.

"What the hell are you two doing here at eight o'clock in the morning?"

Before his first cup of coffee, the mayor is neither sunny nor funderful.

"We apologize for disturbing your sleep," says Ceepak, "but we need to ask you a question regarding a phone call you received early Friday morning."

"What? You're kidding."

"No, sir. Do you recall the telephone conversation?"

"When?"

"Yesterday. Three fifteen A.M."

"And this couldn't wait until I was in the office because . . . ?"

"Because it is related to our ongoing murder investigation. The dismembered body found at One forty-five Tangerine Street."

The mayor steps out on the porch, closes the front door behind him.

"Jesus, Ceepak," he whispers angrily, "didn't Chief Baines talk to you? That poor girl was mutilated by out-of-town mafioso—the crew that runs the Atlantic City escort service she works for—because they caught her skimming off the top, cheating her pimps out of their cut."

"Gee," I say, "wasn't that an episode on *The Sopranos*?"

"Mayor Sinclair," says Ceepak, "Chief Baines has not proffered a theory on the murder of Gail Baker."

"Crap on a cracker! I told Baines to call off the investigation . . . get the State Police out of my town. The FBI organized crime people will look into it. They'll find a woman to wear a wire."

"Adriana," I say. "Christopher Moltisanti's girlfriend. That's from *The Sopranos*, too!"

"Mayor Sinclair," says Ceepak, "we only have one question: Why did Mr. Patrick O'Malley call you at three fifteen A.M. on Friday."

The mayor frowns. Furrows his brow. "Was that him?"

"Come again?"

"Friday morning. My phone rings at some ungodly hour."

"Three fifteen?" I toss in.

"Probably. Yes. I remember seeing the time when I checked the caller ID."

"Was it Patrick O'Malley?" asks Ceepak.

"No. Whoever it was, they had their number blocked. The screen said 'Private Caller.' I think. I was half asleep. Truth be told, I had forgotten all about it."

"What did you and the unidentified caller talk about?"

"Nothing."

"Nothing?"

"Right."

"Then why did he call?"

"Beats me. All I remember is crawling over to the phone. Picking it up. Saying 'hello' about a hundred times. No one on the other end said a word. My wife told me to be quiet, she was trying to sleep. I figured it was a prank caller. Anyway, I checked the caller ID, said 'hello' one last time, my wife kicked me in the shin, and I hung up."

"Interesting," says Ceepak.

"Annoying," says the mayor.

"Thank you, sir. We have no further questions at this time."

"Whoa. Wait a sec. What exactly do you mean by that?"

"Excuse me?"

"That 'at this time' bit."

"Ah. Yes. We will most likely question you later about the activities taking place at number One Tangerine Street."

"The what?"

"The parties," I say. "With the girls. Up in the hot tub?"

The mayor slips into a catatonic coma.

"Danny?" Ceepak is shaking his head.

Perhaps I said too much.

Or perhaps Ceepak wants the mayor to stress about how much we know on the subject of his dalliances with the sugar daddies and how much his wife may soon want to kick him someplace besides his shin. I hope Mr. Sinclair uses extra-strength deodorant. I have a feeling the man is going to be perspiring like the inside of a sweat lodge today.

"We'll contact you later," says Ceepak.

"Wait a minute!" Sinclair wiggles a finger at me. "You can't slander my good name like that, young man. I'm the mayor! You work for me! I can have you fired!"

"Actually," says Ceepak, "Officer Boyle and I work for Sea Haven Township. Unless you can prove we have engaged in conduct unbecoming a public employee or have violated certain departmental rules and regulations, I think—"

The mayor misses the rest of Ceepak's front porch dissertation. He yanks open the front door, runs inside (probably to see if son will let him borrow the motorcycle for a speedy getaway), and slams the door in our faces.

That's when the cell phone starts chirruping on Ceepak's belt.

27

"THIS IS CEEPAK. GO."

He always says that when it's a business call.

We amble away from the porch, head toward our car.

"Hang on. I'm putting you on speaker so my partner can listen in."

The next voice I hear belongs to Dr. Rebecca Kurth, the county medical examiner.

"I called in some new autopsy findings to Bill Botzong and the State MCU team. He requested that I relay the information on to you."

"Standing by," says Ceepak handing me the phone so he can take notes.

"Upon further examination of the remains," Dr. Kurth continues, "two things struck me as peculiar. Number one: although we found the residue of soap underneath Ms. Baker's fingernails, we found no traces of it on any other part of her body. This seemed

191

extremely odd—unless, of course, she was attacked as soon as she reached for the bar, before she had a chance to lather up. However, we found no shampoo residue on her skin, either."

Ceepak nods. So I say, "Interesting" to the phone like he would.

"Sure is. If shampoo was in her hair, some foam should have trickled down to her shoulders, her torso. There should even be a trace amount on her hands. There is none anywhere. Perhaps our killer rinsed the body parts clean after severing them."

This time, I just nod.

"This next part is even stranger," says Dr. Kurth. "When we opened her up and examined her organs . . ."

I do a silent *urp*. My imagination is too vivid. I see this stuff when people talk about it.

". . . we found that a dark blue substance had stained her esophagus and lungs. I'm having a hard time explaining how it got there. If she drank something, say, with a heavy amount of blue food coloring in it, it might explain the discoloration on the interior of her throat but not the lungs."

"Any idea what sort of dye it is?" asks Ceepak.

"No. Not yet. We're still analyzing its composition, running it through the database. First guess—and it is only a guess—I'd say it's some kind of heavily dyed automatic toilet bowl cleaner. Toilet Duck and Tidy Bowl are both the same intensely blue color."

Yep. There's even a Tidy Bowl cocktail: vodka and Blue Curaçao liqueur. Bud makes them at Big Kahuna's for frat boys. Sure, they suck 'em down, but not into their lungs.

"This new evidence would seem to suggest," says Dr. Kurth, "that Ms. Baker was killed somewhere besides the outdoor shower stall. The CSI crew did not find a similar discoloration on the walls or floor."

So maybe Mr. O'Malley drowned Gail in a toilet bowl.

In the bathroom.

In the house at number One Tangerine.

"Thank you, Dr. Kurth," says Ceepak.

"I'll keep you guys in the loop when we find out what kind of dye we're dealing with."

"Appreciate that."

Ceepak clips his phone back to his belt.

"We need to get inside that damn house!" I overstate the obvious because it's what I do best.

"We also need to reexamine the shower stall."

"How come?"

"If Ms. Baker was drowned and, therefore, killed somewhere else, why was there so much blood splattered on the walls?"

———

"I've been asking myself the same thing," says Bill Botzong when we contact him at 9 A.M. "We need to be inside. Now."

Botzong and the entire State Police MCU crew spent the night in their van at number One Tangerine Street. I can hear the crick in his neck over the radio.

"Your warrant will be signed within the hour," Ceepak assures him.

"Good. We'll hit the bathrooms first. Look for discolored toilet water."

"We'll see you at nine thirty," Ceepak says to the radio.

"Bring some coffee," says Botzong.

"Roger that." Ceepak cradles the radio mic back into its bracket. I'm behind the wheel as we cruise down Ocean Avenue toward town.

"Let's swing by The Rusty Scupper," says Ceepak as he stares out the window. I can tell: he's piecing together the jigsaw puzzle in his brain.

I take the next right, head west to Bayside Boulevard. The greasy spoon where Gail Baker used to waitress is open for

breakfast and we still have an hour before we can enter the so-
called Sugar Shack on Tangerine Street. Ceepak's probably figuring we can talk to Gail Baker's co-workers, maybe eat a slippery
egg with a ketchup-encrusted fork and crunch on some burnt
bacon. We can also grab Botzong and his team some coffees—the
kind with oil slicks skimming the surface.

Yep, the Scupper does breakfast even worse than they do
lunch.

We cruise over to the public pier on the bay side of the island
because that's the restaurant's main attraction: it's close to the water
and the boats. The stench of the barnacles on the pilings helps
cover up the foul smells from the kitchen.

Now, when I call The Rusty Scupper a restaurant, I'm using the
term loosely. It's really just this four-table grease pit with a grill. The
décor is simple: red-and-white vinyl tablecloths with tomato-red
rings wherever a dirty-bottomed ketchup bottle has recently resided.

The place is totally empty. No one's sitting in any of the wobbly
chairs. At one table, there's stack of laminated menus polka-dotted
with unidentifiable food splotches.

"Let's grab some chow while we're here," suggests Ceepak, gin-
gerly picking up a menu with his thumb and forefinger. We're
going to need Purell after we order. "No telling when we might
have another chance to eat today."

"Sounds like a plan," I say.

We sit down. First Ceepak wipes the clumps of scrambled eggs
off his chair, the seat of which is ripped and torn so you can see
the spongy yellow foam inside the cushion.

I'd probably drink some of the tepid water sitting above my
bent spoon, but I'm sort of allergic to lipstick when it's rimming
the top of a dirty plastic drinking cup.

"What're you two eating?" a guy in leather pants and a sleeveless
leather vest (no shirt) says when he comes out of the kitchen to

our table. He sports a shaved head, handlebar mustache, nipple rings, and a filthy apron splattered with egg yolks and coffee stains. Well, I hope they're coffee stains. The apron doesn't really match his black leather pants, but I guess, that without Gail, they're going with a whole different look.

"We'd like some eggs and some information," says Ceepak.

"Do I look like a library?"

Actually, now that I examine his tattooed arms, he looks exactly like Peter O'Malley's boyfriend. The biker boy.

"You're Peter's friend," I say. "Peter O'Malley."

He shifts his weight. A hip rises. Bare abdominal muscles ripple. "So?"

"We're investigating the death of Gail Baker," says Ceepak. "She used to work here." He hands the man his card.

Biker boy takes it. Flicks it under his nose. "Is this you? John Ceepak?"

He can read.

"That's right."

"I'm Thomas."

"Pleased to make your acquaintance. I take it you are a waiter here?"

"Chef. We're a little short-staffed this morning. I have to work on the floor and in the kitchen."

And probably on the kitchen floor, too—which is where, I have a hunch, they cook their eggs to make 'em so gritty.

"So, Mr. John Ceepak," Thomas asks shifting his weight so he can flash his washboard abs again, "do you work out?"

"Some."

"Some? You look like you're ripped under that shirt."

Great. Even the gay short-order cooks want to flirt with my partner.

"Was Gail a friend of yours?" Ceepak asks, choosing to remain oblivious to Thomas's manly advances.

"More like an acquaintance. You know—when things were slow, we'd grab an empty table and a cup of coffee. Swap stories about our O'Malley men."

"She told you she was intimate with Peter's father?"

"Uh-hunh. And . . ." Thomas glances around to make certain no one is eavesdropping, which they're not because, like I said, we're the only ones in the joint. "Gail had also been with *two* of Mr. O'Malley's sons. Wild child Sean last winter and, a couple years ago, the one they named after the peanut butter."

"Skippy," I say.

"Is that *really* his name?"

"I think so."

"Anyway, this one day, Gail and I had an absolute hoot comparing certain O'Malley *familial similarities.*"

He leans on the words like we should catch his double meaning. I don't.

"The boys' *physical attributes?*"

I've still got nothing.

"You know—the Irish curse? A red nose and a short hose? All potatoes and no sausage?"

Thomas blinks a lot. Grins.

"What about Kevin O'Malley?" Ceepak asks, somewhat abruptly. "Did Ms. Baker have any sort of relationship with Kevin O'Malley?"

"I doubt it. That boy is his father's favorite. No way would he jeopardize that by chasing after his father's hot little toddy."

"Any thoughts about why Kevin is the only son the father seems to include in his business affairs?" Ceepak asks.

"He's the first-born man-child," says Thomas. "In an Irish Catholic family, that automatically makes you the heir apparent. The other three sons—Peter, Skip, and Sean—all have issues with their dad. Even the sister, Crazy Mary, doesn't like the old man very much. Guess he never took her to a daddy-daughter dance at the loony bin."

I get the feeling Thomas doesn't like Big Paddy O'Malley very much, either. Probably still bitter about his boyfriend being uninvited to last weekend's grand opening at the Rolling Thunder.

"Of course, both Peter and Sean also had problems with their mother—may God bless that tubby old witch's soul. Skippy, on the other hand, Skippy *loved* Jackie O'Malley. Absolutely *adored* her. Frankly, between you and me, I think Skipper is gay—he just doesn't know it yet."

"An interesting hypothesis," says Ceepak, probably so the guy will shut up.

"You wait, John."

Ceepak flinches. Nobody calls him John, except his wife and the chief.

"It's just a matter of time before that boy comes skipping out of his closet in something skimpier than a chariot skirt. He's a straight man and he loves cats? I don't think so."

"Do you have any idea," asks Ceepak, "who in the O'Malley family would gain the most if Mr. O'Malley went to jail?"

"Is that going to happen?" Thomas asks eagerly.

"We don't know. But if it did, who, in your opinion, would benefit the most?"

"Easy. Kevin. With the mother dead and the father in jail, the golden boy would take over everything."

28

WE'RE BACK IN THE CAR, HEADING SOUTH AND EAST TO Tangerine Street.

"You think Kevin killed Gail and then made it look like his dad did it?"

"It's a possibility, Danny."

"Guess it would explain why there's so much evidence pointing to Mr. O'Malley as the murderer."

Either that, or he *is* the murderer. Sometimes a duck is a duck, or however that saying about quacking and waddling goes.

Ceepak flicks on the car radio, I guess for a quick update on the news. Maybe the weather. After all, T.J. has that golf outing this morning. The radio is tuned to WAVY.

"This is the Skeeter buzzin' in your ear. I'm on the Boardwalk where we've set up shop inside the loading shed at Sea Haven's brand-new, all wood, all-wild Rolling Thunder roller coaster. We're counting down the minutes till ten, when Big Paddy O'Malley will come in, head over to the

control room, and bop the button that will send the first train rollin' and
thunderin' around the track. Stop by and say hey. Be the sixth caller and
you could win an all-day, all-access pass to ride all the rides on Bruno's
Fun Time Piers—including the all-new Rolling Thunder!"

Ceepak snaps the radio off.

He doesn't make any commentary.

He doesn't have to.

We're on our way to search Bruno Mazzilli's other Fun Time
enterprise.

As we near the house at 9:29 A.M., I see that the State MCU team
has called in a few more vans. People are milling around in white
Tyvek clean suits. They look like envelopes on a coffee break in a
FedEx drop box. I also see a guy in khaki pants and a polo shirt
handing a sheaf of official-looking documents to Detective Bill
Botzong at the edge of the driveway to number One Tangerine.

"Judge Rasmussen was as good as her word," says Ceepak.

The warrant has arrived. The troops are going in.

Picture a frat house for rich old farts.

Only instead of furniture collected off the street, these guys have
an Ethan Allen showroom of stuffed chairs and shabby-chic sofas.
The kitchen has all sorts of stainless steel gear lining the Italian tiled
walls. Refrigerators, grills, trash compactors, beer coolers with windows in the doors so you can keep an eye on your designer
brewskis. Everything's done up in chrome and black and marble.

In the living room, I see a fully stocked bar with a big mirror
behind the bottles and a battalion of cut crystal tumblers and fancy
beer glasses. No mugs.

Speaking of mirrors, when we check out the first floor bedrooms, there seems to be a mirror hanging over every bed. I think
I'm gonna have nightmares about Bruno Mazzilli's ape-hairy back
jiggling on the ceiling for the rest of my life.

"They wired these bordello rooms with video cameras," says Carolyn Miller, the CSI tech, as she points to a small lens hole in a piece of furniture I think you call an armoire if you have five thousand dollars to spend on a TV cabinet. The hole is aimed at the bed.

"Find the videos," barks Botzong. "Look for photo albums. Any kind of souvenirs or trophies these guys kept of their conquests. It'll help us ID the bastards when they start lying about it in front of their wives."

"Here's a bathroom," says Ceepak.

He, Botzong, and I poke in our heads. We don't want to walk in—not until Ms. Miller crawls across the floor and reveals its secrets: footprints, hairs, fibers. But, gazing through the door, I can tell even the bathrooms were designed to be romantic in that gaudy Donald Trump sort of way. Claw-foot tubs. Gold fixtures. Candles everywhere.

"The toilet water is uncolored," reports Ceepak.

Yeah. Guys hang out here. They left the seat up.

"Carolyn?" says Botzong. "Clear the bathrooms for us first. If you find any kind of blue toilet cleanser—in the bowl or under a sink—give me a holler."

"Boss?" a CSI guys calls from the kitchen.

"What's up?"

"I think I found the shoe polish."

Miller goes into the bathroom, the rest of us hustle back to the kitchen.

"It was in a plain white bag under the kitchen sink," says the tech, who, in addition to his hermetically sealed suit, is fully gloved and handling the evidence with forceps like it's a rod of radioactive uranium. "Kiwi. Liquid Magic Scuff Cover," he reads the label for us. "'Polishes in one easy step for all smooth leather shoes with scuffs that need covering.'"

Scuffs or blood stains.

"Says it's 'water-resistant,'" the tech reads off the back of the label.

Handy. Especially if your bloody scuffs are on a shower stall wall.

"Six bottles of Kiwi, all empty. Four bottles of Stride Rite, one still half full."

"Any receipt in the bag?" asks Ceepak.

"No, sir. Just this."

"What?"

The tech forceps a crisp white rectangle out of the plastic bag.

"A business card. Big Paddy O'Malley, Shore 2 B Fun Enterprises. Lists an address on Ocean Avenue."

"He dropped a calling card into the bag?" says Botzong incredulously.

"It's possible someone is attempting to frame Mr. O'Malley," says Ceepak.

"Yeah. Either that, or this guy is the dumbest killer in history." The lead detective turns to a young blonde in a blue windbreaker. "Okay, Reiss. Hit all the local shoe stores, drug stores, Kmarts and Wal-Marts. Anybody who might have this much white shoe polish on hand. Somebody buys a dozen bottles, maybe a cashier remembers them. If they do, Bunny, dig for security tapes."

"Will do," says the CSI named Bunny Reiss. She heads out the front door and, yes, hops into her sedan at the end of the driveway.

That's when I see Sean O'Malley parked out front in the street.

"Ceepak?" I say. "Sean's back."

"Then let's go have a word with him, Danny—let these folks do their jobs."

"Yeah." I'm already strolling out the door.

Something about smug n' chubby Sean has rubbed me the wrong way since grade school. Okay, *everything* about him. As we head down the walkway, I can hear the radio blaring inside his car. Cliff Skeete and WAVY.

"Nine forty-five in sunny, funderful Sea Haven on W-A-V-Y, the crazy wave of sound for Sea Haven and the shore, and we're just fifteen minutes away from thunder rolling across the sky." The crowd whoops a whoo-hoo in the background. *"Hey, if you want to ride the thunder and feel the rumble of Sea Haven's first all-wood roller coaster, you need to hurry on down. The place is packed—"*

Sean clicks off his radio. Smirks at us.

"What the dilly yo, po-po?"

"Why are you here again, Mr. O'Malley?" asks Ceepak.

He shrugs. "Yo, didn't you hear the man? It's a sunny, funderful day. Figured I should chillax on the beach."

"You cannot park here for beach access. This is a residential street."

"But that be my boss's hizzle."

"Come again?"

"Number One Tangerine is his boss's house," I translate.

"Aw-ite, Danny Boy. You got it goin' on. Anyways, the big man want me to keep an eye on his shit."

"You work for Bruno Mazzilli, is that correct?" says Ceepak.

"At's ite. He owns the boardwalk, brurva. My old man? He just be renting space."

"Well," says Ceepak, "you can tell Mr. Mazzilli that any items removed from his house as evidence will be returned to him at the conclusion of any and all legal proceedings. This area is now considered a crime scene, and I must ask you to move along.

"My old man in trouble?"

"Move along, Mr. O'Malley."

"You dudes takin' him down?" he asks gleefully. "You find some incriminating shit in there? Everybody know he be boning the Baker biatch."

"If you do not move your vehicle, sir, we will be forced to call a tow truck and have it moved for you."

"'Course, I banged her, too. Gail 'Da Ho' Baker. Big Paddy had to settle for sloppy seconds. My big bro Skipperdoodle never did tap that pooty. Crashed and burned, big time. His loss. Girl had her a bumpin' booty—"

"So, Sean," I say, because I'm afraid he'll say tooty-fruity or kooty next, "don't you have a butt to go kiss? Mr. Mazzilli probably wonders where you are."

"Yeah." He cranks the ignition. "You'll see. Mr. Mazzilli gonna put me in charge of the Rolling Thunder when Daddy goes to jail!"

Ceepak rests both hands on Sean's rolled down window.

"I thought your brother Kevin was the designated heir for all your father's business affairs."

"That's what Big Paddy like to see happen. But Bruno ain't gonna deal with Kevin. Calls him a sanctimonious piece of shit on a regular basis. That roller coaster? That baby's gonna be mine, brurva, I guaran-damn-tee it. Later!"

The cocky kid peels wheels and tears up the road because he knows we're way too busy to write him up.

Especially since he just made himself another suspect in Gail Baker's murder.

"You think Sean's the one framing the father?" I say.

"It is yet another possibility, Danny. However, I consider it a remote one at best."

"How come?"

"Young Sean strikes me as rather incompetent."

True. I can't imagine him taking the time to orchestrate the whole deal. He's too busy memorizing hip-hop slang.

"Furthermore, I feel he has an exaggerated sense of his own worth to Mr. Mazzilli, who is brilliant and ruthless when it comes to business. It is highly unlikely that he would turn—"

"Guys?"

Detective Botzong is at the front door, signaling for us to come back in.

"You're gonna want to see this," he says.

We double-time it up the walkway.

"What did you find?" asks Ceepak when we hit the front door.

Botzong leads the way. "Potassium chloride. In the first floor-medicine chest."

Uh-oh.

Potassium chloride is one of the drugs used for executing criminals with a lethal injection.

It stops the heart from beating.

29

WE COME INTO THE KITCHEN AND SEE CAROLYN MILLER hovering over a row of glass vials lined up on the marble island in the center of the kitchen.

They're tiny bottles with bright yellow labels and metal caps, the kind doctors tip over and jab needles into to draw out serum when they give you a shot. Six of them. My eyes are young enough to read the label: Potassium Chloride—Concentrate Must Be Diluted Before Use. Four vials are empty, their lids punctured.

"So," says Botzong, "either one of the men in the house had a serious potassium deficiency or they wanted to jump straight to step three of the lethal injection sequence."

Ceepak nods. "They knock you out with sodium thiopental. Paralyze you with pancuronium bromide. Stop your heart with potassium chloride. A bolus injection of 100 milliequivalents affects the electrical potential of the heart muscle. It simply stops."

"Remember that male nurse in Indiana?" says Botzong. "They convicted him of killing six people by injecting them with potassium chloride to induce heart attack."

"They suspected him of killing a hundred," adds Ceepak. "Mostly elderly patients at the county hospital where he worked."

"Wait a second," I say, confusion wrinkling my brow. "Gail Baker didn't have a heart attack."

"No," says Ceepak. "But Mrs. O'Malley certainly did."

Jeez-o, man.

"He killed them both?"

"We can't make that assumption," says Botzong. "Not yet, anyway. But this?" He gestures at the lineup of little bottles, all of which, I now notice, are labeled as 20 ml vials with 40 mEq, which must be that milliequivalent thing Ceepak rattled off. I do the math: fill a syringe with two and a half bottles and you could stop a condemned man's heart on death row in the thirty-six states where lethal injection is the preferred form of capital punishment.

And, like I said, three of the six ampoules are empty.

"Did you find needles and syringes?" asks Ceepak.

"No," says Miller.

"Were there any other suspicious drugs in the medicine chest?" asks Ceepak. "Anything that might've been utilized to incapacitate Ms. Baker? Chloroform? GHB?"

Miller shakes her head. "No. I'm wondering now if our guy just didn't sneak up behind Baker and bop her on the head with that blunt object Dr. Kurth labeled as the murder weapon. Maybe he tried knocking her out like they do in the movies and ended up killing her instead with the blow that cracked the skull and breached the dura matter."

I guess I look confused again because Ceepak explains, "That's the outermost meningeal layer of the brain, Danny."

Okay. Now I've got a headache to go with my queasy stomach.

"Would the potassium chloride show up in Mrs. O'Malley's

body?" I ask, mostly so I can quit picturing my brain as a squishy layer cake packed inside a Tupperware carrying case.

"Not really," says Botzong. "It's not even a poison. Just a chemical compound you need to live. Too much, it screws with nerve signals in your heart. Plus, now Mrs. O'Malley's body has been embalmed for burial. Embalming fluid wipes out just about everything else that might be swimming around inside a corpse."

"So somebody killed Mrs. O'Malley, and then, the day of her funeral, they killed Gail? Why?"

"Danny?" This from Ceepak. "So far, we have nothing to link the two deaths."

"Except Mr. O'Malley," I say. "He killed his wife and then his mistress, who wanted to become his new wife. He killed her before she had a chance to start nagging him."

"It's a possibility, Danny," is all Ceepak says in reply to my lame excuse for a criminal motive.

"So," says Botzong, "where does Mr. O'Malley—or whoever—get this many vials of the concentrate?"

"We need to check with hospitals, doctor's offices," says Ceepak. "See if any has gone missing from the pharmacy closets."

"Of course," adds Miller, "the majority of the potassium chloride produced is used for making fertilizer."

"Peter O'Malley runs a landscaping company!" I say.

"True," says Ceepak. "But he was nowhere near the roller coaster last weekend and I don't think potassium chloride would be packaged in bottles like this for horticultural purposes. This most likely came from a doctor's office or a hospital, somewhere patients are treated for hypokalemia, low potassium"

"What about Dr. Hausler?" I say to Ceepak, remembering the broken-hearted, monkey-faced dentist. "Would he have access to this drug?"

"Perhaps," says Ceepak. "But, as you recall, Danny, he was jealous of the rich men giving Gail gifts. I do not think he would supply one of them with the chemical compound they needed to induce a heart attack in their wife."

"Who's this Hausler?" asks Botzong.

"A local dentist who was romantically linked for a short period of time with Ms. Baker."

"Marco?"

"Putting him on the list."

"Here is his business card," says Ceepak. "When we interviewed Dr. Hausler, he had a pretty solid alibi for the time of death."

"Any reason he'd want to kill Mrs. O'Malley, too?" asks Botzong.

"None that is readily apparent."

"Okay, let's make Mr. O'Malley and those who might want to frame him our prime targets," says Botzong. "You two guys were there when Mrs. O'Malley died, right?"

We nod.

"Did you see anything up on that roller coaster? Anything hit you as hinky?"

"Not at the time," says Ceepak.

"Could Mr. O'Malley have injected his wife with an undiluted dose without her knowing it?"

"Perhaps," says Ceepak. "If he waited until the ride started rolling. Used the commotion and excitement to cover his actions."

"If he injected a large enough dose," says Miller, "the effects would be almost instantaneous."

Yeah. She'd have a "heart attack" by the time they hit the second hill.

"Kevin O'Malley was sitting right behind her," I add. "He could have jabbed her in the neck. The headrests in the roller coaster cars had those slotted vents—like in a sports car, you know? He could've poked the needle right through one of the openings."

"And why does Kevin O'Malley want us to arrest his old man for murder?" asks Botzong

"With the death of his mother and the incarceration of his father," Ceepak explains, "Kevin O'Malley would assume total control of the O'Malley family empire."

"Maybe Kevin did it when they were climbing that first hill," I say. "Gravity pins his mom's head to the back of the seat. He leans forward like he wants to tell her something. Bam! Pokes her with the poison dart!"

Everybody around the marble countertop is sort of staring at me now. I hypothesize out loud more dramatically than most cops.

"Are their video cameras on the roller coaster track?" asks Botzong.

"Yes," says Ceepak. "I noticed several. The operator in the control room most likely uses their video feeds to monitor the ride."

"We need to track down the digital recordings from last Saturday morning," Botzong says to his team. "Might help us see what actually went on up there."

"Sir?" says Carolyn Miller. "I seriously doubt whether they record the input from those track cameras. After all, they're utilized for operational purposes, not enhanced security."

True. You don't get many shoplifters on a roller coaster ride.

"The dead air," I mumble.

"Come again?" says Ceepak.

"Cliff Skeete did that live remote broadcast on W-A-V-Y. He was riding the ride with the O'Malleys and all the local big wigs. When they all started screaming 'heart attack,' the station took him off the air. But they were probably rolling tape on his feed at the station. Recording it. We could also *hear* what happened."

———

Half of the State Police Major Crimes Unit is working the phones, calling up doctors, surgeons and pharmaceutical supply companies.

Meanwhile Ceepak and I race up Ocean Avenue to the studios of WAVY.

So it's only fitting that we're listening to their live broadcast from the Rolling Thunder on the radio in our police cruiser.

It's 9:59 A.M. One minute to blastoff.

"And so," we hear Mr. O'Malley say into Skeeter's microphone, *"I hereby dedicate the Rolling Thunder to my late wife, Mrs. Jacqueline O'Malley—a woman who loved family and fun more than anything in the world."*

I wait for him to say, "so I'm sorry I killed her," but he doesn't.

"Thank you, Mr. O'Malley," says Skeeter in his deep-and-velvety voice, the same one he used whenever he would intro a Barry White track when we did wedding gigs together back in the day. *"Thank you for those truly touching and inspirational words."*

And then he shifts gears.

"Are we ready to do this thing? Boo-yeah! Let the thunder roll!"

My cell phone starts blaring Springsteen's "Born to Run."

Samantha Starky's ringtone.

I ignore it.

Ceepak, who is currently behind the wheel, punches off the radio.

"Go ahead and answer it, partner."

"It's a personal call. Sam Starky. I'll let it bounce over to voice mail."

Ceepak gives me this pursed-lip look to say, "It's okay this one time."

Bruce is screaming, "tramps like us" as I flip open the phone.

"Hey, Sam."

"Hey, Danny. Where are you?"

"On the job."

"Really?"

"Yeah."

"Oh. Hey—thanks for getting me home last night. I was kind of tanked. Three drinks, you know?"

"Sure."

"So, did that other girl spend the night at your place?"

"Yeah. She had nowhere else to go."

I refuse to say "but I didn't sleep with her." If Sam thinks that, well, it's her problem.

"Hey, a bunch of us are down here at the new roller coaster.

"Sounds like fun."

Roller coasters usually are—as long as no one jabs you in the back of the neck with a hypodermic on that first hill.

"You want to come hang out with us? So far, no one's had a heart attack."

She's making a joke. I'm not laughing.

"Of course, we're stuck in this incredibly long line—longer than last weekend and I thought it might be neat if you came down and rode with us and then maybe you and me could have the talk we need to have if we want to do this the right way."

"Do what?"

She takes a breath. A rare occurrence. "Break up."

"Sam?"

"Yeah?"

"I'm on the job."

"I know, but . . . well . . . it's Saturday."

"So?"

"Saturday is supposed to be a day off."

"Not for a cop running a case. Come on. You know that."

I gesture to a squat and boxy building sandwiched between Pizza My Heart and Captain Video—the not so glamorous WAVY studios. Ceepak sees it, pulls to the curb.

"I gotta run, Sam."

"Okay."

"Have fun with your friends."

"Say hi to Ceepak."

"Yeah."

211

I fold up the phone.

"Problems?" says Ceepak as he slides the transmission into park.

"Sam. She wants me to go hang out with her college pals, ride the new roller coaster, and then have a deep meaningful discussion so she can dump me with a clean conscience."

"Sorry, Danny."

I grab my door handle. "I'll deal with it later. Right now, we need to focus on figuring out who killed Gail Baker and Mrs. O'Malley."

"Roger that."

As we climb out of the cop car it hits me: Damn. I've turned into Ceepak junior. The guy's contagious.

30

ANDREW MEYER, ONE OF THE YOUNG GUYS AT WAVY, escorts Ceepak and me into an audio studio.

"This is where we cut commercials and promos," he says. "You can use the computer there, call up the digital archives."

The walls are covered with gray foam rubber shaped like egg cartons. Soundproofing panels. Out in the hall, we can hear Cliff Skeete at the Rolling Thunder.

"There they go! Whoo-hoo. Listen to that rumble! Like thunder rolling across the clouds!"

Poor guy. He's already running out of material and the ride's only been open for fifteen minutes. Cliff promises to be right back with more *"fun in the thundering sun"* and segues into Springsteen's biggest radio hit: "Hungry Heart," the one about the wife and kids in Baltimore, Jack. Makes me think about Sam. And boardwalk nachos smothered in jack cheese. Guess we should've grabbed those eggs at The Rusty Scupper. I'm starving.

Meyer closes the door to cut off Cliff while Ceepak sits down in front of the microphone and mixer board.

"Can you call up last weekend's live remote?" he says to Andrew Meyer.

"Sure." Meyer leans in. Clacks some keys on the keyboard. Scoots the mouse around. Clicks it.

"Whoo-hoo!" The Skeeter from last Saturday is back.

"Can we fast forward to the point in time where the disc jockey was taken off the air?" asks Ceepak.

"Yeah. Hang on." Meyer slips on a pair of headphones. Skitters the mouse around. I see sound waves scroll across the screen like a rapid-fire lie detector test.

"Here we go." Meyer flicks a switch to put the sound back up in the speakers.

"We need someone to call nine–one–one! Now! Omigod! She's in bad shape! Call nine–one–one. We need an ambulance. Go to music! Go to music!"

A second or two of jumbled screams and shouts.

"What the hell happened?"

"Oh, Jesus Jackie. Jesus."

"We need to go back down!"

"No! She's having a heart attack! Unbutton her blouse."

Ceepak raises a hand. Meyer pauses the playback.

"Any idea who said, 'no,' Danny?"

"I'm not one hundred percent sure, but it might be Kevin. Skippy's definitely the one who said they should go back down."

Ceepak nods. That was his pick, too.

"Please continue," he says to Meyer.

More commotion. Screams. Cliff taps his microphone a couple of times.

"Elyssa?" he says to whomever must've been his engineer/producer last Saturday. *"Listen, sister, we need a goddamn ambulance and we need it fast! She looks bad, man. Bad. Call nine–one–one."*

And then a new voice is heard—closer to the microphone.

"Daddy killed Mommy!"

"That's Mary," I say. "The sister. She was sitting right in front of Cliff."

Ceepak leans in. Me, too. We're straining to isolate Mary's voice from the general hubbub.

"Daddy did it! I saw him! Daddy killed Mommy!"

"Shut the fuck up, Mary." Sean. The sensitive son.

"Daddy did it, Daddy did it."

"Shut! Up!"

"I'm a little birdy and I'm gonna tell—"

"Okay, lady. You're freaking me out." Cliff. *"Just sit down and chill, all right?"*

"Does anybody know CPR?" Kevin.

"Please, God, someone help!" Mr. O'Malley.

"Skip? Help Mom." Kevin again.

"I . . . I . . ."

"You were a fucking cop, for Christ's sake! Help her!"

"I can't."

"What?"

"I don't know how."

"Jesus!"

"They never taught me."

Um, yes they did.

"I'm a little birdy and I'm gonna tell everybody!"

"Sit down, lady. You're rockin' the damn car."

It goes on like that for nearly ten minutes.

Skippy starts crying.

Kevin calls him a worthless sack of shit.

Sean tells Kevin to *"cut Skipperdoodle some fucking slack, man."*

Mr. O'Malley tells them all to *"be quiet, the whole damn lot of you!"*

Mary giggles like a maniac and softly chants, *"I saw Daddy do it,"* over and over and over.

Cliff keeps talking to his producer, telling her it's getting ugly up here and he sees the cop cars and the ambulances and maybe a fire truck and two guys running up the roller coaster track.

"Wait—it's Danny . . . Danny Boyle . . . and . . . Ceepak. We're gonna be okay. Hey, Danny? Yo!"

Ceepak motions for Andrew Meyer to stop the playback.

We know what happens next.

Mrs. O'Malley dies.

31

"Mr. O'Malley is ready to talk," says Chief Baines when he radios us at the radio station.

Andrew Meyer is burning us a CD of what was recorded when Cliff was bumped off the air.

"Big Paddy and his lawyer have already left the Rolling Thunder," the chief continues, "and are currently en route to headquarters to complete their interview with you two."

"We're on our way," says Ceepak.

"Good. The lawyer says he's bringing in a witness to corroborate O'Malley's story."

"Any idea who?"

"Of course not. The shyster's slicker than an eel in olive oil. He's building suspense, trying to play us like he plays the poor saps in the jury box."

"We may need to question Mr. O'Malley about a second death."

More dead air on the radio, this time from the chief. Even

though he's a couple of miles away, I can see him tugging at his mustache, trying to pluck the thing out of his lip. It's what he always does when one of us gives him a new ulcer.

"Second death?" he says finally.

"Yes, sir. New evidence recovered inside the home at number One Tangerine suggests that Mrs. O'Malley's death last week may have been something other than a heart attack."

"What kind of evidence?"

"Numerous vials of potassium chloride, several of which were empty."

"You're telling me somebody poisoned Mrs. O'Malley?"

"No. I'm saying that is what the evidence recovered so far would seem to suggest."

"That's what I just said, John."

"If I may, sir, there is a difference. Until we find evidence linking the drug ampoules to the deceased and/or a suspect, all we have is proof that someone was in possession of a very powerful poison that they, most likely, removed illegally from a pharmacy."

"You're right," says the chief. "Let's take this thing one step at a time." I think that last bit was aimed at himself.

We hit the house, head straight for the interview room.

Big Paddy, Loud Rambowski, and Golden Boy Kevin are seated at the table. So is that fiery redhead from the funeral: the lady I pegged to be Mrs. O'Malley's sister. In this light, her hair looks orange.

"Officers," says the lawyer, standing up, pointing to two chairs, like he's in charge.

Ceepak? He finds a different open chair. Stands behind it.

"I don't believe we've met," he says to the orangehead.

"Frances Ryan."

"My sister-in-law," says Big Paddy.

"She can tell you where Dad was when the girl was murdered," adds Kevin.

"Indeed?" says Ceepak, finally sitting down. So I grab a seat, too. "Can she also explain why we found potassium chloride in the medicine chest at number One Tangerine Street?"

"Huh?" This from Daddy O'Malley.

"What the hell are you trying to pull here?" says Rambowski. "Have you made a connection between this . . . this . . ."

Ceepak helps out: "Potassium chloride. When delivered in a lethal dose, it causes the heart muscle to stop beating, leading to death by cardiac arrest."

"So?" says the lawyer. "Is there any connection between what you found and my client?"

"Not at this time. However, we have established that your client, Mr. O'Malley, was a frequent visitor to the house."

"No you have not," says Rambowski. "Not to my satisfaction."

"You wanna see the videos?" I ask.

Every drop of blood drains out of Mr. O'Malley's face.

"Goddamn that Johnson. Arrogant prick."

"Pardon?" says Ceepak, like we're at a tea party and somebody just farted.

"Keith Barent Johnson! He's the one who wanted the cameras in every bedroom! Said the videos were the only thing that got him through July and August when Bruno rented out the house to tourists and we all got busy making our nut for the year, couldn't screw around with the girls."

Mrs. O'Malley's sister has her purse in her lap and is twisting the straps like crazy. I think right about now she'd like to tear one off and use it to strangle her brother-in-law.

"Gentlemen," says Rambowski, "let's talk about why we're actually here. This morning you intimated that you had enough evidence to arrest Mr. O'Malley for the murder of Ms. Gail Baker. Is that what you intend to do, now that you've uncovered somebody's stash of potassium chloride, even though, if I might remind you, Ms. Baker did not die from a heart attack?"

"We have not yet written up an arrest warrant," says Ceepak, somewhat reluctantly.

"Good. Because my client has an ironclad alibi. Patrick?"

I can tell Mr. O'Malley is still thinking about the lethal injection and the heart attack.

"Hmm?" he says.

"Tell these gentlemen about the telephone call. Thursday night."

Mr. O'Malley sits there. Nods a couple of times.

"Dad?" Kevin prods him.

"Right. The phone. Okay." He reaches into the coat of his seersucker suit. Pulls out a cell, which he places on the table in front of him. "This is my main phone. 609–555–9566. I didn't want to turn it over earlier because, frankly, there are some rather embarrassing text messages and photographs stored in the memory. I should've erased them."

The sister-in-law flings daggers at him with her eyes. When she runs out of those, her eyes chuck spears.

"Anyway, we dug through the folders and, yes, you will find Ms. Baker's final text message," says the lawyer in what I take to be a stupid move.

"It says, 'I need 2 c u now,'" reports Kevin. "It arrived, as indicated in the phone records, shortly after midnight, first thing Friday morning."

Wow. The whole team is helping us out.

"The phone call to the mayor's house is in there, too," says Mr. O'Malley.

This is pretty incredible. I'm leaning back in my seat, they're making this so easy. Ceepak, however, is leaning forward. Elbows on the table. Hand stroking his chin.

"Now, whoever had the phone," says the lawyer, "erased the message they texted back to Ms. Baker from the 'Sent' file."

Ceepak's ears perk up. "What do yo mean by 'whoever had the phone?'"

32

"I MUST'VE GRABBED THE WRONG ONE WHEN I LEFT THE office on Thursday night," says Mr. O'Malley.

"And how could that happen?" asks Ceepak.

"Easy. We have a half dozen of these things sitting in chargers behind the counter at King Putt. Same make and model. We use them like walkie-talkies as we travel around town, managing our properties. Anyway, I just called Skippy at the golf course. Told him to find out who the hell had my phone Thursday night. Whoever it was, he's your goddamn killer."

"Mr. O'Malley," says Ceepak, "while I appreciate your being candid about the embarrassing evidence on your cell phone—"

Big Paddy slides the phone down the table like he and Ceepak are playing air hockey. "Here. Take it. Maybe you can un-erase the text message whoever did this thing sent back to Gail."

Ceepak blocks the shot. Moves the cell sideways. "Rest assured, Mr. O'Malley we will attempt to do just that. However, so far, all we have is your word that you were not in possession of this phone Thursday night into Friday morning."

Mr. O'Malley gestures toward the sister-in-law. "That's why Frances is here."

The big woman crosses both arms over her chest. Her Irish, as they say, is up. She looks like she might explode.

"Frances?" says Mr. O'Malley.

"What?"

"You said you'd tell them."

"That I did, Patrick. However, that was before I heard how you poisoned Jackie."

"Frances, I did not kill your sister."

"Then what're you doing with this heart attack drug these gentlemen are talking about?" she says, flicking a hand in our general direction.

"Ms. Ryan," says Rambowski, "as I told the police, there is no link between the potassium chloride they found in some house on—"

"Bullshit, you fucking goddamn liar!"

As my mother used to say, she has a mouth on her.

"What? You needed the damn insurance money to pay back the shylocks you borrowed from to build that monstrosity on the boardwalk? Mark my words, first nor'easter blows through town, that thing is toppling over like a house of cards made out of matchsticks!"

"Frances, I swear on my children," says Big Paddy, "I did not kill Jackie!"

"Sure you did. You knew she was overweight and smoked and had a history of heart problems so you just nudged things along a little is what you did."

"Ms. Ryan, if I may," says Ceepak. "As Mr. Rambowski has pointed out numerous times, there is currently no link between Mr. O'Malley and the potassium chloride. In fact, I suspect someone may be attempting to frame your brother-in-law. To spoon feed us enough clues that we will rush to judgment and recklessly lock him away for life."

"Who?" demands Big Paddy. "Who's trying to set me up?"

Ceepak's got a good poker face. Doesn't glance over at Kevin. I would've.

"We can't say for certain, sir. Not yet." He turns to Ms. Ryan. "But tell me, Ms. Ryan, why did you come here this morning?"

"Because I'm too goddamn Catholic," she says. "I can't lie. Even when I want to."

Ceepak nods. At least that part of their religious beliefs overlaps.

"I called Frances late Thursday night," says Mr. O'Malley.

Ms. Ryan nods. "Right before midnight."

"Then I went over to where she was staying."

"Place called the Mussel Beach Motel."

The two bitter enemies are completing each other's sentences like an old married couple.

"Here is the record of that call," says barrister Rambowski, pushing a sheet of paper across the table toward Ceepak.

"It's on one of the other lines attached to our Verizon account. 609–555–9567."

Ceepak studies the phone bill.

"He was drunk," says Ms. Ryan. "Bawling his eyes out. Said he had to come see me."

"So I drove over to the motel," says Mr. O'Malley. "Brought a bottle of whisky."

"We split it. Down by the pool. I called Paddy a goddamn son-ofabitch for the way he treated my sister. Whoring around all over town. Jacqueline knew what Patrick was doing all those nights he didn't come home—and it wasn't working at the office, not in the middle of February when no one plays putt-putt, that's for damn sure. In fact, Jackie had known about his chippies for years."

"That's what the trip to Buffalo was all about," Mr. O'Malley confesses, looking down at his hands.

Frances Ryan laughs. "That night before the funeral, oh I reamed Big Paddy but good. Screamed like a banshee at him. We got so loud, we woke up the motel management. Lovely young lady named Rebecca came out in her bathrobe, told me to, and I quote, 'shut my trap.' Said I'd wake the dead, not to mention all their paying guests."

"The motel manager is a friend of ours," I say. "We'll ask her to corroborate your story."

"Oh, she'll corroborate it all right," says Frances. "I don't think Ms. Rebecca will soon forget Paddy O'Malley and me."

"I drove home around four in the morning," says Big Paddy.

"After I made him a pot of coffee in my motel room. He was drunker than a skunk in a barrel of rum."

"And why," asks Ceepak, "did you wait until now to tell us all this?"

"Because," says Mr. O'Malley, "my learnèd counsel advised me not to say anything to the police about any telephone calls I might've made on the night of Miss Baker's murder, no matter how innocent they may have seemed. He also suggested that you gentlemen would have difficulty with my admission of drinking and driving, something, I swear, I very rarely do."

The sister-in-law snorts out a "Ha!"

Guess she won't lie about that, either.

"So," says Kevin, "can we go home now? You know where dad was when Ms. Baker was murdered."

"Please wait here," says Ceepak standing up from the table. "My partner and I need to confer with our chief." He turns to Big Paddy. "We will also need to call the management of the Mussel Beach Motel to confirm your whereabouts for late Thursday into Friday morning. After that, you, sir, are free to leave."

"Thank you."

"Awesome," adds Kevin because I don't think he caught the point Ceepak just made: the father may be going home, but the son who tried to set him up will probably be spending the night in jail.

"This shouldn't take long. Danny?"

We head out the door, hit the hall.

"You buy it?" I ask when we're out of earshot of everybody in the interview room.

"Yes. For some time now, I have sensed that Mr. O'Malley had nothing to do with either death."

"Because so much evidence said he did?"

"So much overwhelmingly obvious evidence, Danny. It's usually rather easy to spot a cheater. They try too hard to convince you that they're playing fair. The business card in the shopping bag was, for me, the last straw."

Yeah. That was definitely a lame move. If you're trying to frame somebody, you can't turn the framee into a complete imbecile.

"So, we're holding Kevin for further questioning?"

Ceepak's cell phone chirps. The personal line.

"Perhaps so," he says, ignoring the phone burping on his belt.

"I'll call Becca, check out the Mussel Beach story."

"That'll work," says Ceepak as I whip out my cell phone.

Then I give him the pursed lips and head bob that he gave me earlier when Samantha Starky called: It's okay for him to answer his personal phone on duty "just this one time."

So he does.

"Hello, dear. Yes. Good. And they're having fun?"

He steps away to get an update on T.J.'s big farewell bash.

I speed-dial Becca.

She definitely remembers Frances Ryan and Big Paddy O'Malley.

"They were boozing it up and screaming at each other until I finally went out there and threatened to call the cops. The fat one, the woman with that rat nest of carrot-colored hair, which, by the way, is a total dye job, she said, 'May heartache and vultures gouge out your eyes.' I think it's an Irish curse. They were drinking Old Busmill's and Jameson whisky—so at least their blood alcohol level was Irish."

She confirms the alibi.

I promise to bring back the towel I borrowed. Tomorrow.

When I hang up, Ceepak is finishing with Rita.

"Right. How's Ms. Minsky? Good to hear. Right. I'll be in touch. Same here, dear." He closes up the phone.

"Everything okay?"

He nods. "T.J. and friends are at the miniature golf course. Ms. Minsky is napping. Apparently, Gizmo is curled up on the bed beside her."

And as soon as he says that, his face freezes into a solid block of focused thought.

I've seen the look before: Ceepak just figured everything out.

33

CEEPAK MOVES LIKE A MAN POSSESSED TO THE NEAREST computer terminal.

I ask no questions. I never do when he switches into his totally focused mode.

He clacks keys. I read over his shoulder.

In the Google search box he is typing "animal euthanasia potassium chloride."

The first entry is for a PDF from the American Veterinary Medical Association.

He clicks to it.

"AVMA Guidelines on Euthanasia. June 2007." He scrolls down the table of contents, past inhalant agents to noninhalant pharmaceutical agents. There it is on page 12: "Potassium Chloride in Conjunction With Prior General Anesthesia."

He moves the pointer to the chapter heading. Clicks again. A new page pops up. Ceepak scrolls down until he sees the paragraph about potassium chloride: "Although unacceptable and con-demned when used in unanesthetized animals, the use of a super-saturated solution of potassium chloride injected intravenously or intracardially in an animal under general anesthesia is an acceptable method to produce cardiac arrest and death."

There's another paragraph listing the advantages: "(1) Potas-sium chloride is not a controlled substance. It is easily acquired, transported, and mixed in the field. (2) Potassium chloride, when used with appropriate methods to render an animal unconscious, results in a carcass that is potentially less toxic for scavengers and predators in cases where carcass disposal is impossible or impractical."

Guess that means you could use it on your pet elephant and not worry about poisoning all the buzzards circling overhead.

Ceepak swivels in the desk chair, grabs for a phone. I glance at the next paragraph: "Disadvantage—rippling of muscle tissue and clonic spasms may occur on or shortly after injection."

Ceepak presses 411. Puts the call on speakerphone.

The chirpy recording says, "Verizon four-one-one. What city?"

"Avondale, New Jersey," says Ceepak.

"Okay. Business or residence?"

"Business!" says Ceepak, kind of tersely. Seems the perky pre-recorded woman asks too many questions for a cop in a hurry.

"Thank you." The voice fakes hesitation, like she's really lis-tening to us. "Um, which business?"

"South Shore Animal Shelter."

"Hang on while I look that up."

When she tells us she found the number, Ceepak tells her, even though she isn't really a person (well, she was a person when she recorded this crap but she's not one now), that she can go ahead and place the call for an additional charge. Hey, we're in a hurry. Whatever Ceepak's just figured out has to be huge or he wouldn't waste fifty cents of the taxpayers' money.

The call rings through. Someone answers. A real person this time.

"South Shore Animal Shelter, how may I direct your call?"

"Dr. Cathy Langston, please."

"Who may I say is calling?"

"Officer John Ceepak. Sea Haven Police."

"Oh. Um. Okay. Just a moment."

Police get that kind of response all the time when we call folks.

While we're on hold, I'm tempted to say, "So, what's up?" But I don't. Ceepak's eyes are riveted on the speaker box like he expects a miniature Dr. Langston to pop out of it.

"This is Dr. Langston."

"John Ceepak."

"Well, good morning, John. How's Barkley?"

"Fine, thank you."

"Good to hear. Rita called. Said you folks just adopted a cat, too."

"Yes, ma'am. Gizmo. He used to belong to Mrs. Jacqueline O'Malley. With her passing, the family decided they were no longer able to keep the animal in their home. Allergy issues."

"Mrs. O'Malley was a wonderful woman," says Dr. Langston. "She was one of our top volunteers. Helped us socialize the feral kittens, get them ready for adoption."

"Did her son often accompany Mrs. O'Malley to the shelter?"

"Skippy? Yep, he sure did. I'm hoping he'll carry on his mother's good works. Maybe he can come out here every Monday, Wednesday, and Friday like she used to do. He did come out this week by himself. Said it's what his mom would've wanted."

Uh-oh. Not if he came out to grab some potassium chloride.

"Tell me, Dr. Langston, have several vials of potassium chloride gone missing from your pharmacy recently?"

"Wow. You're good, Officer Ceepak. We just discovered it last night. An equestrian client called about a horse to be put down at his stables. He, of course, didn't want to bring the sick animal in. We were going to go out there to euthanize the horse in its stall."

"How many ampoules were missing?"

"All of them. We had a half dozen doses. But, we don't use it that often. Just when we're called on to do livestock euthanizations in the field. Of course, we always anesthetize the animal first."

"Yes, ma'am. When was it stolen?"

"You think somebody stole it?"

"Yes, Dr. Langston."

"Well, like I said, we noticed that it was missing last night. But, we use it so infrequently it could have been removed any time in the last month or so. We did inventory at the end of April. All six ampoules were here then."

"Thank you," says Ceepak.

"Sure. Hey, pet Barkley for me. And rub Gizmo's butt. He likes that."

"Roger. Will do."

Ceepak is in total military automaton mode now. He would not typically say "roger" to an order to rub a cat's hiney.

He punches off the speakerphone.

"Skippy?" I say.

Ceepak nods.

"Did he kill his mom, too?"

"Doubtful. He most likely stole the potassium chloride when he went to South Shore this week. I suspect his sister gave him the idea to frame his father, make Mr. O'Malley look guilty for both murders."

"Crazy Mary told Skippy what to do?"

"In a roundabout way. His mother suffered a massive heart attack on the Rolling Thunder due to her underlying health issues. While the family was stranded on that roller coaster hill, Mary started chanting 'Daddy did it.'"

"And Skippy decided to make it look like he really did do it!"

"Exactly. He knew about the potassium chloride because, as Dr. Langston just confirmed, he often accompanied his mother on her visits to South Shore Animal Shelter. After what he considered a lucky lightning strike on Saturday, Skippy formulated a plan to frame his father."

"Why?"

"Because, as he told us, he and his father weren't very close. In fact, I sensed a great deal of animosity between the two men. As you might recall, Skippy felt that I would be sympathetic to his anger, given my own strained relationship with my father."

Yeah. Ceepak's dad's an a-hole, too. But, I don't think Johnny C would ever try to frame the dirty bastard for murder.

"Skip must've felt totally humiliated," I say, "when he learned that his dad was dating his ex-girlfriend."

Ceepak nods. "I am quite confident his obnoxious younger brother Sean, who is in the employ of Mr. Mazzilli and privy to everything that goes on at number One Tangerine, teased Skip mercilessly about his father having relations with Ms. Baker. Lightning struck a second time late Thursday when she texted Skippy."

"You mean when she texted Mr. O'Malley."

"Danny, I am quite confident that, last Thursday, Skippy was the one with the cell phone usually assigned to his father. Remember when we were there last Sunday?"

"The battery on Mr. O'Malley's cell died and he asked Skippy to toss him a fresh phone."

"Exactly. I should've realized sooner that Mr. O'Malley and his businesses would employ numerous cell phones. I should've also paid closer attention to the fact that Skippy was the one in charge of maintaining the phones, handing them out."

"Hey, I should've seen it, too," I say so Ceepak will quit shoulding all over himself, something he always advises against.

"We are where we are," Ceepak says with a sigh.

"But why would Skippy kill his old girlfriend? Jealousy? Revenge?"

Ceepak shakes his head. "Patricide."

"Huh?"

"It means killing your father. Skippy was hoping to trick us into doing what he himself could not: make the father he hates go away."

Okay, I've heard of suicide by cop, where a whacko deliberately does something so outrageously hostile it provokes a lethal response from law enforcement officers, gets them to kill him because he can't pull the trigger on himself. This is something new: patricide by cop. Getting the police to haul away your old man when you're too chicken to deal with him yourself.

"We need to talk to Mr. O'Malley," says Ceepak, who's up and out of his seat so fast, the chair goes rolling backward and knocks over a wastepaper basket.

Yeah. Big Paddy needs to know his third son has the worst Oedipus complex since, well, Oedipus, the Greek dude who killed his father and married his mother and became his own stepdad. Hey—it was on *Jeopardy* once.

34

WE BARGE BACK INTO THE INTERVIEW ROOM.

"Mr. O'Malley?" says Ceepak. "We need your permission to search your miniature golf establishment. Immediately."

"What?" fumes the lawyer just because he's a lawyer and we're cops who asked for something. "Why?"

"We have reason to suspect that your son may be involved in the murder of Gail Baker."

"Now wait a goddamn minute," sputters Kevin, the only son currently in the room.

"Sorry," says Ceepak. "I should have been more specific. Your son Skippy."

Mr. O'Malley actually laughs. "Skippy? A murderer? Impossible. The boy's too soft. It's why he washed out with you guys." He flaps a hand to take in the entirety of the Sea Haven Police Department.

Ceepak presses on: "Do we have your permission to search the King Putt premises?"

"You're wasting your time, but sure—go ahead."

"Be careful," says Kevin. "Skippy's there right now."

Mr. O'Malley laughs. "Careful? Dealing with Skippy? Kevin—the boy's a wuss. A washout."

"He has guns, dad."

"Since when?"

"Since they kicked him out of that police academy."

Because he cheated on an exam. Skippy. Always looking for a shortcut. For somebody else to do his dirty work. Probably why he stuffed that business card in the bag with the drug bottles. Thought we'd appreciate a big hint on the final exam, too.

"Are they legal?" Big Paddy asks Kevin, as if proper gun permits are Skippy's biggest problem right now.

"Yeah."

"Mr. O'Malley?" Ceepak says to Kevin. "Do you know the number and type of weapons your brother may possess?"

"I know he has a couple of shotguns. Something he called FN SLPs. And a semiautomatic pistol. A Beretta."

"What the hell is an FN SLP?" asks Mr. O'Malley.

"FN is a manufacturer and distributor of firearms including the Winchester and Browning brands," says Ceepak while unclipping the radio unit from his belt. "SLP means self-loading police."

"It's the shotgun SWAT teams use," I add, because I got to fire one the last time I was on the range.

"This is Ceepak for Detective Botzong," he says into his hand-held radio.

We wait for Botzong to respond.

"Give me the goddamn phone," Mr. O'Malley snarls at the lawyer. "I'm going to tear that boy a new asshole."

Ceepak holds up a hand. "No phone calls, sir."

The lawyer actually nods. Wow. He's on our side?

"You don't want to tip him off, Patrick," Rambowski mumbles. "Let these gentlemen take care of it."

"He tried to make it look like I killed that girl and my wife!"

"Let them handle it."

There's a burst of static out of the radio. "This is Botzong."

"John Ceepak."

"What's up?"

"We require further forensic assistance at a new location."

"Where?"

"Ocean Avenue at Oyster Street. Miniature golf course called King Putt. We're on our way there to apprehend a prime suspect in the murder of Ms. Gail Baker."

"Who?"

"Mr. O'Malley's son Skippy."

"When do you need us there?"

"As soon as we secure the location."

"Okay. We'll stand by."

"Quick question: would the signature of the rake used to cover up the footprints near the garbage cans where the two suitcases were discovered correspond to the tines on a sand trap rake?"

"Probably. We know it wasn't a leaf rake. Teeth were too far apart. I'll check with Carolyn Miller. She'll be on the go team to the golf course."

"That'll work. Hang tight. We hope to be back to you in five minutes."

"Ceepak?"

"Yes?"

"Be careful."

"Roger that." He clips the radio back to his belt. Sticks his head out the door. "Forbus? Bonanni?"

Officers Jen and Nikki, gun belts jangling, hustle into the room.

"Sir?" says Jen Forbus.

"Stay with these gentlemen. They are not to make any phone calls or leave this room until we confirm that we have our suspect in custody."

"We're gonna make the collar?" I ask.

"We'll call for all available units, but I'd like to be the first unit on the scene, Danny."

Right.

The golf course. King Putt.

The place where T.J. and his buddies went for that Farewell to Sea Haven party.

35

"LIGHTS AND SIRENS?" I ASK.

"Negative."

Yeah. I didn't think so.

We're peeling wheels out of the parking lot, spewing a flume of gravel back at all the guys' personal cars lined up behind us. Ceepak's at the wheel. I'm riding shotgun as we race off to apprehend Oedipus Skippy, who actually has a shotgun, a tactical shotgun, one with ghost-ring sights for easy acquisition of targets at short distances, not to mention the ability to dump a full magazine of seven rounds before the first empty shell casing hits the ground.

We don't want a man pumping that kind of shotgun to know we're coming because we blared our siren and swirled our roofbar.

We stopped by the locker room on our way out of the house. Pulled on our level III body armor before we jumped into the car—heavy vests that go on over our shirts and have POLICE written across the front and back with reflective yellow lettering, I guess to turn us into light-up targets.

"All units, all units. Code eight." On the radio, Dorian Rence, our dispatcher, is putting out the call for backup. "Ocean Avenue and Oyster Street. King Putt Golf. Suspect is considered armed and dangerous."

She could've added the word "extremely" in front of both armed *and* dangerous.

We fly the nine blocks up Ocean Avenue from police head-quarters.

I work my personal cell. Call Ceepak's house.

"Rita says the guys finished their game, went across the street to grab a burger at The Pig's Commitment."

Ceepak nods. His immediate family is safe. Now he just has to save the rest of the world.

He slides the vehicle into an empty parking place near the entrance to the pink pyramid. For the first time in his life, he's parking in a handicapped space.

We're both up and out of the car. Fast.

"Office," says Ceepak, going for his sidearm.

Mine's already up and aiming at the door. I use the two-hand cup-and-saucer grip—wrapping the nonfiring fingers around the back of my firing hand. I get more bull's-eyes that way.

Ceepak does a series of hand signals that, after working with the guy for a couple years, I finally understand. He'll kick open the door. I'll cover him.

He kicks.

The front door flies open.

"Down!" I shout.

Three kids, about eleven years old, picking out their putters, hit the deck. Three colorful golf balls bounce like bouncy kangaroos across the wooden floor.

"Clear!" shouts Ceepak.

Skippy is not behind the counter, but a row of blinking chargers and cell phones sure is.

I'm also figuring one of the hundred or so putters lined up in the wooden racks along the walls might be the "blunt force impact" weapon Skippy used to bash in Gail Baker's skull. He puts it back in the rack, we'd never find it. Be like trying to find one particular needle in a needle box. And, if we do, it's covered with a week's worth of teenaged boys' fingerprints.

A second patrol car screeches into the parking lot.

"Murray," says Ceepak.

He strides out the door.

I talk to the three kids lying on the floor. One's whimpering, one's breathing hard, and the third guy's horrified eyes are about to gumball out of his head.

"Everything's going to be okay," I tell them. "We're just looking for someone."

"Did he do something bad?"

Figuring *"Well, duh!"* would be an inappropriate answer, I go with, "Yeah. Just keep down."

Ceepak returns with Dylan and Jeremy Murray, the only brother act currently serving on the force in the Sea Haven. Guess Santucci, Murray's usual partner, is working his side job, running Italian Stallion security for Mr. Mazzilli at the grand opening of the roller coaster.

"Secure this area," Ceepak says to the Murrays, chopping the air with his hand as he spells out the master plan. "We'll direct any golfers still on the course down to this location."

"Got you," says Dylan.

"Watch those windows."

Jeremy Murray nods, takes up a defensive position at the plate glass window overlooking the course. As he crouches down, I scan the horizon. I can see the River Nile and Victoria Falls—a sculpted

mountain with foamy blue water bubbling up out of the peak—
but no Skippy.

Just a tumbling ribbon of blue, blue water.

"Ceepak?" I say.

He cocks an eyebrow.

"He did it here!" I say. "In the river."

Ceepak peers through the window. "Why is that water so
blue?"

"They probably dye it," says Dylan Murray. "To fight algae and
weeds. My uncle has a pond up in Pennsylvania. He dumps in this
stuff called Aquaclean. The blue blocks the sunlight."

"Thank you, Dylan."

"No problem."

"We'll call our supposition into the medical examiner," says
Ceepak, adding, "as soon as we get a chance."

"Roger that," I say. Holding a locked and loaded pistol always
makes me talk much more militaristically.

"We need to clear the course, Danny."

"You want to split up?"

"Swing right, I'll head left. Any golfers you encounter send
them down here to the Murrays."

The pink pyramid is about to become Fort Apache.

We dart through the back door, the one that takes you out to
the first hole.

"We'll want to search inside that utility shed," says Ceepak,
head gesturing toward the smaller pyramid tucked behind a clump
of fake palm trees. "Later."

"Right."

He heads to the eighteenth hole.

A family foursome is clomping down the hill to play the final
hole, where if you can run your ball up the ramp so it flies into the
crocodile's snout instead of his wide-open mouth, you win a free
game.

"Sir? Ma'am?" says Ceepak. "You and your children need to head into the office. Immediately."

They give him no guff. People seldom do when you're wearing what they'd call a bulletproof vest and have your semiautomatic weapon out and up.

The mom's good. She calmly ushers everybody down the winding concrete path before they have time to panic. While Ceepak clears the back nine, I make my way up to the front. It's a little after noon so King Putt isn't very crowded. In fact, it's almost deserted. Must be why T.J. and his pals opted for an early tee time: They'd have the course to themselves.

I cross a sand trap (more like a kidney-shaped sandbox, but it goes with the whole Sahara Desert theme) and come to the Python Pit. Hole number six. Three high school girls are giggling every time the cobra head pops up out of his basket.

"Girls?" I say.

They shriek. I came up behind them.

"You need to head back to the office. Now."

They squeal and scamper away.

"In here, girls!" Jeremy Murray screams from the office doorway. "Now! Move!"

Guy could be a lacrosse coach.

I swing around holes seven and eight, remembering when I came here as a kid how much fun I had. Hoping I don't see it all again when my life flashes in front of my eyes two seconds after Skippy pops out of the cave with one of his tactical shotguns. Or his Beretta. Or whatever else he's got.

A towering mountain sculpted out of plaster on chicken wire looms at the center of the course, linking holes nine and ten. Up top is the fake Victoria Falls, with tons of water the color of windshield washer fluid fountaining up through its crater top, then tumbling down over craggy outcroppings until it splashes into the mighty blue Nile snaking through the labyrinth of holes.

There is a tunnel cutting through the fake mountain. It's dark and dank.

It's where I'd hide if I were Skippy.

The civilians on my side are all safe. I see Ceepak gesturing at an elderly couple at the eleventh hole. Both seem to need new hearing aid batteries.

Meaning I need to take the cave alone.

I suck down a deep breath and grab the Maglite off my utility belt. I use what some guys call the Arnold Technique when juggling a flashlight and a Glock: Maglite coming out of the bottom of my left hand, fist held to my collar bone, gun pointed at the ground when searching, at the target as needed.

I'm pretty fast on the upswing.

I creep forward, shine the light into the darkness. I see nothing but slick walls. I step into the mouth of the mountain.

"Skippy?" I shout.

My voice rings off the sculpted rock.

No answer.

I swing the flashlight left, to where I know there's a recessed nook, a ledge where you can sit and make—out with your date in the dark.

Nothing.

I swing it right.

The blinding beam bounces back at me.

Reflected off the POLICE letters on Ceepak's chest.

This is why I like to keep my gun pointed at the ground in the flashlight searching situations. You shoot fewer partners.

Ceepak radios in a BOLO APB.

That's a "be on the lookout" all points bulletin. We assume Skippy hightailed it off the golf course two minutes after his dad called him up to ask who had the magic cell phone on Thursday night. He knows we're onto him.

"Request all available assistance, local and state, police, fire department, sanitation workers: anyone with eyes on the street. We need to locate Skip 'Skippy' O'Malley. Male Caucasian. Sandy hair. Freckled face. Approximately six feet tall, hundred and thirty pounds. Slight build. Stooped shoulders. No known distinguishing tattoos or scars."

Although sometimes he wears a chariot skirt.

I check out the parking lot on the other side of the fence penning in the golf course.

"He might be in the King Putt pickup truck," I say because it isn't parked where it was parked the last time we came by to stop Mr. Ceepak from harassing folks picking out their tiny pencils and score pads. "It's got the logo painted on the doors."

Ceepak nods. "Suspect could be driving a Dodge Ram pickup truck with King Putt Mini Golf signage painted on the doors."

Ceepak is, of course, one step ahead of me. I say pickup truck, he says Dodge Ram, because he remembers those tire treads Carolyn Miller found over on Tangerine Street.

"Please be advised, suspect is thought to be heavily armed and mentally unstable."

Wow. Dr. Ceepak. Much tougher than Dr. Phil.

We listen in as Mrs. Rence broadcasts the bulletin.

"Should we hit the road?" I ask when she's done.

"Not just yet," says Ceepak. "I want to investigate that tool shed."

We head over to the smaller pyramid in the stand of artificial Egyptian trees.

I reach for the handles.

"Danny?"

I look over. Ceepak has assumed a firing stance, weapon aimed at the split between the twin doors.

"Do you think?"

"It's a possibility. Jump clear as you open."

I nod. Damn. Would Skippy really hide in the shed?

"On three," says Ceepak. "One, two, three . . ."

I pull the door open, fly to the right.

But nobody discharges their weapon.

"Suitcase," says Ceepak who, in the time it took me to wince, already has his flashlight up and is working it around the storage hut's clumpy shadows. "Matches the color and style of those found at the crime scene."

Now his beam hits a sand pit rake.

Then a hacksaw hanging on a hook. The blade is too clean. It's brand-new.

"He did it here." He turns around. Surveys the bright blue river. "He crept up behind her, whacked her in the head with a blunt metal object—"

"A putter," I suggest.

"Yes. A putter. Similar impact pattern to that of a hammer. Good going, Danny."

I'd say thanks but we are talking about a creep bashing out a bathing beauty's brains here.

"Realizing she was dead, he most likely dismembered her body in the river, knowing that the water would wash away most of the evidence, that the blue dye would cover up the blood."

"Especially if he dumped more in when he was done."

"We should check the filtration system. We may find traces of Ms. Baker's blood and bone matter trapped inside."

"Wait a second," I say. "If Skippy killed Gail here, how come we found blood splattered all over the shower walls?"

"Because he wanted us to. I suspect, Danny, that Skippy took some of Ms. Baker's body parts out of the suitcases when he arrived at number One Tangerine. That he pressed the bar of soap up under her fingernails. It's why there was so much green residue trapped under her nails yet no soap on the rest of her body."

I hate to ask but I do: "And the shampoo?"

Ceepak grimaces and looks a little queasy. "Skippy took Ms. Baker's decapitated head into the shower stall, lathered the hair with shampoo and then, when he noticed that the recently severed neck was still dripping blood, spun around, and, holding the head out, splashed blood droplets on all four walls."

Like a little boy making a spiral-art painting at summer camp.

"It would explain the unusual spatter pattern," Ceepak continues. "He then went to the twenty-four-hour CVS and purchased the white shoe polish, knowing that it would further implicate his father. He took the empty bottles and the potassium chloride vials, three of which he emptied, into the house."

"How'd he get in?"

"Perhaps he had learned from his father or his younger brother where the spare key was kept."

Yeah. Guys that rich probably bought one of those plastic key-hiding rocks they sell in "People With Too Much Money" catalogs.

"Hey, Dad!"

It's T.J. and Dave Tranotti. They're coming into the golf course sucking on milkshakes from the restaurant across the street.

"You looking for your father?" T.J. asks.

"Come again?"

"The skeevey old guy with the wild greasy hair," says Tranotti, who must not have studied international diplomacy during his first year at the naval academy.

"He said he was my grandpa," says T.J. "Well, stepgrandpa."

"My father was here?"

"Yes, sir. Joe Ceepak. But the other cop already hauled him away. Told your father he was in direct violation of an active restraining order."

"Who was this other cop?"

"Freckle-faced dude," said Tranotti. "Had on a cop cap, black cargo pants, uniform shirt."

"Holster and pistol," adds T.J.

"He works the counter here on his days off," says Tranotti.

"You know him, Danny," says T.J. "Skippy O'Malley."

36

"WHAT DID MY FATHER WANT WITH YOU, T.J.?"

T.J. shrugs. I'm still not used to his buzz cut. I keep expecting to see his bouncing bundle of dreadlocks bobbing up and down.

"Said he wanted to 'get to know me.' Talk to me about my grandmother. I know you and mom want to keep him way from Grams."

"So T.J. told the old wino to take a flying fuck at a rolling doughnut," says Tranotti.

"Yeah," says T.J., looking down at his sneakers. "Sorry about that."

Ceepak nods. "An understandable reaction, son."

"Next time, I'll be nicer."

"Let's hope there isn't a next time. Did Skippy O'Malley put my father into the King Putt truck?"

"Yeah. He slapped him in cuffs and everything. Sort of shoved him into the vehicle, held down the top his head—did it just like the cops do on TV shows. When I told him to take it easy on the old fart, dude flashed me his badge. Said I shouldn't interfere with police business unless I wanted to take a ride, too. Oh, there was a rifle in the truck. I saw it on the floor. Wicked-looking shotgun."

"Do all auxiliary cops get to carry that much firepower?" asks Tranotti.

"Auxiliary cops?" says Ceepak.

"That's what O'Malley said he was when I asked him how come he worked at the golf course all the time if he was a police officer."

"T.J., David—young Mr. O'Malley is in no way affiliated with the Sea Haven Police Department. It is very important that we locate and apprehend him ASAP. Could you tell what direction he headed with my father?"

"Not the jail," says Tranotti. "He peeled wheels out of the parking lot and headed north on Ocean."

Cherry Street is south.

"The causeway is north," says Ceepak.

True. And it's the only road off the island.

My partner reaches for his radio. "Dorian, this is Officer Ceepak."

"Go ahead, Officer Ceepak."

"We need a roadblock. . . ."

"Ten–four. The Causeway. Chief Baines already ordered one."

"We have confirmation that Mr. O'Malley left the golf course in the King Putt pickup."

"A Dodge Ram," T.J. tosses in.

"A Dodge Ram," Ceepak says to the radio, even though he already knew that.

"Ten–four. You told me that already."

"Sorry. Dorian?"

"Yes, Officer Ceepak?"

"We've just been informed that O'Malley has taken a hostage."

"Copy that. Any ID on who he grabbed?"

"Yes. Joseph Ceepak. My father."

There is a beat of dead air.

"Ten–four." I can hear our new dispatcher straining to remain professional. She cracks. "Hang in there, hon, ya hear?"

"Yes, ma'am. Will do."

Down comes the radio mic.

"Danny? We need to be mobile. Fortunately, the vehicle is easy to spot. We should get a hit on it soon." Then he turns to T.J. "I need for you to go home, in case Skippy, for whatever reason, decides to come after you, your mom, or Marny."

"Yeah," says T.J.

"I'll hang with you, man," says Tranotti, who, I can tell, has put in some serious physical training during his first year at Annapolis. "We can play Battleship."

T.J. laughs.

"Sorry about this, son," says Ceepak. "Guess I ruined your big day even more than we had anticipated."

"Nah," says T.J. "I ruined it myself. Shot six over par on the back nine. Did even worse on the front of the course. Go on. Go rescue your old man."

"Will do. Tell your mother I love her."

"Hey, tell her yourself. Tonight. After you come home safe."

"Roger that."

Then they hug. Seriously. I don't think I ever hugged my dad. Not even when I graduated high school, which, by the way, many people considered a mathematical impossibility.

"Dylan? Jeremy?" Ceepak breaks out of the father-son embrace and marches into the office where the Murrays are guarding the golfers. I'm right behind him.

"Keep this location secure. Young Mr. O'Malley might roll back this way if we corner him and he has nowhere else to run." He turns to the kids and parents we hustled off the golf course earlier.

"King Putt is officially closed for the day due to ongoing police activity. Come back tomorrow and the management will gladly offer you a free game or a full refund."

Having seen all our weapons and heavy-duty body armor, they scurry out the door in a clump. Guess playing putt-putt tomorrow sounds like an excellent idea.

We're crawling north on Ocean Avenue in our patrol car.

I'm in the passenger seat, scoping out every pickup truck I can spot. They're all legit. Landscapers. Brick masons. Guys helping their buddies move a couch.

"Why'd he grab your father?" I ask.

"Perhaps he hopes we will negotiate with him if he has a hostage."

I laugh a little. "Leave it to Skippy to grab a hostage nobody wants."

"Danny, right now, my father is simply a citizen being held against his will in need of our assistance. It is our sworn duty to protect him."

"Right. Sorry."

Tomorrow, Joe Ceepak can be the sorry asshole we all wish would curl up and die. Today, we have to save his wrinkled old butt.

"All units, all units . . ."

Ceepak's behind the wheel so I twist up the radio dial.

". . . Joseph Thalken of the Sea Haven Sanitation Department reports seeing the King Putt pickup truck heading north on Beach Lane near Kipper Street."

Joey T. The man deserves a medal for all he's seen this week.

"The boardwalk," I mumble. "It starts at Kipper. He could be heading to Pier Four. If he takes that shotgun to the roller coaster he could seriously ruin his dad's big day."

"Is your friend still broadcasting from the Rolling Thunder, Danny?"

I snap on the dashboard radio while Ceepak hits the lights and sirens and jams the accelerator down to the floor.

"Hang on."

We slalom our way north through heavy traffic, occasionally borrowing a lane from the terrified cars trying to head south.

"*. . . and what's your name, young lady?*" Cliff Skeete chatters out of the car radio.

"*Layla.*"

"*Like the song?*"

"*Hey, that's the first time anybody ever said that.*"

"*Well, Layla, you ready to climb aboard a lightning bolt and roll like thunder?*"

"*Not really. I came here for the roller coaster.*"

I like this Layla. She's got sass. 'Tude.

Cliff moves on down the line. "*And you are, mi'lady?*"

"*Samantha Starky. My friends call me, Sam.*"

Jeez-o, man. Sam's still there.

"*How long you been waitin' on line, Sam?*"

"*Three whole hours, Skeeter! I listen to you all the time. You used to hang out with my old boyfriend, Danny Boyle.*"

So. The breakup is official. I heard it on the radio.

"*You know Danny, right?*"

"*Indeed I do.*"

"*Well he makes me listen to you and WAVY all the time!*"

Impossible as it seems, she sounds even perkier on the radio.

"*Well, you're almost to the front of the line,*" says Cliff. "*Hang in there.*"

"*Hey, we wouldn't miss this for the world!*" says some guy. "*We'll tell our grandkids about this someday!*"

"*And your name, sir?*"

"*Richard Heimsack.*"

Dead air while Cliff soaks in the name and I realize Richard and Sam are already contemplating grandbabies.

"Well, Richie—"

"Richard."

"It is one awesome ride, brutha."

Now the police radio crackles.

"This is unit six. We have suspect's vehicle in sight. Approaching parking lot to Pier Four on the boardwalk."

"The Roller Coaster," says Ceepak. "Hang on."

I grab the handle you're supposed to use to climb out of the vehicle, because when Ceepak stomps on the gas our Crown Vic Interceptor flies faster than the runaway mine train at Disney World.

I grab our radio mic.

"This is A-twelve. We are en route to Pier Four. Anticipate suspect will be headed toward the Rolling Thunder."

"Roger that" and "Ten-four" come in from all over the place.

Every cop in Sea Haven is on their way to the roller coaster to try and stop Skippy O'Malley from being free enough to ride that ride.

"This is Unit Six. Suspect is exiting vehicle with hostage . . . we will follow."

"Do not aggravate the situation." It's the chief. I guess everybody's in on this thing. "Wait for backup, Unit Six. Wait for backup. Tail the suspect but do not engage him. He is armed and dangerous. State Police are on the way. They're calling in a hostage negotiator."

"Give me the ears on the ground," says Ceepak.

He means I should turn up WAVY. Right now, Skeeter is our best source of potential intel on Skippy's movements.

"Comin' up, 'Love Rollercoaster' from the Ohio Players . . . but first . . . hey, have you tried Big Bruno Mazzilli's brand-new Stromboller-Cruster Italian Sandwich? Available exclusively at Big Bruno's Stromboli Stand right here on Pier Four. Thick layers of . . ."

"Yo! Douchebag!" somebody yells close enough to Cliff's microphone for us to hear it. *"There's a freaking line here."*

Dominic Santucci. I'd recognize that obnoxious voice any-where.

Ceepak presses even harder on the gas while yanking the steering wheel hard to the right. Tires squeal, and we tilt through a careering turn into the parking lot for Pier Four.

"...*provolone, salami, prosciutto and melted mozzarella* ..."

"*I said get back. You, too, old man.*"

"*Back off, Dom.*" Skippy. "*This is Ceepak's father. He's my fucking prisoner.*"

Jeez-o, man.

"...*rolled in a flaky crust and baked to golden perfection* ..."

"*Skippy?*" Santucci again. "*Jesus—why you wearing a fucking rain-coat, dipshit?*"

Oh, man. He's doing it Columbine style. Weapons hidden under the flaps of his long coat. Santucci needs to back off. Big time.

But he doesn't.

"*You can't come up here, you stupid wuss. These people have been waiting all morning to ride the ride.*"

"*My father owns this fucking piece of shit. I can do whatever the hell I feel like doing.*"

We hear Cliff's hand muffle the microphone with a thump. "*Hey, you guys?*" He's still audible. "*We're goin' out live.*"

The hand comes away from the mic.

"*Elyssa? Listen, girl—we need more security down here on the loading platform ... there's this dude in a trenchcoat. ...*"

Then there's this big explosion.

"*Ohmigod!*" Cliff yells. It sounds like he dropped his micro-phone.

"*Get down, motherfuckers!*" we hear Skippy yell. "*All of you. Down!*"

Our car speakers rattle with high-pitched wails. Shrieks. Squeals of terror.

"Get down, people," says Cliff, staying incredibly calm. *"Do like the man says. Be cool, man. We're cool."*

"Shut the fuck up!"

"Yes, sir. Oh, man . . . that dude's bleeding . . ."

"No, dipshit. He's dying."

"We need an ambulance."

"I said shut the fuck up!"

We hear nothing more from Sergeant Santucci.

Ceepak slams on the brakes.

We yank open our doors and hit the asphalt on the run.

This time, we're close enough to hear the shotgun blast in person.

37

ONE HOUR LATER, THE STATE POLICE SWAT GUYS DOT THE roller coaster scaffolding like black crows scoping out a cornfield with high-powered rifles.

Skippy O'Malley has about three dozen hostages inside the loading shed—the place where you climb into the coaster cars on one side, exit on the other. The shed has walls and an angled roof that completely covers the final waiting line switchbacks and the train tracks. It also shades the control room, about the size of a boxy camper, on the far side of the rails.

In other words, none of New Jersey's best snipers, even the guy at the peak of the highest hill, has a clean shot at wacko O'Malley. They might've put on their black Kevlar, camouflage clothes, and battle helmets for nothing. A couple of the guys even rappelled down ropes out of helicopters so they could be at the peak of that first hill and have a clean shot at everything below.

But all they can shoot at right now is a metal roof.

Fortunately, Skippy's last shotgun blast was fired as a warning shot and did its job: He dispersed the several thousand people waiting in a line snaking from the ramp up to the loading platform all the way back to the boardwalk and Pier Two, half a mile south. When Ceepak and I came charging up the access steps to the boardwalk, we were met with a thundering herd of panic.

On the radio, Cliff Skeete haltingly confirmed that *"a man working roller coaster security has been shot and killed."*

Skippy helped out by letting the folks at home know *"the asshole I took down is police sergeant Dominic Santucci. He's been riding my butt since day one on the job."*

He said it like he was still a cop. Who knows. Maybe in his mind, up there in Skippy Dippy Land, he still is.

After that newsflash, Elyssa the producer, or the program director, or maybe even Mayor Hugh Sinclair, decided it was time to take the live remote off the air. They played "Love Roller Coaster" because it was all cued up and then moved on to non-theme-park themed tunes.

Ceepak and I are in the improvised Situation Response Command Center where local and state authorities, tactical and support teams are trying to figure out what the hell we do next. We're borrowing the food stand where they deep-fry the Oreos and Snickers bars. Nobody's nibbling or noshing. We're all too pumped up. You get around this many special-tactics guys and you feel like you're in a marauding army of black-clad ninja warriors, only with better weaponry than curved swords and nunchucks. In fact, every weapon in the arsenal has been called up. Sniper rifles, submachine guns, flashboom and tear gas grenades, battering rams, ARVs (Armored Rescue Vehicles), not to mention our own stockpile of tactical shotguns like the one (or two) Skippy is toting.

"There's a camera on the loading platform," says Big Paddy O'Malley, whom Officers Forbus and Bonanni hauled down here from headquarters. We need his technical expertise and inside

knowledge about the Rolling Thunder. We don't need his bad attitude. "What the hell does my idiot son think he's doing?"

"Mr. O'Malley?" says Ceepak, trying to get the man to focus.
"How can we access that video?"

"Kevin?"

Kevin O'Malley plops a briefcase up on the counter of the food
stand. "We swung by the office. Grabbed the plans."

When he snaps open the briefcase, the first thing I see is a
wadded-up T-shirt stuffed into a plastic bag. It's stained with blood.

"Whoa," I say. "What's that?"

"Something you people probably need. A Sea Haven police
officer who moonlights as a security guard for Mr. Mazzilli
brought it by our offices earlier in the week."

Ceepak's turn: "What?"

"He claimed to have removed it from your initial crime
scene—the suitcases with Ms. Baker's dismembered body parts. He
expected us to pay him for it."

"We did," says Mr. O'Malley. "But not as much as he wanted."

Santucci. That slimy weasel. He did snatch Gail's Sugar Babies
T-shirt. We'd crawl up his butt about it, only he's already dead.

"Why are you just now turning this over to us?" asks Detective
Botzong. He sounds pissed.

"Because," says Big Paddy, "it—"

"Dad?" advised Kevin. "Don't. You're without legal representa-
tion."

True. We didn't ask Forbus and Bonanni to bring Louis Rambowski along for the ride. He didn't figure to be much help.

"I don't need a goddamn lawyer, Kevin! Why didn't we turn
this bloody T-shirt over to the police? Because it would have mis-
takenly linked the dead girl to me and further misled you gentlemen in your efforts to track down the real killer—my goddamn
son Skippy."

Detective Botzong is still furious. "Where is this goddamn

patrol cop you got that boosts evidence from a murder scene? What's his goddamn name?"

"Dominic Santucci," says Ceepak solemnly. "The off-duty police officer whom Mr. O'Malley's son just murdered."

That stops Botzong like a canon blast to the chest.

"Oh." He stammers a little. "My condolences on your loss."

Ceepak nods, turns to Kevin O'Malley.

"The video cameras?"

"Right." Kevin unrolls a schematic. "The feeds go directly to the control room."

"The small building directly across from where Skippy is currently holding his hostages," says Ceepak, just so he's clear.

"Yeah. That's right. So, obviously, we can't go over there. However, if I remember correctly—yes, there's a junction box right there." He points to the flashy neon sign over the entryway. "The lightning bolts on either side of the lettering are practically pointing to it. Behind the illuminated Entrance sign."

"On it," says the head of the T.E.A.M.S. crew. That's what New Jersey calls the unit of the Technical Response Bureau that's prepared to deal with what they call "extraordinary police emergencies" such as a psycho putt-putt ball washer holding three dozen innocent civilians hostage on a roller coaster loading dock. The T.E.A.M.S. unit is "a multifaceted entity" that maintains an "all-threats, all-hazards" methodology.

In other words, these guys know how to steal cable TV.

In about five minutes, three bruisers in battle gear have us hooked up to the feed from the wide-angle camera taking in Skippy and his hostages; we can see what the snipers can't.

First of all, Skippy is up and pacing back and forth, completely shielded by that arched steel ceiling.

He has most of his prisoners sitting on the concrete floor, huddled up against the rear wall. I see a lone blob I take to be Mr. Ceepak tied or chained to one of the railings where you line up in twos to take your seat in the next roller coaster car. I figure one of the blobs in the clump on the floor is Samantha Starky. She was too close to Cliff Skeete and the action not to have been swept up in this thing.

Skippy is waggling his Beretta 92FS, a semiautomatic pistol, in the air like he's making a speech. Who knows what he's ranting and raving about. Maybe his dad, and Ceepak's dad, and how Father's Day sucks.

I notice two rifles lying on the ground near the bumpy yellow tiles that tell you you're too close to the track. He brought both shotguns.

There's also an empty roller coaster train parked behind Skippy. It came down about the same time he blew Santucci away. Everybody escaped because Skippy was too busy corralling the people trapped in the final switchback barriers.

The second train got stuck about halfway around the track when the guy pushing the buttons decided it was better to leave the people stranded than to bring them down here where they might get shot. The fire department, with help from the SWAT helicopter, rescued everybody. The roller coaster operator also escaped from the control room right after he shut the thing down.

"Can we still access the deejay's feed?" asks the SWAT team leader.

"We're working on it," says the guy who rigged up the TVs. "Just now completing a patch into the W-A-V-Y studios. They've been keeping the disc jockey's microphone open for us and are, of course, recording everything."

"Jesus, what the hell is he saying?" demands Big Paddy.

"When you get the feed," says the SWAT leader, "put it on speakers."

"Here we go, sir." He flips a few switches on a portable console.

"*. . . what you people don't know is, my father, Big Fucking Paddy O'Malley, killed my mother. That's right. That heart attack she had? That* *wasn't just a heart attack, okay? No way. He did it to her. How? Oh, I don't know. Maybe he shot her up with potassium chloride, which, by the way, is what Kevorkian used in his suicide machine, okay? It's what they use when they do lethal injections and need to stop a prisoner's heart, okay?"*

This is creepy. We now have sound to go with the picture.

"Okay?" Skippy screams.

Thirty-six terrified heads start nodding.

"It's true. But you know what? My dad didn't even need to Kevorkian my mom. Nah. He just needed to keep sleeping around with every stinking slut in town. Girls half his age. Then, you know what? He'd come home. Rub my mom's face in it. 'You're an old, fat cow,' he'd tell her. 'That's why I'm banging a waitress from the Rusty Fucking Scupper on a regular basis.'"

"I said no such thing!"

"Easy, dad," says Kevin. "It's just Skippy."

"Dammit to hell, if your snipers don't kill the lying son of a bitch, I surely will!"

"Your son, sir," says Ceepak, "is teetering on the brink of insanity. These are the ravings of a madman."

"Just like his goddamn sister, Mary. It's from his mother's side, the Ryans. They're all loony."

Chief Baines steps forward. "Patrick? You need to calm down. Let the professionals handle this."

"He's my goddamn son!" he screams.

On the TV, Skippy freezes.

Mr. O'Malley shouts even louder. The man is a human bullhorn: "You're a goddamn disgrace, Skippy O'Malley!"

Ohmigod. We're only about one hundred feet away. Skippy can hear him.

He looks up.

Directly at the TV camera.

"Is that you, Daddy?"

"Get that man out of here," barks the SWAT commander, pointing to Mr. O'Malley. "The other one, too! Now!"

Big guys with tinted goggles grab hold of Kevin and Paddy O'Malley. Lift them up off the ground and forcibly haul them out of the food stand, knocking over a couple of fifty-pound sacks of powdered sugar on the way.

"Hey, Daddy? Big Paddy?"

Skippy doesn't know his father isn't watching him on TV anymore.

"This one's for you, you murdering piece of shit!"

He wades into the clump of hostages.

One guy takes a swing at him. Tries to trip him up.

He misses.

Skippy turns. Squeezes the trigger on his semiautomatic. Pop!

The young guy's head explodes.

"Does anyone have the shot?" the SWAT Commander shouts into his headpiece's microphone.

"Negative" crackles back from every sniper up on the coaster track.

Pop! Skippy puts a second bullet in what's left of the brave kid's brain.

"Let him know we're fucking watching!"

A fusillade of gunfire erupts up and down the wooden scaffolding. Steel pings on steel as the snipers nail the train tracks just outside the cover of the shed roof.

Skippy freezes. Pulls back his pistol.

"Cease fire," shouts the SWAT commander.

Skippy turns slowly to the camera. "That one was for my fucking father! But if any of you assholes shoot at me again, or toss in a flashboom, or teargas me, I'll kill as many of these motherfuckers as I can! Do you hear me, Ceepak? I'll fucking kill them all!"

And then Skippy opens up a pocket on his cargo pants and pulls something out.

He wiggles it over his head.

He brought a gas mask.

38

"WHAT THE HELL IS HE DOING NOW?" SAYS CHIEF BAINES.

On the video monitor, we see Skippy marching up and down in front of his hostages. He looks like a demented insect in his gas mask. His voice comes out nasal and whiny.

"You? What's your name?"

"Ken Erb."

"Get up."

The guy stands. It's Mr. Erb. The one who used to fly the bird kites on the beach. Neat guy. Artistic. Into adventures. Figures he'd want to be one of the first to ride the Rolling Thunder.

"You?"

A girl stands. Jeez-o, man. It's Sam.

"What's your fucking name?"

"Samantha Starky."

"Do I know you?"

"Maybe. We met once. I was with—"

"*Shut up. Sit down.*"

"*You . . .*"

"Ceepak?" says the chief. "What the hell is he doing?"

"I'm not certain, but it appears as if he is culling the hostages."

"What?"

"He is picking a handful of his prisoners."

"I can see that! But why? What for?"

Ceepak shakes his head. "Unclear, sir."

"How come he knows you're here, Officer Ceepak?" asks the SWAT commander, shifting his weight, jostling his gear. He's giving Ceepak the hairy eyeball.

"Skippy O'Malley, at one time, served with the Sea Haven Police Department."

"You're kidding me, right?"

"Part-timer," says Chief Baines. "One summer only. Auxiliary cop."

"He correctly assumes that I would be here," adds Ceepak, "given the severity of the situation."

Yeah—me and Ceepak. We're always there when the solid waste hits the rotary blades.

"John's here because he's my top guy in crisis situations," says the chief. "We're gonna make him a detective. Have him head up a new division. A detective bureau here in Sea Haven."

We are?

"We need one," said Baines, as if none of this would've happened if we all had different titles.

Wow. Ceepak's getting bumped up to detective. I'd say we should go out and celebrate, grab a beer, but we're kind of busy.

"*I want your name!*" Skippy screams at what looks like the sixth victim he's picked out of the crowd. "*I want them to know whose lives they're fucking with if they fuck with me again!*"

"*Layla.*"

Skippy points his pistol at the girl's head.

I swear: she does not flinch.

"You're fucking making that up!"

"No, I'm not. My parents liked the song."

It's the sassy girl from the radio.

"It could've been worse. They could've named me Ruby Tuesday or something."

Skippy grabs her by the arm, flings her over to the group he is quickly assembling on the loading platform, close to the roller coaster cars and the spot where Mr. Ceepak sits on the ground, hands behind his back, the handcuff chains looped around a pole.

"Fine! They can carve Layla on your fucking tombstone if those SWAT assholes shoot at me again! I want one more. You."

"No!" The guy on the ground is cowering. Holding up his hands to block the bullets.

"Get up, you fucking pussy! What's your name?"

The guy mumbles something.

"Louder! So John Ceepak and the snipers climbing the monkey bars and every fucking cop in the goddamn Garden State can hear your name!"

"Richard."

"Richard what?"

"Heimsack."

"Heimsack? That's your fucking last name?"

Sam's friend from Rutgers just nods.

"Okay, Richard Heimsack, unlock that old fart." He tosses him the handcuff keys. *"His name is Joseph Ceepak. That's right, everybody listening. It's Officer John Ceepak's father. But he's not the kind of dad who'd be proud to have a son like Officer Ceepak, the biggest fucking Eagle Boy Scout in the goddamn world. The jarhead that jumped in my face for calling my girlfriend on the phone when I was supposed to be directing traffic around a goddamn sewer pipe. He was right. He was right. My bad. But his father? This worthless sack of sleazy shit? He's no father. He's a fucking bully and a blowhard. Get him on his feet."*

Two of the hostage guys help Mr. Ceepak stand. He teeters on wobbly legs.

"Yes, Mr. Joseph Ceepak, just like Big Paddy O'Malley, is a disgusting excuse for a father. He's so awful, his son had to take out a restraining order against him! But that's okay. That's okay. We can make the bastard pay even if the State of Ohio couldn't. Oh, yeah. I read up on you, Joseph Ceepak. I know what you've done. I know you ruined both your sons' lives. See, folks, the Bible got it wrong!"

Man—shy, skinny Skippy sure loves having an audience. He's ranting and raving like one of those sweaty Sunday morning television preachers.

"The sins of the father should be visited on the fucking father, not his unfortunate son."

Skippy sidles over to his rifles. Picks up a shotgun with his free hand. Aims it at the main group of hostages. Holsters the Beretta. Picks up the other shotgun. Aims it at the group closer to the train.

"You people with Mr. Ceepak, you and he are coming with me. Walk across the roller coaster cars. Go into that fucking trailer on the other side of the tracks. Move it."

When they don't as move quickly as he thinks they should, Skippy fires another shotgun round over their heads. The blast punches a hole through the ceiling. Buckshot rains down. The seven hostages and Mr. Ceepak hurry across the seats of the stationary roller coaster, climb out on the other side, and head for the control room. Except one guy who thinks about running down the exit ramp.

Skippy fires a warning shot two inches in front of his feet.

The guy throws up his arms and shuffles over to the control room.

"Move it, people," Skippy shouts. They all scramble and bob through the door of the trailer, and I'm reminded of all those horrible images of Nazi soldiers herding Jews onto boxcars bound for Auschwitz.

"We got to do something," I say to Ceepak. "Where the hell is the hostage negotiator?"

"Five minutes out," says the SWAT Commander.

"You!" Skippy turns to Cliff Skeete, who's sitting just in front of the bigger bunch of hostages on the loading dock. He's still wearing his headphones, still at his dinky little card table with the vinyl WAVY banner flapping off the front. *"Skeeter. Your microphone still open?"*

Cliff tosses up both hands. *"I don't know, man."*

"Yeah. Sure. Get up out of that chair, you lying black bastard. You're coming with me. Bring your gear. We'll use it to broadcast my demands."

"We ain't broadcasting no more."

Skippy raises the barrel of his shotgun. There's no need to pump another load into the chamber; the tactical weapon autoloads it for him.

"Be cool, man. Be cool."

Skeeter picks up his cordless microphone and his backpack full of gear.

"Move it!"

Cliff walks through the parked train. Skippy cuts across the roller coaster, using the seat behind the one Cliff is crossing so he can move sideways and keep one eye on Cliff, the other on his clump of twenty-some prisoners still sitting on the wooden loading deck.

They reach the platform on the other side of the tracks. Skippy slings one rifle over his shoulder, prods Cliff with the muzzle of the other.

"Give me that fucking microphone."

Cliff hands Skippy the microphone.

"Where's the goddamn wire?"

"It's cordless, man. Beams your voice back to the wireless transmitter in my bag, which sends it to W-A-V-Y."

"Good. Get into the trailer with the rest of them. Stay away from the windows, my man. Snipers are always looking for assholes stupid enough to stand in front of a window. Think they can disarm me with a well-placed

shot. I learned about that one at the police academy. Some jerk in the Midwest actually did it. Better shot than Danny Fucking Boyle."

Great. He's dragging me into his tirade, too.

Cliff goes into the control room.

Skippy squints up at the arched ceiling.

"I'm so glad my daddy put in the roof! Aren't you guys? You poor SWAT bastards. Up there freezing your nuts off on top of a rickety goddamn roller coaster and you can't shoot me because my daddy didn't want people to demand refunds if it started raining after they bought their tickets. He built them a shed so he could steal their money, rain or shine!"

He faces the crowd on the far side of the tracks.

Raises his shotgun.

They scream and squirm backward.

Skippy laughs. Lowers his weapon.

"And my father thought I was a wuss! You people are all fucking pansies! Each and every one of you! But guess what? This is your sunny funderful day! As soon as I am safely inside that door, you are all free to go. Now, I'm sure the police will want to ask you a lot of questions. Please tell them that justice will soon be served. And, when it's time to go, kindly exit the way you entered. No pushing or shoving or I might have to shoot you. Also, try not to trample Mr. Santucci or that brave little asshole whose head I blew open like a watermelon on your way out the door, okay? And, finally, and this is the most important part. On behalf of my entire family, Daddy and Kevin and Peter and Mary and Sean O'Malley, I hope each and every one of you will tell your friends about Sea Haven's exciting new thrill ride: Big Paddy O'Malley's heart-stopping new wonder—the Rolling Fucking Thunder!"

39

As soon as Skippy closes the door to the control room, his hostages stampede off the platform.

They're pushing and shoving at the bottleneck where they have to squeeze through an opening to run down the ramp that takes them back to the room full of stanchions and barriers like they have at airport security so you can wait in line for an hour and keep doubling back on yourself.

The mob treats the stockades like hurdles to be knocked over in an Olympics trial gone wrong.

Ceepak and I are running toward the entryway. So is the rest of the SHPD and several of the state police.

We'll try to make the evacuation as orderly as possible.

"Sam!" I shout when I see her.

"Danny! He has Richard!"

"I know. Don't worry. We'll get him out of there."

"How?"

"We're working on it." I grab her by the arm. "Come on. Run. I've got you covered."

We dash from the roller coaster entrance to the side of the fried-food stand.

"Okay. You're clear." I gesture toward the staircase leading down to the parking lot. "Is your car down there?"

"Yeah."

"Good. Go. Call your mother. Let her know you're okay." I practically shove her toward the steps.

"What about you, Danny?"

"I gotta go back to work."

"Be careful, okay?"

"Yeah."

"Danny?"

"Huh?"

"Thanks."

I think she wants to kiss me. Part of me wishes I could kiss her, too. I'm so happy Skippy didn't randomly decide to blow a hole through her head. Hey, I've seen what those tactical shotguns can do. On the range, they let me fire one at an old TV set. Shattered the whole thing. Blew out the front and turned the metal at the back into a spaghetti strainer.

"I'll call you later," I say.

"Promise?"

"Promise."

She runs down the staircase to the parking lot. I race back to the Rolling Thunder, reflexively keeping my head down like I expect Skippy to be the one up on the crossbeams sniping at me.

"We're clear," says Ceepak when I meet him in the entryway. "They're all out."

"Except the ones he took with him."

"Roger that. We'll get them next."

———

A quiet ten minutes passes.

Maybe the longest ten minutes in my life. I'm thinking about how quickly Skippy could kill all his hostages. Boom, boom, boom. The shotgun reloads itself.

"Ceepak? Boyle?" The chief signals for us to join him.

"New development?" asks Ceepak.

"Negotiator's here. He's made contact with O'Malley via the radio gear."

"Any demands?"

"Yeah. He wants to talk to Danny."

"Okay. Where's the microphone or whatever?"

The chief shakes his head. "He wants to talk to you inside. In person." He gestures toward the Rolling Thunder. "In the control room."

Now he leads us around a bank of cold deep-fat fryers to the communications center the tech guys hastily set up in the rear of the food stand. I see a very serious man in a short-sleeve New Jersey State Police shirt holding a yellow legal pad, a set of head-phones strapped across his flat top haircut.

"Do you need food, Skippy?"

"Nah." Skippy's answers are coming out of a pair of portable speakers. "I had a big lunch. Of course, I wouldn't mind trying one of those, what'd you call 'em, Cliff? The Stromboller Crusters?"

"We can try to get you one."

"Nah. Forget it."

"How about water?"

"Nope. Water makes me pee."

"How about your guests?"

"It'll make them pee, too, and I'm not about to start handing out hall passes."

"How many people are in the control room with you, Skippy?"

"Eight. Nine if you count Old Man Ceepak, which I don't because I'm not convinced he's actually human."

269

I'm trying to listen actively like Ceepak told me to do when I asked him how we were going to get Skippy and everybody else out of this thing alive. He gave me a crash course in hostage negotiations. Never lie. Ask open-ended questions. Remind Skippy who he used to be. Junk like that.

So when I listen actively, what I hear is a guy who has never had the chance to blow off steam and is now spouting off like a geyser.

"Send in Danny," Skippy demands. *"He's the only one I'll talk to."*

"We're attempting to locate Officer Boyle right now."

I tap my chest.

The tall man nods.

"Is Ceepak there?"

Ceepak raises a hand.

The tall man sees it.

"Yes. Officer Ceepak is here with me in the command post."

"Oooh. You've got a command post. I must be important."

"You are, Skippy."

"Well, if Ceepak is there, then Danny Boyle's there, too. The two of them might be queer for each other, you know what I mean? They're always so far up each other's butts they could be a pair of hemorrhoids."

I'm tempted to shake my head, say, "No we're not."

Then I remember: Skippy is a lunatic. I need to just listen, not react.

"Okay," says the negotiator. "I see Boyle. Sorry. I'm from up in Rahway. Didn't recognize him. Where are you from, Skippy?"

"What is this, Negotiating for Dummies 101? Are you trying to establish rapport with me or something?"

"I'm just here to help us all get what we want."

"Yeah? Well, what the hell do you want, Officer Tom Parkhill from Rahway, New Jersey?"

"For you, your guests, and us to all get out of this thing the best way possible."

"Oh, really, how would that work, Tom?"

"What do you think would be the best ending, Skippy?"

"For you to shut the fuck up and send in Danny."

"Why do you want Officer Boyle to come join you and the others?"

"Because he's my only fucking friend in the whole world, okay? Sorry about that homo crack, Danny. I know you and Ceepak aren't queers. He's married, right? Ceepak?"

I nod. I'm not sure why.

"Hey, Skippy?"

"Yeah, Tom?"

"Here's what I'm gonna do. I'm gonna take a minute to talk to Mr. Boyle. You think about what you're willing to give me if he comes in."

"What?"

"We need to make an exchange."

"Bullshit. I don't need to do anything."

"If I send in Officer Boyle."

"Then I promise I won't blow the brains out of this fucking douchebag Richard Balls Sack or whatever his fucked-up name is. That's my deal. You send Danny in, I don't send another dead body out the door."

"Give me a minute."

"Sure. And get me that fucking sandwich. That fucking Stromboller Coaster."

"Okay, Skippy. I'm sending somebody over to grab you one. I'll be back in two minutes."

"Who the fuck cares?"

Officer Parkhill presses what I suspect is a mute button on the wire dangling off his mouthpiece.

"Boyle?"

"Yeah."

"Your friend is irrational. Lot of pent-up rage."

Ceepak's nodding. He agrees with the diagnosis.

"Sir?" I say.

"Yes?"

"He's not really my friend."

I just had to get it on the record.

Parkhill, who is even more stoic than Ceepak, cracks a thin smile. "Pretend he is for today, okay?"

"Yes, sir."

"He's already killed two people. We need to make him feel like a human again, a man with connections to reality, or I guarantee he'll kill every one of those hostages."

"We went to school together. We were part-time cops the same summer."

"Good. Use that. Let him know somebody remembers the guy he used to be."

"Okay."

Parkhill picks up what looks like a very cold cup of coffee. Gulps some down. "Here's our situation: We know nothing about his setup inside that control room. There's no security camera in there. If you go in, we don't know what we're sending you into."

"He has three weapons," says Ceepak. "Two rifles, one sidearm."

"He probably has extra ammo," I say. "The pockets of his cargo pants looked pretty stuffed."

"And," says Ceepak, "he is already wearing a gas mask."

"Ruling out tear gas," says Parkhill.

The SWAT Commander steps forward. I still don't know his name but with all his black armor and black helmet and bulging black weaponry he reminds me of Robocop. "However, he has put himself in a very tight box. Literally. The control room is tiny. Maybe two hundred square feet. If Officer Boyle goes in, distracts him for a few minutes, my men can initiate a vertical assault and rappel down to that building from the girders up above, toss flashbooms through the windows, here and here."

He points to the side windows of the rectangular trailer on the blueprint of the control room.

"He'll see you coming," says Ceepak.

"How? My men move quieter than cats on goose down pillows."

"Video monitors. Kevin O'Malley told us earlier that all the camera lines feed into that control room. We can't see him because there are no cameras inside the coaster operations center, but he's receiving real-time information from cameras covering every inch of the track. You launch a vertical assault, the civilians all die before your men reach the end of their lines."

Robocop nods. Guess he hadn't thought about that.

"There is one point of entry he may not have covered on his video monitors," says Ceepak, tapping the train track between the loading platform and the exit platform in front of the control room building. "I could crawl in under here."

He points to what looks to be an access panel to the crawl space under the elevated area on the schematics.

"And come out the other end underneath the train tracks."

"Can you fit through the railroad ties?" asks Parkhill.

"Roger that. Danny and I had the opportunity to walk the track last weekend."

Right. When Mrs. O'Malley had her heart attack.

"The space between ties appeared to be a little less than their width. I'd estimate there is fourteen to sixteen inches of clearance between ties. I have a thirty-inch waist. I should be able to squeeze through, once I remove my Kevlar vest. I'll carry the flashbooms and my weaponry in a gear bag that I can haul through the tracks after I'm clear."

"He'll see you," I say. "The cameras have to cover the loading platform."

"Correct. But, as you see, the camera is positioned up here in the rafters. The stranded train is here." He taps the track on the blueprint. "If I come up here." Now he taps to the front of where the stranded train's front car would be. "And stay low, the camera won't see me. I can toss in the flashboom; the blast of light and noise will disorient Skippy long enough for me to make my entrance."

"But you won't know where he is," I say.

"No. But you will, Danny."

True. I'll also have a splitting headache and be blind.

"You can spot me, call out his coordinates. You may also have a chance to grab one of his weapons yourself."

I nod. "Yeah. It might could work."

"It's a good plan," says Robocop. "A little on the Lone Ranger side of things for my taste, but it looks like our best option. I'll get my best man."

"Sir? I already volunteered."

"Commendable, Officer Ceepak. But my guys train for this sort of thing every day."

"So does Ceepak," I say. "Besides, he's my partner. We know how to communicate with each other. I don't want some total stranger shooting at me when I shout out where the hell Skippy's hiding."

"Son," Robocop starts in but I raise my hand to let him know he can spare his breath.

"Look, guys—I'm only going to do this if Ceepak is the one covering my back."

40

CEEPAK STRIPS DOWN TO HIS T-SHIRT AND CARGO PANTS—
he needs to be less bulky to squeeze through the ties on the roller
coaster track.

Robocop packs a gym bag for him. In goes Ceepak's Glock,
with an extra mag.

"We're putting in two XM84 Stun Grenades," says the SWAT
team leader. "You know their capabilities, correct?"

"Roger that. They should effectively neutralize and disorient
enemy personnel. We tossed a few into insurgent strongholds when
I was over in Iraq. Proved quite effective. I'll, of course, need protective eye gear."

"Yeah," says Robocop, stuffing a pair of goggles into the bag
with the bombs. I think the guy finally gets it that Ceepak understands what they call "tactical intervention strategies," even if he
doesn't wear a helmet to work every day anymore.

"You ready, son?" Officer Parkhill asks me.

"Yeah. I'm good to go."

I'm actually scared shitless, but Parkhill and the gang of manly men in combat gear don't need to hear that right now.

"Okay. I'm gonna contact Skippy. Let him know you're coming over."

My mouth is so dry it feels like I licked the salty bottom of a pretzel bag.

I just nod.

Parkhill slips the headphones back on and flips the switch on his microphone.

I catch Ceepak's eye. He gives a slow nod, the kind that says, "It's all good," even when we both know it isn't. Time to embrace the suck, as his soldier friends say.

"Skippy? This is Tom Parkhill. Skippy? You got your ears on? Skippy? This is Officer Parkhill. We're ready to talk."

Great. No answer. Maybe Skippy went home and this was all a horribly bad dream.

"Hello, Tom."

"Hello, Skippy."

"Skip. I prefer Skip. Skippy sounds like a baby name."

"Okay, Skip. Danny's good to go out here."

"Hiya, Danny!"

I wave. Don't ask me why, but I do. A little fuck-you finger wiggle coupled with a sideways eye roll. It cracks some of the tough guys up. Ceepak, too. They don't laugh out loud or anything. But tension is momentarily eased.

"He can't bring a gun," Skip shouts into his microphone.

"He won't."

"And no bullet proof vests or anything either."

"Now, Skip, Danny's a professional. You remember what's it like on the job. He's got to wear the uniform or he'll catch flak from his bosses."

"No! He could sneak in a Glock or a dagger or something under the body armor. No pants either."

276

Parkhill, probably the most patient, unflappable man on the planet, looks flapped.

"Come again?" he says.

"No pants. No shirt. No weapons and no wire. I want him in swimming trunks and flip-flops! Like when we were kids on Oak Beach. Remember that, Danny? Oak Beach? We were the shits back then."

I hold up my hands, looking for a little guidance.

"It's going to take a few more minutes to find Mr. Boyle a swimsuit."

"Steal one from that shop across from the Fried Oreo Shack. There's nobody minding the store, right? You can take whatever the hell you want. Grab a couple bikinis for your girlfriends."

Parkhill glances at me. I shrug.

What the hell. I'll do it.

"Okay, Skip. Give Danny a second to change."

"Sure. No problem. Take your time, guys. I'm sorry to put you through the wringer like this, Danny, but shit, man, you know?"

Parkhill shoots Ceepak a knowing look. I heard it, too. Skippy sounds semihuman again.

"It's okay, Skip," says Parkhill. "We're getting the beach gear for Danny right now. Thanks for the tip on the shop. We sent someone over there. . . ."

"Stay away from the T-shirts, man. They'll rip you off on the tees. Of course, I guess you guys don't have to pay."

"Not today, anyway," says Parkhill, sounding like the jolly uncle he probably actually is when he isn't on the job dealing with wingnuts like Skipper Doodle. "Okay. We've got the gear. Give us a couple of minutes."

I turn around and a guy in more padding than a middle linebacker for the New York Jets is standing in front of me holding a stack of Hawaiian print swim trunks.

"I figured you were a medium, sir," she says.

Okay. The guy is a girl. In their SWAT getups, it's hard to tell.

"Yeah. Medium. Thanks."

About six guys in black body armor form a circle around me. They face out so I can change in private. While I slip out of my shoes, lose my Tyvek vest, my shirt, my pants, my socks, and my underwear, I hear Parkhill bargaining with Skippy.

"Skip, Danny's getting changed."

"Cool."

"He's going to a lot of trouble to give you what you want."

"I know. Tell him thanks. I'm just a little freaked out in here, okay?"

"Sure. Understandable. Hey, why don't you give Danny something?"

"Like what."

"Let a couple of hostages go when he gets there. Seems like a fair trade."

"Fine. I'll let one of the girls go."

"Great. You want that sandwich, Skip?"

"Nah. I'm not really hungry. Besides, you guys would drug it. Put crushed sleeping pills between the fucking meat and cheese. And no fucking water, either!"

And crazy Skippy is back.

"You must think I'm a fucking moron, Asshill. I know all the fucking tricks. I went to the police academy, remember?"

I tug on a baggy pair of swim trunks: Tommy Bahamas that hit me mid-thigh. White tropical flowers and green ferns on washed-out black fabric. It could be worse. The SWAT team lady could've brought me a Speedo.

"I'm good to go," I say.

My dressing circle parts.

"Okay, Skip. Danny's dressed. He's coming over."

"Put Ceepak on the line."

"I'm not sure if Officer Ceepak is here right now."

"Put him on the goddamn line or I'll send one of the fucking girls out the door dead."

"Hang on."

Ceepak steps forward. Parkhill unclips his tiny microphone, hands it to him.

"This is Ceepak."

"That motherfucker tried to lie to me. Said you weren't there."

"How can I help you, Skip?"

"You have to promise me something."

"What?"

"That you will not follow Danny! That you won't sneak up behind him so you can bust in here and ream me out again like you did that time in the middle of goddamn Ocean Avenue where everybody and their brother could see what a dipshit you thought I was."

"I will not follow Danny."

"You still live by that stupid code? The one Santucci used to rag you about?"

"Affirmative."

"So you can't lie to me, right?"

"Correct."

"So when you say you won't follow, Danny. . . ."

"You have my word. I will not follow Danny."

"Okay. Good. You're a good cop, Mr. Ceepak. I could've become a good cop, too. Right?"

"Yes, Skip. You could have."

"Could" being the operative word in that sentence. Hell, any-body *can*. Skippy, however, didn't.

Parkhill gives us a "let's move on" hand signal.

"Danny is on his way," says Ceepak. "Here is Officer Parkhill." He hands the microphone back to the negotiator.

"Okay, Skip. Danny's coming over."

I make my way out of the food booth, hit the boardwalk, pause, and take in a deep breath. I've got twenty yards of open planking to cross before I enter the Rolling Thunder. I've also got goose-bumps—and not because it's 65 degrees and I'm half naked.

What if Skippy's still jealous about me getting the cop job he always wanted? What if this swim trunks deal is just his twisted way of making me an easy, unarmed target?

I'm about to start walking again when somebody taps me on the shoulder.

Ceepak.

"Which way are you going?" he asks.

I point at the entryway to the Rolling Thunder roller coaster. The jagged thunderbolt neons are dead ahead.

"Good. I'll go out the back way, crawl underneath the board-walk, find that access panel. I just wanted to make sure you and I weren't taking the same route."

In other words, he's keeping his word.

He's not following me.

He's just covering my ass.

41

I HAVE TO STEP OVER DOMINIC SANTUCCI'S BODY.

I also have to not puke.

Skippy blew open the poor guy's guts. I'm reminded of how Santucci was there the day I saw my first dead body ever, on the Tilt A Whirl in Sunnyside Playland. Now, I'm looking down at his. There's a swarm of flies flitting over his black and bloody intestines.

I have to keep moving.

I climb up the short ramp to the covered waiting shed and I see Skippy's second victim. This time I want to cry. The guy was just a kid in a black heavy metal T-shirt who watched too many movies and, to mangle some Springsteen lyrics, tried to walk like the heroes he thought he had to be.

Guess you could say the same about me.

I keep walking. Toward the stranded roller coaster.

Toward the control room.

The door creaks open. There's nothing but blackness on the other side.

"Danny?" It's Skippy.

"Yeah."

"You look ridiculous, man."

"Thanks."

"I'm just yanking your chain, pal. Try wearing a skirt to work everyday."

Right. Mr. O'Malley never missed an opportunity to humiliate his son on a daily basis.

"I'm like Ceepak," says Skippy. "I never lie. So, as promised, I'm sending out one of the girls."

"Cool. Thanks."

"Go," he yells. "Now!

Richard Heimsack stumbles out of the dark doorway. I think Skippy shoved him. He shields his eyes with a hand. Guess Skippy doused the lights inside the control hut so the snipers couldn't see him, even though they probably could with night vision scopes. Anyway, the darkness in the metal box means the flashbooms will be more effective than the sunshine blinding Richard Heimsack right now.

"Keep moving," I say to the college kid through clenched teeth.

"I . . ."

"Keep moving, man. Don't look back. Take good care of Sam, okay?"

"Yeah. Okay. Thanks."

He rushes past me.

"Look at him run. Biggest pussy in the bunch. Heimsack. What a name. I called him Ballsack even though he doesn't have any. Come on, Danny. Come on in."

He gives me a big smile and a happy hand gesture like we're both ten again and he's inviting me to climb into the giant sand castle he just built on the beach.

I make my way across the parked roller coaster. I chance a

glance under the tracks. I don't see Ceepak. Then again, he had a much longer distance to travel, most of it on his belly.

I go through the open door in the middle of the twenty-foot-long, ten-foot-deep aluminum-sided rectangle.

Ceepak's gonna need good aim to toss a grenade from the front end of the first roller coaster car into this three-foot-wide door.

"Close it."

I shut the door behind me. Jeez-o man. We didn't think about that. The grenade's just going to bounce off the door.

But then I notice two tinted windows over the control console. They look out at the loading dock. Okay. We're still good to go. Ceepak's just going to have to have to use his hook shot and smash out some glass.

"Grab a seat, Danny."

My eyes haven't adjusted to the darkness, but from the sound of his voice, I think Skippy just hunkered down in a corner.

"Where are you, Skip?" I say as I knee into a rolling chair.

"Over here." He flicks on a small flashlight.

Yep. He's crouched in the corner at the south end of the room. Mr. Ceepak is right beside him. I have never seen so much fear and hate colliding in one man's eyes before. Of course, Skippy has his Beretta 92FS pointed at the side of the old man's skull, which might have something to do with his sour mood.

There's a girl huddled against the wall, maybe two feet down from Skippy and Mr. Ceepak. I can see better now. In fact, I can tell that Skippy has his seven remaining "guests" lined up along the wall, their knees tight to their chests. I see Cliff Skeete in his bright red doo rag. Ken Erb. People I don't know. Mostly young. They all look scared to death.

Except that one girl. The one closest to Skippy.

She's short, maybe five-one, 100 pounds. Cute librarian glasses.

And now I see the shotguns. Skippy just laid them down. On the floor. Right in front of his feet, their barrels pointing in my direction. He could pick one back up and blow my brains out whenever he feels like it.

"Sorry about the swimsuit," says Skippy.

"You like it? I think it's last year's model."

"I think it's cute," says the girl.

Skippy snaps around to face her. "Shut up!"

She flips up her hands to say, "Whatever."

"Meet Layla," says Skippy. "She mouths off from time to time like that. Makes her number two on my hit list."

"Am I number one?" I ask. I'm seated in a backless swivel chair. I guess it's what the guy who runs the ride uses to slide around and punch buttons. The console is behind me, its padded leather bumper nudging me in the back. When I was feeling around for the chair in the dark, I noticed that the video monitors displaying security camera feeds are mounted on the walls. Skippy can see everything from his vantage point in the corner. His eyes flick from screen to screen. So far, the snipers haven't budged. They're still birds on a wire, perched on the coaster's crossbeams.

I roll sideways. Closer to the corner.

Skippy's maybe four feet away. The guns maybe two.

"Am I number one?" I ask again.

"Nah, Danny. You're my witness."

"For what?" I think I'm asking open-ended questions like Ceepak told me to. I'm not exactly sure what the term means. I wish I'd had more time to study this stuff. I might be doing it wrong.

"The government's witness to the execution of Mr. Joseph Ceepak."

"Whoa," I say, like Skippy and I are playing beer pong. "Hang on, buddy . . . time out."

Mr. Ceepak tilts his head sideways. Skippy is burrowing the muzzle of his Beretta deeper into the soft spot at his temple.

"Your partner? This piece of shit's son? He never really thought

I'd make a good cop. But I would. I am. I can bring the justice, which is what a good cop does, Danny. He brings the goddamn justice. And in a just world, this old drunk definitely deserves to die. I know what he did, all those years ago. He should've gotten the needle. Lethal injection. I wish I still had some of that potassium chloride but I left it all on Tangerine Street."

"Yeah. That was clever, Skippy."

"Thanks. But, you want to know the truth?"

"Sure."

"I got lucky. I was just gonna plant the drugs on Dad, but I couldn't figure out how to get you guys into the house. Then, boom! My father's whore texts his phone while it's sitting in my pocket. Talk about meant to be. God wanted me to kill her, too. After that, everything just fell in place, you know?"

"Sure."

"So how'd I blow it?"

"Huh?"

"How'd you guys figure out I was the one who killed Gail?"

"You know . . . this and that." I am trying so hard not to piss him off.

"Yeah, right. You got fucking lucky, too." He jams the gun even tighter against Mr. Ceepak's skull. "The prosecuting attorney's office in Ohio cut this dirty old bastard a deal. He got off easy. Then he got out early. That's not fair. He cheated the system. So, if I can't kill my dad, I figure I'll kill Ceepak's for him and maybe someday, when I'm dead and gone, which, you know, could happen any fucking second now, Ceepak will return the favor and pop a cap in my old man's head."

"Hey, Skippy—remember Mrs. Fabricius?"

Skippy looks at me like I'm the crazy one. "What?"

"Sophomore year. She taught us math."

"Oh, yeah. Her. She was okay."

"Okay? Jeez-o, man, Skip—you were her favorite."

He shrugs. "She made it interesting. Not dry and dull, you know?"

I inch forward.

"You aced every exam."

"You remember that?"

"Sure. You blew the curve, bro."

I roll closer.

"Hey, how about Mr. Skaggs?"

"Who?"

"Monkey man. The gym teacher. Remember how he'd hang off the chin-up bars chomping on a banana?"

"Danny?"

"Yeah?"

"You're wasting my time."

"I just thought—"

"I've got work to do." He uses his thumb to slide the hammer drop, take off the Beretta's safety.

"Whoa, easy."

Now his thumb pulls back the hammer spur. His finger quivers on the trigger.

His hand is trembling.

Where the hell is Ceepak?

"For fuck sake, don't shoot me, kid!" All of a sudden, Mr. Ceepak is begging. "Come on. I never did shit to you. Cut me a fucking break!"

"Shut up!"

"Come on! You don't really want to kill me!"

Incredibly, Layla laughs. "Uh, *yeah*—he does."

Skippy looks stunned. Lowers his pistol a couple inches. Turns to glare at the girl.

As he turns, she kicks out her foot.

Sends one of the shotguns skittering across the floor to me.

I pounce on it. Flip it up and twirl it over. Aim it at Skippy's heart.

"Freeze!" I shout.

He swings back, Beretta aimed at me.

"Danny?" His eyes go wide.

Everything shifts to super slo-mo.

Skippy's trigger finger twitches.

Mine twitches faster.

The shotgun in my hand explodes.

The wad slams Skippy in the shoulder. Shrapnel freckles his face with blood.

Reflexes swing him right.

The muzzle of the Beretta is now aimed at Mr. Ceepak's gut.

A round goes off.

Mr. Ceepak recoils, clutching his stomach. An artery is spurting.

Skippy wheels around to squeeze off another round.

But I already have his head in my sights.

I have to kill the crazy bastard.

That's when glass shatters, the whole world explodes, and we all go blind.

Ceepak finally tossed in the flashboom.

42

My ears are ringing as a battalion of heavily armed ninjas swarms into the control room.

I see four silhouettes of soldiers grab Skippy's arms and legs and lift him up off the ground. His pistol rattles to the floor.

He's screaming.

"My arm! Jesus, my fucking arm!"

Through the blinding white burning my retinas I can see a rump roast of raw beef where Skippy's right shoulder used to be.

The SWAT guys drag his ass out the door. Fast. All around me, it's smoky bedlam. People screaming. Crying. Wailing. Soldiers shouting, "Out, out. Go, go."

Mr. Ceepak is somewhere on the floor, wheezing. I smell the metallic scent of blood.

"We need a medic over there!" I stumble toward the door. "There's a wounded man in the corner."

"Good work, Officer Danny!" a voice cuts through the panicked din and the alarm clock bells jangling in my eardrums.

It's the girl. Layla.

"Out, out, out!" Robocop is in the house, hustling Layla and the other hostages out the door.

My temporary blindness finally fades.

"Keep your legs down, Dad!"

It's Ceepak. In the corner. Working on his father, who is gurgling and rasping and gushing blood.

"Johnny," the old man groans. "You gotta fucking help me . . . don't fuck this up, you stupid shit."

"Danny?"

"Yeah?"

"Can you see?"

"Yeah."

"I need more sterile gauze." He tears off his T-shirt and stuffs it into his father's abdomen. "Stat. Alert the medics, then grab the AED out of the ticket office. He's going into v–fib."

Ceepak starts pumping on his father's chest.

As I'm running out the trailer door, I hear Ceepak shout, "Don't die on me, you goddamn son of a bitch! Don't you dare die!"

43

I DON'T KNOW IF ANYBODY'S GOING TO GIVE HIM ANOTHER Distinguished Service Cross for it, but Ceepak saved his old man's life.

Brought him back from the brink, just like he did for that soldier over in Mosul, although I'm guessing the soldier deserved to live more than Joe Sixpack did.

But who am I to judge?

They took him to the hospital in the second ambulance.

Skippy got the first ride. He's going to live but he'll never play tennis or badminton. Apparently, my shotgun blast seriously dislocated his shoulder— like into the next county.

I don't think he'll be getting many visitors. The O'Malley clan is conveniently forgetting they ever had a boy named Skipper. Maybe Mary will drop by. Maybe they'll end up in the same psych ward after the trial.

I called Samantha like I promised I would. She was at her

mother's house. After Sam thanked me for saving Richard Heim-sack's life, her mom got on the phone and told me what a hero I was and how she always knew I'd do something heroic because I was such a hero and blah, blah, blah. Then she asked me whether I wanted to come by for Sunday dinner because she wanted to bake me a cake and introduce me to some of her friends who she'd already told what a hero I was.

I said thanks but no thanks, as I had prior commitments for Sunday afternoon.

First, Ceepak and I are going to his father's apartment and toss his things into a U-Haul so he's ready to head back to Ohio or wherever he wants to call home when he's released from the hospital. In grudging gratitude for his son's lifesaving administration of CPR and expert use of the AED, Joseph Ceepak has promised never to darken his son's door or life again. He has also taken a solemn vow to leave Ceepak's mom the hell alone.

After we pack up the old man, we promise Marny Minsky we'd check out her apartment. Make sure none of the sugar daddies booby-trapped it or planted miniature video cameras in her ferns. What can I say? She's still a little paranoid. But starting Monday, she's turning over a new leaf. Rita made a few phone calls, got her a job at Santa's Sea Shanty. Less bling. More jingle bells.

When Marny's settled, we'll head back to Ceepak's place and the little patio behind the Bagel Lagoon.

We're going to give his stepson T.J. the Farewell to Sea Haven/Hello, Annapolis party he truly deserves. There will be no putt-putt. No roller coaster rides. We'll simply crack open a couple of beers, toss some meat on the grill, eat some of Rita's potato salad, and tease T.J. mercilessly. Then we'll let him know how proud we all are of him.

You see, when Ceepak and I first met T.J. Lapscynski, he was a punk kid with a paintball rifle and a bad attitude causing trouble up and down Ocean Avenue just for the hell of it. But Ceepak saw something in him that maybe nobody else ever did. Talent. Character. The way he looked out for his mom, Rita. Over the years, Ceepak helped turn the kid around, saved his life, probably, the same way he saved his father's today.

My partner's pretty good at that.

Hey—look how far he's come with me.

Oh, by the way, Layla will be at the cookout. We bumped into each other again at the house when I went there to put on some warmer clothes after the medics checked me out. I thanked her for the assist. She said I looked cute in my swim trunks.

Layla Shapiro is her name.

Jen Forbus, the officer who'd been debriefing Layla, said the two of us made a good team.

Who knows. Maybe we do.

Maybe we will.

Acknowledgments

FIRST AND FOREMOST TO ALL THE READERS AND FANS, especially the mystery mavens on DorothyL, who would not let Danny and Ceepak die.

To Claiborne Hancock, Jessica Case, Michael Fusco, Ann Kirschner, and everyone at Pegasus Books for offering the Jersey Boys a fantastic new home. It's particularly great to have Michael designing the covers again! This one makes me think of orange-and-white swirl cones down the shore.

To Otto Penzler for his help in finding Ceepak a new home.

To my fantastic agent (and roller coaster aficionado) Eric R. Myers, who keeps finding Ceepak and Danny nice places to live.

To Chief Michael Bradley of the Long Beach Island Police

Department and Lee Lofland (author of *Police Procedure & Investigation*) for helping me get the cop details right.

To Kathy Williams, Capt. Dave Morkal, John Broadwater, Nikki Bonanni, Karen Corum, Jen Forbus, and Lynne & Rhys Fraser—my terrific early readers.

To Lisa Knauf and Steven Smith, who made generous contributions to the Artemis Project animal rescue group in New York City so they could name Gizmo (a.k.a. Hideous Gizmideus) and Puck.

And, most especially, to my beautiful and extremely talented wife J.J. She is the first editor of every writer's dreams.